DREAMS MANIFEST

Book Two in The Depths of Memory Trilogy

CR BUNDY

Lusios Publishing, LLC

For my Son

CONTENTS

CHAPTER 1

Gazing into the mirror Brague surveyed the work of his colorist, ensuring all of the details were perfection. Brague had had his sigil improperly applied once before, and to his great embarrassment, it had taken almost a full season to grow out. He'd killed the colorist as soon as he'd seen the flaw to prevent anyone else from being scarred...no, *maimed* as he'd been. The offending colorist had gotten the yellow background swirl a whole tone darker than normal, throwing off the overall harmony of the design. Spending another few moments checking over the placement and color choices, Brague gave a perfunctory nod to the colorist, signaling his acceptance of the proposed work.

He held very still while the colorist activated the chemical heat-set, and felt the radiating warmth of it through his thick, insulating shell. At that inopportune moment, his communicator chimed. He waited impatiently for the process to finish, lest he mar the design. It took only another few moments, and then the colorist moved in to polish and shine the crisp new lines. Brague waited patiently, knowing that this step was necessary to seal in the colors. The colorist finished and then backed away, deferentially exposing the vulnerable cleft of his neck to Brague.

Brague raised himself to his full height and examined every detail of the finished work in the mirrored wall. It satisfied him to discover all elements met his exacting attention to detail. His communicator chimed again, reminding him that there was an urgent message awaiting his attention. The colorist waited, frozen, waiting for Brague's judgment.

"It is ... acceptable," Brague graciously intoned.

The colorist eased his submissive posture and bowed. "I am honored to please you. I will endeavor to exceed your expectations in the future."

Brague caught a quick, caustic whiff of emotion lacing the air, entirely at odds with the colorist's demeanor. He took another, deeper breath, but Brague no longer scented the affront. Brague chose to ignore the cheeky colorists moment of indiscretion and strode back toward his research facility. Keying the security algorithm into the communicator on his left arm, Brague accessed his systems. Bringing up the messaging relays, he found a communiqué from Princess Qwell awaiting his review. He'd heard she was working on a particular project, and this was her request to have *him*, Selector Brague, placed on this assignment. He keyed off a quick acceptance note, full of the requisite honorifics and gratitude. Brague had assumed he'd be chosen for the project and would have been greatly disappointed if his assumption had been proven incorrect. Still, this gratifying moment of acceptance was a unique thing to be savored.

Brague adored his job, but he had no cause to find it anything less than exceptional. His illustrious career as a Selector had earned him full autonomy over all aspects of his research, from the specimen labs to the computing systems. The Hegemony had endowed his recent projects with generous resource budgets, both monetary and material, much to the chagrin of lesser-ranked Selectors. Due to his proven and dependable results, Brague had been granted great freedoms with his Selection process and staff allocations. He had a reputation as one of the best available, with no errors in Selection and an Evaluation rate of over 96%. Accurate Selections avoided losses of resources and time for the Queens, allowing the territories of the Hegemony to expand at a calculated and consistently planned pace. His most recent assignment to Princess Qwell was surely a sign of the Hegemony's enduring faith in his abilities.

Entering his research quarters, Brague noted everything was precisely as he'd left it. He strode to the main terminal interface, not wanting to delay starting on his new assignment another moment. He reviewed all of his current projects and found none of them at the level of Princess Qwell's priority or status. Brague foisted the rest off onto lower rated Selectors, (He gave them) nothing above their abilities but quite beyond their prestige.

After taking care of reassigning his current project load, Brague searched through the databases for candidate planets. His carapace hummed faintly in excitement, for this was no ordinary Selection.

Princess Qwell's directive was to create a new breed of Juggernaut that would be adapted to submerged, aqueous environments. With the resources required for proper growth margins, utilizing partially or wholly aqueous planets opened up a much wider range of options for future expansion. Presently specialized equipment was needed for their race to operate underwater. This raised the cost of extracting needed minerals and chemicals from the oceanic floors to prohibitive levels. Logistics wasn't the only problem. Such operations experienced a worker loss in the mid-fortieth percentile as well, which was wasteful and inefficient. This Selection might prove to be the most exciting, interesting, and hazardous challenge of Brague's entire career.

Failure to Select an appropriate planet would be a disgrace with the potential to ruin his career. Although he'd never botched a job, this assignment brought with it the highest risk of failure to date. Erroneously

Selecting a planet that led to Princess Qwell's failure would, of course, mean his immediate extermination, a possible but highly improbable outcome in consideration of Brague's exemplary record.

There were plenty of water worlds out there, but as always, the trick was in Selecting the one that would allow for the best success for the future Queen's goals. All Selectors created their own search and filtering algorithms, and Brague had the utmost confidence in his methods. Selecting the right planet for this mission would ensure the highest of honors for Brague--the ability to contribute his genetic material to future generations.

Brague's first step was to compile a listing of possibilities for Evaluation. The needs of this particular case opened up an entirely new range of planets and criteria most often excluded from common searches. A humid, primarily oceanic world with some swampland would be ideal, to provide a transitioning zone for Princess Qwell to experiment with different genetic variations of Juggernaut pupae. Caves were also desirable for this type of work, as they lent shelter, safety, and privacy to the Queen's activities.

Brague was familiar with all steps in the Juggernaut life cycle and Juggernaut physiology. This extensive and exhaustive standard training was required of all Selectors and would play heavily into this assignment. The database filter netted a variety of initial possibilities, many of them inevitably inhabited by lower beings that were often more suited to such climates. Brague had noted over his many cycles of research that the less-than-sentient races often gravitated towards wetter climes, but he'd never cared enough about them to find out why. Upon brief reflection, he discovered he still didn't care.

Brague mused that when this initiative proved successful the expanded range of the Juggernaut's territory would mean fewer "safe" colonization options for such pathetic life forms, which was as it should be. Species who couldn't compete due to a lack of intelligence or hardiness should do the universe the favor of extinguishing themselves or at least cease their predictably incessant breeding.

Perhaps it would be preferable to Select a planet already colonized by one of the more disgusting races? Choosing an already inhabited world would send a message that their infestations on proper Juggernaut territory would no longer be tolerated. Expanding Juggernaut territory options in this manner would significantly limit colonization options for a variety of inferior species, especially the invasive species of primates. All affected lesser races would have no choice but to accept their subsequent reduction of position within the celestial hierarchy.

The idea of bringing home to the substandard races the gravity of their mistake in colonizing Juggernaut lands pleased Brague immensely.

Brague updated the database filters to include only

planets colonized by lower beings. The enormity and significance of this project made good, solid supply lines (and frequency of transit within them) of paramount importance, so he added another filter, one that specified planets with proximity to military outposts and agricultural distribution points. Soon a preliminary list of a few hundred planets ranked in descending order of relevancy appeared in his result set.

At this point, his real work began. Just because the database listed a given world did not mean it still met the necessary qualifications. The experienced Selector knew that the real determinant of a planet's usefulness lay in one key factor above all others: toxicology. Especially with colonized worlds, frequently the new inhabitants had introduced toxins or chemicals into the ecosystem that were difficult or time-consuming to remove, and these potential hurdles didn't always get into the database promptly. Not all settlements were reported as required to the Hegemony, and some species of lower beings foolishly continued to ignore Hegemonic mandates.

To maximize the efficient use of scientific resources, inspections of distant planets didn't occur with any real frequency, at least not until they were needed. Thus was the need for skilled Selectors, to sniff out problems and challenges well in advance of any resource commitment.

For instance, the fourth planet on the list looked particularly promising. Topping the list were its extensive cave complexes, deep oceans, vast mineral deposits, sizable areas of swampland and a humid but mild climate. It fit all the major criteria perfectly. It also matched with Brague's secondary requirements, having a small colony of primates, who were clinging to a meager existence and plagued by disease.

Primates were still a relatively new species, and as such, hadn't won the Hegemony's formal Acceptance of Sentience ranking. Based on what he'd learned of the species, Brague doubted they ever would. Weak races that couldn't adapt to life off of their home world were doomed to failure in the goal of galactic expansion. The primate species current circumstances didn't bode well for their future. Primates should have taken the hint in the beginning and given up!

It was evident they weren't up to the task. After all, the database showed primate numbers across all of their colonized worlds were in a slow, steady decline. How primates kept fighting without any discernible forward progress was beyond Brague, and he idly wondered what possessed such a lowly race to attempt seemingly impossible things beyond their means. It would be a charity to release them from their problems, and it genuinely pleased Brague that he might be the one to do so.

Brague sent a communiqué to Princess Qwell, presenting the current list of options. Even for a well-respected Selector like Brague, frequent demonstrations of progress were essential. He included a timeline for narrowing down the attached list to a few dozen for Evaluation, setting an aggressive goal of a mere three Latnes for this task. He also noted that comprehensive progress reports would be sent every sub-Latne. This was more detail than necessary, but Brague preferred to keep Princess Qwell as involved as possible. This meant assignment completion would occur in the Nithe Tor-Latne of the Sun Trine, always an auspicious time for accomplishments involving new growth and Juggernaut expansion. Of course, with the importance of this task and what was at stake, Brague would Evaluate each of the final options personally.

Brague swelled with pride over the Queens' enduring faith in his abilities. He only hoped to be rewarded with the highest of honors for success in this venture. The competition was brutal amongst his caste for the limited breeding rights available. Surely the enormity of this task would secure his privileges?

Quickly cross-checking his personal lab's roster of available specimens with the initial list of planets he'd forwarded to Princess Qwell, Brague was pleased to find some matches for initial testing and research. He found it quite remarkable what one could learn about a planet through its evolved fauna, especially when those creatures experienced certain ... *stressors*. Heading off to his lab, Brague considered that this part of his job was by far the most interesting and certainly the most entertaining.

Selector Brague Research Notes,
Princess Qwell Assignment,
Kacke Prime-Latne of the Dark Trine.

UPDATE FOR THE FIRST SUB-LATNE OF THE project. Initial re-screenings of the top 200 identified prime pre-Selection planets have been ordered and scheduled. While waiting to receive the re-screening reports, I have spent my time in my formidable lab researching flora and fauna specimens that correspond to planets on the pre-Selection list. Specimen research is always most gratifying, but I'm anxious to begin reviewing pre-Selection reports so a visitation schedule can be set. It's most important to keep up the pace! Princess Qwell will be expecting status reports soon.

Specimen research has proved educational, yet I cannot fully apply it until the present stage of the project is completed. I have placed orders for new sample retrievals from the top 25 planets on the list, as I found some of my stocks lacking. I expect these to arrive within days. It's frustrating to have to wait that long, yet I can't waste my time doing the scut work myself. Better to take full advantage of my status and staff by delegating such work to them.

Also of note for this log entry is that Princess Qwell's personal guard and assistants have supplemented my staff. Extra ships from her fleet have been placed at my disposal. Although I could, of course, have managed with current resources, it is a generous gift nonetheless. Resources are clearly not an issue for *this* Princess. She wants results and seems quite free with her assets to help make it happen.

I must have the final Selection listing for Princess Qwell's review by the next Latne as promised in the initial project plan, which would be Perith Prime-Latne. Although I'm not comfortable spending an entire full Latne just to narrow down the search and conduct specimen studies, with what's at stake for this project I consider it necessary. Failure to properly screen out planets not matching Princess Qwell's requirements would only add precious sub-Latnes to this project.

Best to keep myself busy in the lab while I await the re-screening results. Besides, I find lab work can be quite gratifying, second only to hands-on fieldwork. Experimentation sometimes yields the most surprising results, often giving clues to a creature's native environment and culture. Dealing with specimens during fieldwork in their natural habitat elicits more precise responses.

Although it is not related to the current project for Princess Qwell, I must note progress on one particular experiment I've had underway for some time. The species known as Taska of the Hunchen galaxy will continue to care for injured individuals within the breeding group, even when it is evident that the person's wounds are beyond all repair. They even allocated a portion of their already limited rations to the dying member! This demonstrates an inability of this species to think clearly in the face of crisis. No truly rational--and certainly never any true sentient being--would ever behave so foolishly!

CHAPTER 2

THE LOUD SCRAPING OF THE BARN DOOR OPENING startled Terem, making him look up from oiling the saddle. Treus entered against a backdrop of fading sunset. How was it already dark outside? With the lanterns lit in the barn, Terem hadn't noticed the hour.

"Still hard at work, I see?" Treus smiled at him, leaning against the doorframe.

"I'll be in for dinner in just a moment, sir. I'm almost done getting the saddles cleaned."

"I doubt they've ever been cleaner, Thad. Still, you have to eat sometime, son."

Terem smiled at being called his pseudonym 'Thad,' a reminder of his success in recreating himself post Zebio Sept and after the horrors of the Temples. "Oh, I will. The cook always sets a little aside for me," Terem replied.

"I'm sure he does. Look, you should know that all

the Jonquin have noticed how dedicated you are to your work, and how impressed everyone is with you because of that," Treus stated. "It's rare to find hired help with such dedication."

It was pure self-interest, although Treus didn't need to know that. The harder Terem worked, the less often he noticed the voices. They were the only reminders of the nightmares he'd suffered.

"Thank you, sir. That's very kind of you to say so," Terem replied.

Treus nodded. "It's a simple truth. There's just one problem."

Terem felt a sinking feeling inside. "What's that, sir?"

"It's just that you work so hard and such long hours, no one has had much of a chance to get to know you very well," Treus replied.

Which I have to do, Terem thought to himself, to protect the Jonquin and myself. *"You aren't kidding,"* whispered the unbidden voices. The weirdest ideas would come into his head when he was with people. He would feel with total and complete certainty that there was something wrong with them and that they needed to be eradicated permanently. Not engaging others, avoiding talking, and staying busy seemed to ameliorate the problem.

"I guess I'm a bit shy, is all," Terem offered, a pitiful excuse even to himself.

"I understand," Treus continued. "Just break for

meals with everyone, that's all I ask, okay? You don't even have to say much, just be there, smile back at people, and make some small talk. It'll help you fit in better."

"I'll make an effort," Terem replied, unsure if he meant it.

"You'll do great," Treus smiled at him. "I'm gonna leave you to it. I still have to make sure we're locked up for the evening."

"Have a good night!" Terem replied.

Treus started to close the barn door and then stopped. "Oh, I almost forgot! A Guardian is inside the main hall, catching everyone at dinner for a quick scan. Should I tell her you'll be right in?"

Time's up. We told you it wouldn't last. "Is there a problem in the area?" Terem asked.

"No, no. Sorry, I didn't mean to alarm you. We have a Guardian stop by every few weeks and check up on us all, make sure everyone's healthy and what not. Do they do it differently in the cities?"

"Yeah. People are scanned on the street while they're going about their business. You'd never even notice unless you were watching the Guardians. Sometimes, when someone hasn't been logged with a scan for a few weeks, they'll come by your Sept Hall," Terem explained.

Not that you'd know anything about that, Terem, would you?

"Makes sense," Treus explained. "They visit us in

the evening because we're all accounted for and in one spot, so it's easier and quicker for them."

Terem nodded understanding. *"You know, I'm going to be just a little bit longer on this. Do you think it'd be too much trouble to ask the Guardian to come out here?"* Terem felt one of the voices ask through his mouth.

"Sure, I can ask. Doubt it will be a problem. Just stay here until the Guardian comes and finds you, all right? I don't want her having a fit cause she has to hunt someone down."

"I'll wait right here," Terem replied. "Have a good night, sir."

"Good evening, Thad," Treus answered and then pulled the door shut behind him.

Terem waited, pacing back and forth in the barn.

"What am I going to do?" he asked himself. "I like it here. I don't want to have to hurt everyone."

There is another way. Trust us.

Minutes later the door scraped open again, revealing a short, blonde female Guardian, dressed in their standard green and gray multi-hued garb. Terem noted that she didn't have her scanner in her hand at the moment. Luck was with him.

He smiled broadly at her. "Thanks so much for stopping by out here. I just managed to get everything finished up."

She shrugged. "Makes no difference to me. This barn is on my way out."

Terem watched her pull out a device from her pocket. *That's a medical scanner. She'll know you're infected within three or four minutes of activation.* "So, you travel back to ... wherever ... from here?" he asked.

"I'm stationed out of an outpost to the south of here. It's a few hours by horse," she explained.

"You came on horseback?" he asked. "Why didn't you stable the mare for the day?"

"No bother. I don't ever stay long. I just let her graze a bit inside the front gate while I get things taken care of." She waited for the scanner's results.

No more time. "I was wondering if you could do something for me?" the voices asked.

"What?" asked the Guardian.

"*I need to get a message out to an old acquaintance.*"

The Guardian looked up at him, a confused expression on her face. "I don't usually handle mail, but as the Jonquin have always been nice to me, I'll see what I can do for you. Where's the message?"

"*Well, it's not something for them to read, per se. It's something they need to see an example of to understand.*"

Terem noticed a red light began flashing on the scanner's screen. The Guardian glanced down, and then back up at him. All of her lassitude was suddenly replaced by a keen, calculated stance.

"An example of what?" she asked, sliding the scanner back into her pocket. She started to slowly reach for her pulse weapon with her left hand.

He reached out and grabbed her by the throat, while also pinning her left arm to her side with his right hand. The thing that once was Terem acted, well beyond the reaction speed the Guardian possessed. She struggled but was unable to move or breathe as his digits elongated, encircling the Guardian's neck. She lost the ability to breathe as he crushed her windpipe. He smiled, watching her eyes fill with agonizing panic.

"*Death. Would you like to help me?*"

CHAPTER 3

As Brague took a deep breath, he tried to classify the rank smell of planet Oncorko. This was the first planet on his Evaluation list and the only planet in the Oncor solar system. As he stood on a small hill surveying the local landscape, he reflected that it had not lived up to his expectations. There were elements of musk to the air, which would not in and of themselves have qualified for the 'rank' descriptor. However, to the musk was added a stale, sulfuric smell that unfortunately managed to mask all other possible odors. According to Juggernaut cartography, the last time the planet had been surveyed it did not have this problem with disagreeable odors. Some less sensitive species might not have noticed the smell, but to Brague it was overpowering.

He'd been on the planet nearly two full local solar days and had decided to abandon it as an Evaluation option. However, since he was here, Brague directed a regiment towards identifying the problem. Their base camp was at the far end of the hill, and Brague could see troops working to solve the puzzle. It wasn't his job or responsibility to research the situation, but he took it personally and wouldn't leave without correcting the planetary record's error. Inaccuracies in the database made the already difficult Selectors work even harder. Besides, this gave him an opportunity to discover what had modified this planet's ecology. This newfound curiosity motivated Brague beyond only pleasing the Queens, not that he'd ever admit to such a breach of decorum publicly, of course. Politically speaking, satisfying the Queens was always the top priority of all Juggernaut.

Something most Juggernaut didn't know was that the job of the Selectors went beyond an affinity for complicated math and an eye for detail. Selectors were also bred to be hypersensitive to their environment, much the same way the Queens were. Knowing what would offend the sensibilities of a Queen was just as important as meeting all of the technical specifications of a given project. Aesthetics mattered to them, even though it wasn't widely known, much less discussed openly. The issues of Queens were never discussed in polite company, lest one not show proper respect for their pre-eminence.

Brague noticed Sergeant Wul approaching and hoped this meant he had something worthwhile to report. Brague had threatened to demote Wul if he attempted to inform him of more local geology or climate patterns, so this must mean a real breakthrough. Brague took a few moments to imagine reassigning Sergeant Wul to a sanitation crew, chittering in amusement to himself. Wul's utter humiliation would be a life-long sentence. Sergeant Wul stopped a few steps respectfully away, waiting for Brague's signal to report.

After a satisfying pause, Brague addressed Wul. "Sergeant. I take it you have something useful to report?"

Instead of talking, Wul activated the handheld projector he carried. Immediately a globe appeared, representing Oncorco's land and water masses through color-coded topographical markings. The planet rotated, stopping on the eastern hemisphere, drawing Brague's attention to a point near the coastline.

"As I mentioned before, the Huzzen attempted colonization of this planet two hundred and thirty Hegemonic cycles ago. The Hegemony's last survey here took place just four years after the Huzzen arrived. No particular interest was taken in them at the time, which as it turns out, was unfortunate," Sergeant Wul narrated matter-of-factly. He paused briefly, giving Brague a chance to ask questions without interrupting. As none of this was new news, Brague awaited the rest of Wul's discovery with marked impatience.

"At some point in their travels, they picked up food

or durables that were infested with dormant pukka eggs." Wul changed the display to a series of pukka images at differing stages of their life cycle. Pictures of tiny eggs morphed into small, adolescent worms, then altered into giant slug-like creatures. The graphics displayed their razor-sharp front claws, which they used to attach themselves to their prey so they could eat at a leisurely pace. "This wasn't an immediate problem, as you have likely guessed. Pukka eggs require a short period of dry heat to mature, and on this planet, the humidity wouldn't allow for the cycle to complete. This is a threat that could have been quickly eliminated while still in dormant form, but the Huzzen had neither the technology to detect the eggs nor the ability to destroy them."

At this point in the story, Brague was smiling. He had adult pukka in his labs, having extensively studied the species. Their ability to proliferate wasn't bothersome but combined with teeth that could gnaw through both metal and stone coupled with a carnivore's appetite--a formidable threat to an unprepared and simple settlement.

"At some point after our last survey, the Huzzen retrieved sealable storage units from their transport vessel. This may or may not be when the pukka eggs were introduced; the infested goods could have been transported at that time or earlier in their colonization. Regardless, items containing pukka eggs were placed inside the storage devices."

Wul's narration paused as he adjusted the projector, displaying a small domed storage unit with a hinged door. The image spun, showing the rather bland device. Brague waited for Wul to continue, not liking time spent on storage units, which he considered a rudimentary inclusion in the report.

"These containers not only seal the contents for freshness and added life expectancy, but also work to reduce moisture content. This is generally a good thing for storage units, but most likely, combined with Oncorco's hot days, provided the ideal environment for the pukka eggs to mature. It was only a matter of time until some witless Huzzen opened one of the units, releasing countless adolescent pukka onto Oncorco. It's likely that the entire settlement was consumed within a few days. Perhaps they lasted as long as a sub-Latne, but that isn't likely. No Huzzen remain on Oncorco, so if the pukka didn't annihilate their numbers, something else must have soon after that." Wul spoke all of this in a flat monotone.

Brague laughed heartily at this, liking a tale where a race of lower beings unleashed a veritable plague upon themselves. He'd observed pukka's eating behavior and knew they preferred eating live prey. Wul switched the projected image back to the globe of Oncorco. Brague didn't care about the details on how the Huzzen had destroyed themselves. After all, lower beings brought about their own downfall. It was just a matter of time.

"Mature pukka have a reputation for their voracious appetites and a tendency to avoid other adults except while breeding, so it isn't too far of a stretch to assume that the adults quickly spread out in search of other food sources and territories," Wul continued. The image displayed red dots, showing how the species spread across all adjacent landmasses. Brague noted that his present location was included in the red areas of pukka infestation. Species like pukka were not a threat to the Juggernaut, just a mild annoyance.

"Some time has passed since this infestation," Brague interjected. "How widespread are the current pukka populations, and how does this relate to the current stench?"

Wul adjusted the image to answer Brague's request, showing pukka clustered around seashores. "Field research has found some old pukka surviving off of crustacean life, as it is abundant in this world and there are no large land animals suitable as its prey. A brief analysis has shown an unusually high level of sulfur in the crustacean's shells. As pukka elimination is primarily gaseous, that would account for the smell," Sergeant Wul concluded.

"The smell is an unfortunate consequence of the Huzzen's blunder," Brague replied, still smiling. Sergeant Wul didn't react. He stood, as befit his station, awaiting additional orders. Infantry were incredibly useful but also incredibly dull.

Brague considered his options. It was regrettable

that no Huzzen had survived long enough to be destroyed for their impunity. The Hegemonic policy was all encompassing, even handling foreign infestations that ruined planetary ecosystems. The offending invader and any species introducing it, whether deliberately or not, were both ruled toxic to the environment, and thus had to be removed. Prime real estate was just too valuable to waste on giant bugs and the like. Brague would have to be content with ordering the sanitization of Oncorco. With luck, the planet could be certified pukka-free within the next hundred and fifty or so Hegemonic cycles.

"Sergeant Wul," Brague turned to Wul and addressed him formally. Wul turned off the projector and snapped to attention. "Prepare Oncorco for cleansing. You have two regiments at your command to complete the gross decontamination. Place a warning beacon alerting others to steer clear of this location. Also, send word to Hegemonic command, summarize all that we have discussed and request a science vessel to complete the cleansing process. I think five days should be more than enough time to accomplish this simple task. One ship will stay behind to assist your efforts and return you to the main search force. Do you have any questions?"

"Only one, Selector Brague," Wul replied confidently. Brague imagined Wul would have an enjoyable time killing full-grown pukka. It would possibly mean the loss of a few troops, considering the limited time-frame and manpower. "May I know the locations and timelines of your subsequent Evaluation candidates so we may catch up with you in as timely a fashion as is possible?"

Brague guessed Wul hoped to finish the task early, and by knowing Brague's timeline over the next five days could better anticipate the rendezvous location. Although Brague liked Wul's proactive attitude, guessing at a Selector's timeline was useless. Each Evaluation took as long as it took, and the planets were a bit spread out. Transit times alone could double the Evaluation schedule.

"It won't likely help you, but the next four planets are Bawna, Taloos, Az'Unda, and Keriu. I may stay at each less than a day or over a sub-Latne. There's no way to know in advance. Your best option to catch up with us will be through communiqués to the Fleet Captain." Brague then returned to his personal transport pod, not waiting for additional questions. He had more important things to consider than pukka, amusing though the pest had proved.

As he returned to the fleet awaiting him above Oncorco, Brague checked his messaging queue. Finding no response from Princess Qwell, he grew anxious, not sure if this was a sign of her faith in him or of disinterest on her part. Brague started drafting another communiqué to Princess Qwell, including a full status report of Oncorco, so she could see he was making progress on her project and even going out of his way to ensure this planet would be purified for future Hegemonic use. He could only hope she'd maintain confidence in him. In the meantime, he had a mission. Arguably the most important mission of his career: pleasing Princess Qwell.

CHAPTER 4

#BEGIN TRANSMISSION#
#ROUTING CODE: UNREGISTERED ID,
ROAMING COM S8-628#
#ENCRYPTION: HIGH#

Bauleel,

I'm relieved to hear you're on the mend. I'd wondered why I hadn't heard back from you before now, but never imagined something could have happened to you. I can relate that you feel responsible, at least in part, for Terem's escape. Come to think of it, I'm the one that bagged him and brought him to the Technicians when he first started showing signs of plague mutation. It's a shame I didn't just kill him then, eh?

And Natre, where to begin? You've got to know she's been waiting to assume your post for what, twenty, thirty years now? Although why you gals like to tie yourselves down to those dull Temple walls, I'll never understand. Once you've been away a few days, I'm sure you'll find the change of pace invigorating.

I wouldn't worry too much about what Natre thinks she knows. She's always been more ambitious than technically competent.

Be careful what you do share with your wayward Technician Rilte. Sure, he saved your life and kept you from having to deal with Natre face-to-face, but don't forget he's a Temple man first and foremost. If he decides you're not acting in the best interests of Az'Unda ... I'm just saying: have a cleanup plan.

Keep me updated on your search, and I will assist as soon as I am able. At the moment I'm escorting the Durmah along the Northern Road to Resounding Cliffs. We're about two days out. With Raza's recent orders I will also likely end up accompanying them all the way back to Raven's Call, as I doubt any other Guardians will be available to make the trip.

I did end up having a frank conversation with the girl and explained some things to her. Turns out she's been having dreams of the past and had the wherewithal to try and hunt down concrete proof with the Durmah in tow. Who knew her subconscious mind would be so tenacious? Then again, most of her dreams would be better described as nightmares, and much more accurate than I'd admit to her.

Anyway, I believe I've persuaded her to keep her

dreams and the scant information of her past to herself, and hopefully, I'll see if she's heeding my advice by the time we reach Raven's Call. Otherwise ... Well, I'll worry about that when we get there.

Happy hunting,
Graeber

#END TRANSMISSION#

BAULEEL TURNED OFF THE MESSAGE TERMINAL and slid it into her backpack.

"How am I not surprised?" Bauleel whispered. She took a long drink of water from her canteen, deliberately using her left arm despite its painful protests. The crèche had done an excellent job of knitting the bones in her shoulder back together, but the bruised joint hadn't yet forgotten being shattered in Terem's attack back at Raven's Call temple.

"Did you get your reply?" Rilte asked. He sat next to her on a felled pine tree on the outskirts of the forest surrounding Raven's Call. The heat of the midday sun beat down upon them, making Bauleel feel like every pore on her body was oozing sweat.

"Yes, I did, and I'm afraid the person I'd like to have to help us is, how should I put it, otherwise engaged?" Bauleel explained.

"Will that be a problem for us?" he asked. Bauleel

could sense the anxiety pouring off of him, almost thicker than his sweat.

Bauleel shrugged and then winced at the pain that shot through her back, hampering her awareness of his emotions. "Let's hope not. The good news is Raza has put out an alert to all Guardians calling for a comprehensive search for Terem, so we're not on our own."

"I like the sound of that," he replied, smiling hopefully. "Does that mean we'll be teaming up with some *actual* Guardians then?"

"I'm not planning on it," Bauleel replied.

"But wouldn't that be smarter than running around after Terem alone?" Rilte asked.

"I'm not alone. I've got you." Bauleel flashed him a smile, wincing quietly as her bruised flesh protested.

Rilte rolled his eyes. "Honestly, like I'll do you any good? I have no combat training, and I somehow doubt that knowing how to run statistical models is going to help defeat Terem in the flesh."

"You saved my life once already, Rilte. You're my good luck charm."

"With all respect, Revered Matriarch, you need a lot more than good luck right now."

She could sense his confusion, after all, how could a Technician and an ex-Matriarch take on Terem? Bauleel knew she would have to explain who she was, sooner or later, if he stayed with her and stayed alive long enough.

Bauleel frowned. "Don't call me that. It's not who I am anymore."

Rilte nodded. "Sorry. I guess I still don't understand what we're doing out here. Or should I say, what *you're* doing out here."

Bauleel stood up, not yet ready to explain herself to him. "If you've had a chance to catch your breath, then what *we* should be doing is going."

"I'm ready whenever you are," Rilte replied, standing up and shouldering the backpack and canteens.

Bauleel started walking, with Raven's Call behind her and the forest looming ahead.

"How are you holding up?" Rilte asked, walking alongside her.

"Not too bad, considering. I am sorer than I ever thought possible in about every fiber of my being. If I'd been thinking any more clearly, I would have taken some painkillers from the lab before we left."

"Perhaps when we get to where we're going, wherever that is, you can pick some up?" Rilte asked.

"I'm planning on it," Bauleel replied.

"By the way, where exactly are we going?" he asked.

Bauleel smiled. "There's a Guardian outpost about four more miles north of the city. I figure we can stock up there and also see if there have been any sightings reported."

"So the plan is to just walk into a Guardian outpost,

take what we want, ask them how things are going, and then leave?" Rilte asked.

"That's about it, more or less," Bauleel confirmed.

"Then you'll be telling them you're Mat ..." he asked.

Bauleel cut him off, holding up a finger in admonishment. "No. I won't, and you *certainly* won't." She shook her finger at him for emphasis.

"Okay, then on whose authority will they open their doors and let us take anything we want?" Rilte asked.

"We're Guardians," Bauleel replied.

"Uh, right. Except we're not, you see. These outfits might convince the average citizen, but don't you think real Guardians will suspect something?" he asked.

"Let me spell it out for you: I've impersonated a Guardian before today, on more than one occasion. Just do what I tell you to do, and they won't even raise an eyebrow," Bauleel explained.

Rilte was silent for a moment, and Bauleel could feel him struggling with disbelief. It was a testament to his faith in her or his curiosity that he'd come this far.

"I think I'm just beginning to appreciate how complicated a person you are," Rilte stated.

Bauleel let out a laugh: he had no idea. "I'm flattered, really I am."

Rilte smiled. "I can only hope you're flattered enough to add your past impersonating a Guardian to the story of how you acquired your Methuselah treatments."

Right, her life extension treatments. Had she expected he'd let that finding go unexplained? Bauleel still hadn't decided whether she was going to honor her promise to Rilte to explain the treatments. "I'll consider it," she replied. "But for now the stories will have to wait, as we're almost at the outpost."

"With your extensive background in Guardian impersonation, do you have any advice for me on what to expect?"

"Don't speak unless spoken to. Like the Technicians, the Guardians don't keep to the standard Sept system. It's more of a military-style structure. Keeping your mouth shut will fit in with their expectations. Plus, it'll keep you out of trouble and match the story I'll be feeding them," Bauleel advised.

"Which is?" he asked.

"You'll know when you hear it," Bauleel replied with a wink. "But from here out keep your mouth shut."

"Yes ma'am," Rilte replied.

Bauleel found the narrow road which led upwards to the outpost, located on the top of a small mesa. The grade of the path was steep, and soon they were both panting from the exertion. A good half-hour later they reached the top of the mesa, encountering no other traffic along the way. A high wall stood as an added protection to the outpost, with one single doorlock-accessible gate allowing entrance into and out of the compound.

The gate stood half open, doorlock blinking red.

"How does this not fill me with confidence?" Bauleel said. Rilte looked back at her, nervous tension radiating from him. Bauleel pushed the gate open, walked into the compound and surveyed the area. Rilte followed close behind. She motioned for him to shut the gate behind them.

Everything appeared normal at first glance. The flat top was devoid of all trees and undergrowth, allowing space for not only the square outpost structure but also stables and training yards. Was a natural occurrence, or did the Guardians prefer to keep the area clear as a safety measure? Bauleel didn't know for sure. The outpost stood a full four stories tall, with windows only on the top two floors. She remembered the view from the top being awe-inspiring as well as practical. The picture was missing one essential element.

"Where is everybody?" Bauleel asked, stopping to catch her breath.

"Am I supposed to answer that, or keep my mouth shut?"

"Don't be a smart-ass," Bauleel sniped. "This is bad. Normally there are a couple Guardians' on sentinel on the roof, and another two or three walking the perimeter fence."

"Could they be in a staff meeting?" Rilte asked.

Bauleel stared at him blankly for a moment. "This isn't a Technician's Guildhall. Even when there are meetings, there are those who stand sentinel at their posts."

"All right," Rilte replied. "So what should we do?"

"We need to search the premises. Be alert for any signs of movement," Bauleel advised, pulling the gun out of her backpack.

"You wouldn't happen to have a second one of those handy, would you?" he asked.

"Sure," Bauleel replied. "Wait a sec; do you even know how to use a blaster?"

"No, but I'd still prefer having one. Where is it?" Rilte asked.

"Inside the outpost storeroom, located in the basement of the main structure," Bauleel replied.

"Doesn't do me a lot of good then, does it?" Rilte replied.

"And you'd be so much better off with a weapon you don't know how to use, right? For now, keep quiet and stay behind me," Bauleel ordered.

"Yes, ma'am."

Bauleel rolled her eyes at him, and then started out her search by sweeping the perimeter of the compound in a clockwise pattern. The training yards looked empty; dummies and targets were lonely fixtures punctuating the space. They passed a weapons rack filled with wooden swords and staves. Nothing appeared to be missing.

Rilte pulled a dark wooden staff of his height from the rack. "If it's all right with you, I'll hang onto this. I've spent some time training with these before, mostly agility and speed exercises, but I like the feel of them."

"Sure."

They continued around the compound to the rear of the stables. Bauleel slowly opened the back door. A high-pitched creak echoed up to the rafters, unsettling a group of barn owls and drawing admonishing squawks for disturbing their sleep. Bauleel walked through the barn with Rilte close on her heels checking every stall, but there were no horses. In fact, so far the only sign of life were the grousing barn-owls.

"Even the horses are gone," Bauleel whispered. She focused her awareness, trying to pick up any uncharacteristic scent, but the place smelled only of horse, birds, and dung.

"From the smell, they haven't been gone long," Rilte replied, pointing to muck in the back of the closest stall.

"Agreed, and yet they left behind their bridles and saddles, so it appears they weren't ridden out. This isn't right. Any self-respecting Hall Master would keep a cleaner stable than this. Let's check out the outpost itself." They exited via the stable's front door, which was standing wide open.

They approached the Guardian Guild Hall's closed front door. Bauleel raised her hand to the doorlock and paused. By touching this, her handprint and access would be logged. Anyone in the Core who might be looking for her and had placed a watch on her access codes would know her location within mere moments. Bauleel had to remind herself that if the Core wanted to find her, with the resources they had at their command, they would. She shook off this horrible thought and pressed her hand to the doorlock. Within seconds it flashed a green sensor light, and the door swung open.

A light breeze blew out through the door, carrying with it the thick smell of blood.

"Shit," Bauleel muttered under her breath. She stepped away from the doorway, pushing Rilte back against the outpost wall next to her.

"What's wrong?" Rilte asked.

Bauleel dug in her vest, locating the locator beacon hidden deep in a concealed pocket. She pulled it out and input the codes for 'multiple men down; approach with caution' and then activated the beacon.

"What's that for?" Rilte asked.

"It's a locator beacon. I just sent out the alert for casualties."

"What did you see in there?"

"It's not what I saw. It's what I smelled."

Rilte drew in a deep breath of air. "Are you sure?"

Bauleel just stared at him, raising her left eyebrow even though it hurt to do so.

"Okay, so who'll pick up on that beacon?"

"Any Guardians in the vicinity who aren't otherwise coping with emergency situations will come here without delay. That could be minutes or hours, it's hard to say for sure. Most likely the latter, because anyone stationed here would have put up an alarm before now. All of the Guardian Sept Halls have receivers, so the closest Hall will organize a rescue party."

"How does this stick with your 'stay out of trouble' plan?"

"Guardians are dead. Something killed them, and my guess is Terem did it. If there are survivors, we have to help them. Trying to hide my location from Natre and the others is a fool's errand at best anyway."

Rilte's face paled. "If it was Terem, how do we know he's not still here?"

"By the moons, I've gone completely daft!" Bauleel replied. She would have slapped her hand against her bruised forehead, but Rilte managed to block her motion with his hand on her wrist.

For a moment she was swept up in his emotions. Fear for his safety, concern for hers, anxiety over what lay hidden within the outpost's walls, disbelief over the entire situation, curiosity about who she was, guilt over the bruises on her face, the memory of finding her lying, beaten beyond recognition in a pool of blood and the deep, almost physical pain he'd felt as he picked up her broken body and believed her dead ...

Bauleel pushed his hand away brusquely, unwilling to digest more of Rilte's psyche. She kept her eyes diverted as she took a deep breath, searching through her backpack.

"Are you all right? For a moment there I thought you were about to pass out," Rilte said.

"No, no, I'm just not used to thinking like a Guardian." Bauleel pulled the scanner out of her backpack and turned it on.

"What's that?" Rilte asked.

"It's a life form scanner," Bauleel explained while calibrating the device. "It can be calibrated to detect a variety of things, based on creature size, movement, humans versus non-humans, you name it. It also overlays topographic maps and building structures, making it easier to locate whatever you're scanning for."

"So you're saying all Guardians carry those, or is it something you have special access to because of your position?"

"All Guardians have these." Bauleel had the device scanning for all life signs of any kind. She waited impatiently for the results, her eyes darting back to the outpost's open door.

"That must be expensive."

"The handheld units are relatively cheap. It's the network of expensive satellite orbiters that do the real work. These devices access their data core." A red blip appeared on the scanner's screen. "I've got something. One target with faint life signs, located on the roof." Bauleel walked into the dark doorway and strode down an unlit hallway. She tried the light switch, but no lights came on. Either the lights themselves were broken, or the power was out. She had no way of knowing for sure.

"Wait!" Rilte hoarsely whispered, trailing after her. "Are you sure it's safe?"

"No, I'm not. That's kind of the point." Bauleel stopped and turned to meet his gaze, trying to contain her irritation. "You're welcome to stay here if you'd like."

Rilte frowned. "With all due respect, I think we should both wait until a *real* Guardian arrives to handle the situation."

"Fine. You stay here and escort the Guardians up to the roof when they arrive. It could be days. I'm going to go and make sure that their one survivor is still alive when they get here." Bauleel turned and headed back down the dark hallway, using the scanner's display to provide enough light to see by. The stench of decaying blood was overwhelming to her keen senses.

Within a few steps, Rilte was hot on her heels. Bauleel guessed he either didn't want to wait alone or wasn't comfortable allowing her to go alone. She didn't care either way. Having him close by would make it easier for her to protect him. But must he argue with her about everything?

They reached the stairwell at the back of the building, and Bauleel took a step into something gooey and black by the light of the scanner. Undeterred, she advanced up the stairwell, not investigating further what the substance was.

"Ugh, what's that?" Rilte asked.

"Dried, or more specifically, coagulating blood. Watch your step. It's still sticky in spots."

Rilte groaned but heeded her advice. Each step was covered in the sticky, smelly substance. They reached the first landing, which led to the next flight of stairs as well as providing access to a room full of couches and tables off to their right. Light streamed in through the second story windows broken by sporadically illuminated patches of carmine. Generally, Bauleel would have welcomed the light, except it revealed a cruel story painted upon the walls, ceiling, floor, and furniture.

Bauleel remembered back to her days of studying both medicine and mathematics. There was what, five, six quarts of blood in the human body? This room was about fifteen by thirty feet, with walls ten feet high. That would mean around 1,800 square feet in total, Bauleel calculated, including the ceiling and floor.

"Based on the amount of blood covering, well everything, I'd have to guess at least four people died here," Bauleel stated. "Most of the floor is dry, with isolated puddles remaining tacky." She pressed a finger against a couch cushion, thick, wet blood coating her skin. "These cushions are sopping wet, I can't begin to calculate how much has been absorbed within their fibers. No, there had to be more than four killed here."

"This looks just like the Technician's Guild did after Terem was done with us."

Bauleel remembered all too well. "Including the missing bodies. I wonder how many ..." Bauleel began, unable to finish the question.

"I'm sure the Guardians have records of who was stationed here, so figuring out who's missing shouldn't be too difficult?"

The stench was overwhelming. Not for the first time Bauleel wished she could dull her senses on command. "True. Let's keep going."

Bauleel continued up the stairs. She didn't stop at either of the next two landings, preferring to just scan the rooms as they passed. Each was the same: blood covering everything, yet no bodies. "What did he do with them?" she muttered to herself.

"We never found the remains of those killed at the labs," Rilte replied.

Bauleel didn't want to think of what that might mean, particularly since she had a pretty good idea of what Terem had done with them.

They reached the top of the staircase and found the door to the roof wide open. The outpost's last remaining Guardian sat motionless at the far corner of the stone, bent over and gripping the pike embedded in his chest. She wondered if the blood covering him was his own, or someone else's.

Rilte grabbed Bauleel by the shoulder. "How can

you be sure this isn't a trap, and that it isn't Terem over there disguised as a Guardian?"

Bauleel showed him the results on the scanner. "It's a human male, infection free, weak vital signs. Besides, I seriously doubt even a Terror could run himself through with a pike," Bauleel replied. "Come on, he needs our help."

She walked over to the man, pocketing the scanner and pulling out her medical scanner, activating it as they approached the injured man.

"Now *that* I recognize," Rilte said. Bauleel wasn't surprised. "How's he look?" he asked, looking over her shoulder at the screen.

"Not good." They reached the man, and Bauleel knelt in front of him. She pulled out her emergency first-aid kit and handed it to Rilte. "His right lung is collapsed, he's got a list of assorted broken bones, and he's severely dehydrated. Can you prep a high-dose anti-plague injection, as well as a general antibiotic and a painkiller?"

"Sure, if you've got all that in here," Rilte replied, opening the kit. "You sure keep this well stocked," he said, prepping the shots.

"You can never be too careful." Bauleel handed the scanner over to Rilte and wetted a washcloth from her canteen. She wiped the blood off of the man's face and neck, revealing a number of bruises and cuts. She thought she recognized the man. Captain Tiine, wasn't it? Rilte administered the injections into the man's neck, who let out a quiet groan in response.

Bauleel felt behind his back. "Well, that explains why he's sitting here. This pike is driven into the wall itself." She dug through her backpack for a moment, then pulled out a loop of wire with wooden dowels attached to each end.

"What's that?" Rilte asked.

"Standard issue wire-saw." Bauleel looped it around the pike within an inch of the Guardian's chest. "Can you move his hands onto his lap and hold the end of the pike for me?"

Rilte obliged, managing to keep the pike steady while also watching the scanner for any changes in the Guardian's condition.

Once he had the shaft stabilized, Bauleel pulled back and forth on the dowels, and the razor-sharp wire sliced through the shaft of the pike. Rilte laid the massive pole to the side as Bauleel stored the saw.

"Now comes the tricky part," Bauleel said. "Has the painkiller taken effect yet?"

"I can't say for sure," Rilte replied, consulting the scanner. "But his breathing and heart rate have slowed."

"Good. Okay, now you get a firm hold around his waist, and I'll get under his arms like this," Bauleel instructed, running her hands under his armpits and gripping her fingers around his chest.

"You're serious?" Rilte asked. "This could kill him."

"If we don't get him proper medical attention soon,

he'll die. Now, put your hands around his waist. Then on my count of three, pull. We'll lay him down and see if he survives the extraction," Bauleel explained.

Rilte did as she'd instructed, although Bauleel could tell from his dubious expression that he didn't think this was the best course of action. "I'm ready when you are," he said.

"All right then. One, two, *three!*" Bauleel said.

They pulled the Guardian off of the pike, producing a long, sucking sound as the haft ripped from his chest inch by inch, chunks of blood and tissue embedded in the wood. Blood flowed out of the wounds in front and in the rear of his torso as they laid him flat on his back. He groaned, and for the first time since they'd arrived opened his eyes. Although he was too far gone to focus on them, he muttered "no, no, no" under his breath.

"It's okay, he's gone now. You're safe," Bauleel reassured. She watched Rilte rescan him. "How does he look?"

Rilte frowned and shook his head. "Unless you've got a med lab in that backpack, I doubt he'll be breathing much longer," Rilte replied.

"If you're up for carrying him, he might have a shot," Bauleel answered.

"Where to?" Rilte asked.

"There's a med facility on the second floor. At least there used to be a few years ago, and assuming Terem didn't smash every piece of equipment in sight ... "

Rilte handed her the med scanner and canteens. "You seem to know this place well," he commented as he sat the man back up, and then hoisted him over his shoulder. The unconscious Guardian groaned.

"I've been here a few times before," Bauleel replied as she followed Rilte back inside and down the staircase. "Besides, Guardian outposts are all built based on the same floor plan. So if you've seen one, you've seen them all."

To his credit, Rilte didn't stop once to catch his breath. When they reached the second-floor, Bauleel led him past the blood-encrusted room and down a short hallway to the medical facility. The door was wide open, revealing more blood covering shards of glass and overturned tables. There were four crèches along the outside wall of the room. Bauleel inspected them, noting that the first one's cover had been smashed in by a nearby chair, the second one's cover was cracked, and the third's cover was open, displaying an unfortunate combination of miscellaneous debris from the room's destruction. The last one was in the corner of the room, and besides some blood spatter and dents to the metallic casing, it appeared to be in good working order.

Bauleel used a towel from her backpack to wipe off the crèche and then opened it. It appeared untouched on the inside. "Go ahead and lay him down. I'll get it running."

Rilte carefully laid the Guardian in the crèche.

"But the power, it's still off?" he said, breathing hard from carrying the man.

"Not a problem. Although these units need occasional recharging, and thus why you often see them plugged in as a matter of course, their batteries are designed for extended periods of autonomous use. See!" She exclaimed as the interface loaded on the access panel screen. "Can you help me cut his clothes and pull his boots off?"

Rilte once again assisted her, and the Guardian was nude in short order. Bauleel then checked the crèche's stats. Everything looked to be in order, so she keyed the diagnostic and triage setting, and the crèche's cover slid closed. "Let's see what survival percentage he rates today," Bauleel mused.

Bauleel could see red lights flood the interior of the unit as the sensors kicked in. Soon enough a number of gauges on the screen displayed orange and red colors. A red light started flashing, accompanied by a soft beeping. Bauleel investigated. "Let's see ... he's dangerously dehydrated, which we already knew, but what we didn't know is that this crèche is low on saline."

"So, what, we get some from the other units?" Rilte replied.

Bauleel laughed, invigorated by the prospect of saving the man. "No, silly. We get a new cartridge from their medicinals supply pantry, which should be in that room," she pointed to a nearby secured door.

Bauleel walked to the door and pressed her hand to

the doorlock. After flashing green, the door swung inwards. The small room was pristine with supplies neatly stacked and set in rows.

"Luckily for us, Terem doesn't have security clearance," Rilte quipped.

"Yeah, real lucky," Bauleel replied, her right hand rubbing her sore left shoulder. "I guess he didn't have the motivation to borrow it from someone this time." She walked into the pantry and located the stack of saline cartridges.

"Sorry, I didn't mean it like that," Rilte said.

Hefting a cartridge up under each arm Bauleel walked out of the pantry and back to the crèche. She opened the service panel and keyed in the appropriate sequence which caused the supplies drawer to slide outward from the base of the unit. Bauleel lifted the empty cartridges out of the drawer and replaced them with the full ones. She tossed the empties onto the floor as she pushed the drawer shut and then closed the service panel. The crèche stopped beeping.

"I know, Rilte. I'm just feeling a bit worn out," she replied.

"Understandable. I'd recommend we have a seat but ..." Rilte gestured at the filthy furniture.

Bauleel had an idea. Walking back into the supply cabinet, she located some thermal waterproof blankets and threw them over a nearby couch. "It doesn't make it go away, but at least we can sit for a moment without getting bloody."

"For which I'm in your debt," Rilte replied, sitting down.

Bauleel checked the gauges on the crèche again. "Good news. He's got a whopping eighty-five percent survivability rating. Some systems still orange, but no more reds. It seems to think he might regain consciousness within a few hours even. Hopefully, he'll feel like talking."

"Fantastic. I've always been amazed at how effective the crèches are."

"That's Juggernaut technology for you. There's a reason they live at the top of the food chain."

"Why don't you sit down?" he suggested.

Bauleel dumped her backpack on the couch and flopped down, suddenly very weary.

"So, what's the plan?" Rilte asked.

"Ugh, I'm too tired to have a plan."

Rilte smiled. "Right, how is it I don't believe you? So, what's the plan again?"

"Simple. We rest up and wait for the Guardian to recuperate. In the meantime we'll beef up our supplies a bit, get a few maps, food, etc., assuming of course that Terem didn't manage to destroy everything he could get his hands on. I would have preferred a pair of horses to help us carry what we need, but as we're fresh out of those, we'll have to make do. I'm hoping the Guardian wakes up before we leave so we can find out what happened ..."

CHAPTER 5

Bauleel jolted to awareness, her head resting against Rilte's shoulder. She'd been having the nicest dream of eating pancakes with thick, sugary syrup and blackberries on top. Her head felt thick and dense, and she wondered why Rilte was slumped next to her on the couch. Orienting herself, Bauleel remembered where they were and realized it was morning again. She looked over to Rilte, his gentle smile warmed her.

"Sleep well?" he asked.

"I guess I did. I must have passed out right after collapsing onto this couch," Bauleel replied.

"You sure did. And before you're taken unaware, you should know we have company."

"What?" Bauleel exclaimed, shooting up and scanning her surroundings. The pain in her shoulder and back reminded her to add painkillers back on her to do list.

"They arrived in the middle of the night. I didn't wake you because you were so tired, and they seemed willing to wait until morning to get answers," Rilte explained.

"So you said nothing?" Bauleel asked. Please, please, *please* tell me you kept your mouth shut!

"Nothing. I motioned to you and begged off, making it clear that I didn't want to wake you up," Rilte replied.

Bauleel took a deep breath and sighed heavily. "Good. Thanks for following my advice."

"Hmm, I didn't know that was just advice. I wonder what an order sounds like from you then."

They heard footsteps outside the door. "Shut up, or you'll find out," Bauleel warned.

A moment later three Guardians stormed into the room, two men and a woman, all looking upset. Bauleel recognized the short, black haired man in front but not the other two. Rilte stood up, standing next to her as the arrivals approached.

"If I remember correctly, it's Lieutenant Commander Leelu?" he addressed Bauleel.

"That's correct. And you're Sergeant Baryu, right?" Bauleel replied.

"It's *Master* Sergeant Baryu now, but that's affirmative," he answered, extending an arm in greeting.

Bauleel grasped his forearm in the traditional

Guardian greeting. "Congratulations. This is Corporal Rilte, my trainee."

The Master Sergeant shook arms with Rilte. "This is Sergeant Taine," he motioned to the tall blonde with him, "and Private Jarua," he pointed to the red-haired man behind Taine.

They all exchanged brief greetings. "Now that that's out of the way, can I suggest we dispense with rank and get down to business?" Bauleel requested.

"As you're the ranking officer, Lieutenant Commander, it's up to you," Master Sergeant Baryu replied.

"Then please, call me Leelu. Down to business. You're still stationed here at the outpost?"

"Yes, all three of us are. We left a few days ago to deliver medicinals to the farms north of here and check their fortifications. There was nothing out of the ordinary to report. We were headed back this direction when we received the alarm yesterday afternoon. I assume you sent it?" Baryu asked.

"I did," Bauleel confirmed.

Baryu dipped his head. "Once we received your signal we picked up our pace, watching for signs of anything unusual. We came across nothing on the way back except a couple of the horses that had escaped. Jarua insisted we collect and bring them back with us despite the time lost."

"It didn't take much time to round them up, Lieutenant Commander," Jarua explained. "And I worried what might happen to them out there on their own like that."

"Jarua is our stable master," Baryu replied. "And it seemed a practical conservation of resources at the time, but now I doubt the wisdom of that decision. I'd guess we spent about an hour rounding up the eight horses we found."

"Let me assure you that you made the right decision," Bauleel replied. "Trust me, by the time we'd arrived, discovered the state of things, and then activated the beacon, it was already too late for those who perished here. Getting back an hour earlier wouldn't have made any difference."

"We're lucky you showed up when you did, Leelu. Otherwise, I doubt Captain Tiine would still be with us," Baryu replied, glancing in the direction of the crèche.

"Speaking of the Captain..." Bauleel approached the crèche, assessing the readouts. All of the gauges displayed green and yellows now. A dark red keloid disc on his chest was the only external evidence of the hole the pike had torn through him.

"Why don't we revive him and get a first-hand tale of what happened here during the attack?" She activated the awakening routine. His immune factors were sky-high, so instead of opening the crèche and slowing his healing, Bauleel turned on the speaker. The sound of his breathing filled the room.

"Can I ask what made you stop?" Baryu asked.

"It wasn't luck, I'm afraid. We're part of Commander Graeber's special task force dealing with the Terem Zebio situation. We tracked him going in this general direction and needed to restock our supplies. I'd thought Rilte and I could rest up here overnight and get a pair of horses to continue our search."

"Anything else you need to add to that list?" Captain Tiine's weak but gravelly voice sounded tinny and artificial over the speaker.

Bauleel's lip curved up into a half-grin before she could stop herself. *Ow.* "Yeah, now that you mention it, I need some updated maps of the settlements in the area, travel rations, a clean change of clothes, and enough meds to restock my kit from all the juice we poured into you yesterday."

"You're welcome to anything you and your two new horses can carry," he replied. "Hey, why not take a third horse and load it up with extra supplies. There's even a fresh batch of sweet rolls in the larder, which someone should eat. Not like I'm gonna be stopping you."

"It's good to see you're feeling better, Sir." Baryu stepped closer, into Tiine's line of sight.

"You too. And let me tell you how good it is to see some of my team still alive," Tiine replied. "Baryu, could you draft a message to Chieftess Raza for me, summarizing what I'm about to tell you?"

"Yes sir," Baryu replied, digging out his comm unit.

"Can I assume I haven't been unconscious in this contraption for a few weeks?"

"No Captain," Bauleel replied. "I found you yesterday afternoon and put you straight into the crèche. You've only been in there for...sixteen to eighteen hours now?" She glanced at Rilte, who nodded agreement.

"Thanks for that, Lieutenant Commander. I was serious just now, about the horses. Not the sweet rolls though. I've changed my mind about those."

"I'll restrain myself when it comes to selecting our travel rations," Bauleel answered, reminding herself to not grin again.

"Good. If I remember correctly, I was only outside on that pike overnight...I think. It's hard to be certain when you're in that much pain. Anyway, I'll start at the beginning. The night before you found me everything was business as usual. We'd had a nice dinner, some had already retired for the evening, while others of us sat playing a friendly game of poker in the main room on the first floor. Hmm, Baryu?"

"Yes, Sir?"

"Omit that last part, about the poker, from the Chieftess' report."

"Already done, Sir," Baryu replied.

"Where was I?" Captain Tiine continued, exhaustion evident in his strained features. "Oh yes, I'd just gotten dealt a royal flush when Private Verine came running down the steps. She'd been keeping watch on the roof, and said that someone was approaching the gate on horseback, carrying what appeared to be an unconscious person with them. As you can imagine, everyone jumped up eager to investigate. I never got to finish that hand." He sighed. "A bunch of us ran to the perimeter fence, and we opened the gate for this boy carrying an injured Guardian."

"With the efficiency of a finely-tuned machine, soon the unconscious Guardian was up in the medical facility receiving treatment, and the boy was wrapped in a blanket with a cup of hot tea. He'd been quiet through all of it. We'd assumed he was in shock. It never occurred to anyone to scan him, not with the injured man to treat. After all, who'd ever heard of a terror being able to maintain their sanity or solidity for minutes at a stretch? Much less playing the part of a hero?"

"When he does finally speak, he asks, 'Who's in charge here?' I answer, tell him I'm the Captain of this outpost and how impressed I am that he managed to bring the Guardian in for treatment and would he like to tell us what happened to both of them? He then looks me right in the eye, and I swear I felt a chill slide down my spine all the way down into my toes. He says to me, 'you've got to understand if you'd left me alone none of this would have been necessary.' I stupidly asked him, 'what wouldn't have been necessary, son?'"

"That's how it started. He was on the attack and Guardians were falling like leaves in autumn. Multiple sleeper darts hit him, but I couldn't say whether they had any effect. I jumped into the fray, managing to land a single blow on his neck before he knocked me unconscious. I came to sometime later, up on the roof. It was down to the two of us and that pike he had in his hand. Blood oozed from his clothes, and I remember seeing Bruoh's moonlight reflected in the puddle at his feet. He explained to me everyone was dead. I had no reason to doubt him. He said I should pass along a message for him to whoever came looking." Captain Tiine paused.

"What was this message he wanted you to share?" Bauleel asked.

Tiine ignored her question. "This special task force you're on, dealing with Terem Zebio... Does what I've described sound like your man?"

"It does. And from what I've seen of this place it looks like Terem's style too," Bauleel replied.

"Can I assume your recent and not yet altogether healed injuries are also due to a previous encounter with Terem, and perhaps this mission is a bit personal for you?" Tiine asked.

Bauleel clenched her jaw, causing pain to radiate across her face from the still-healing fractures webbing her bone. "They are, and you can." Bauleel already had their respect, but now sensed waves of awe layering into the intense emotions around her.

"Understand this: nothing we used had any effect on him," Tiine replied.

Bauleel felt everyone's eyes on her. "I appreciate your candor, but I'll be leaving today to track him down."

"He wants to live a normal life. Just to be left alone like any other average person. He said if anyone interferes with him again that he'll kill us all. And he didn't mean all of us Guardians. He deliberately twisted the pike in my chest as he explained himself. He meant *all Az'Un*."

Bauleel felt a righteous rage rise within her belly. Who did Terem think he was--threatening everything she'd worked all her long life to accomplish? She would never allow his threats to be realized. "Thank you, Captain Tiine. Let me assure you I'm not on some petty vendetta. The Chieftess and Commander Graeber and I are all of a like mind that Terem needs to be dealt with as quickly as possible." More importantly, Bauleel knew how the Core would want things resolved. Terem's desire to 'just be left alone' would never be enough for the Core.

"I hope you're right about that, Lieutenant Commander."

"And *I* hope your recovery is a speedy one. Thank you again for your generous hospitality, but we need to get going."

"Private Jarua," Bauleel addressed the short man. "Please ready two horses for Corporal Rilte and myself. We'll leave within the hour. Make sure and pack some extra grain in the saddlebags for them too."

"Yes, ma'am," Jarua inclined his head and then left.

"Master Sergeant Baryu, could you please include my departure in your message to Chieftess Raza?" Bauleel asked. "I'm not sure when I'll get the opportunity to write her again."

"Yes, Lieutenant Commander," Baryu agreed. "Is there anything else you'd like me to include?"

"Copy Commander Graeber. I'll catch his ire if he has to hear it from the Chieftess second hand."

"Will do, Lieutenant Commander," Baryu replied.

"Corporal Rilte, you're with me. Good day, Guardians." Bauleel marched into the still open medicinal supplies pantry and filled her backpack with various vials. Rilte stood by. Once she had a reasonable variety and quantity of everything she could imagine needing, she exited the pantry, pausing only long enough to nod at Master Sergeant Baryu and Sergeant Taine.

They got to the base of the staircase on the main floor when Rilte stopped her. "Can we talk about this?"

Bauleel glared at him. "You will *not* question my authority!"

"I'm not! I'm questioning your sanity. Didn't you hear what the Captain said? *Nothing* they used worked on Terem. Nothing even *slowed him down.* Shouldn't we at least wait and see how Chieftess Raza wants to handle this?"

"Trust me, I know what she'll think of the message Baryu is about to send."

"And what are we going to do when we find him? It's not like your superior negotiating skills are going win the day!"

Bauleel barked out a laugh, and pain sparked across her face. "You don't know that."

"Yeah, I think I do," Rilte exhaled, his voice sounding strangulated by his frustration. "Seriously, what's the plan?"

Bauleel glimpsed Baryu hiding at the top of the stairs around the doorway, attempting not to be seen. "I have a secret weapon," she stated and then strode off to the kitchens to locate the travel rations.

A few seconds later she heard Rilte run to catch up with her. He muttered a soft "You have *got* to be kidding me!"

Except she wasn't.

CHAPTER 6

From: Selector Brague
To: Princess Qwell
Latne: Perith Prime-Latne of the Dark Trine

Revered Transmitter of the Hegemony Princess Qwell:

I am pleased to announce that the Evaluation of possible candidates has been going more quickly than expected. The team I've assembled--including your gracious additions to my staff--to aid me in this task has exceeded my expectations by identifying inconveniences that might otherwise hinder your divine plans.

I will share for your Grace's amusement the disposition of the last two planets Evaluated. The second planet on our list, Bawna of the Bawna Minas system, had developed sudden electrical storms since our last routine planetary survey some few hundred cycles ago.

Unfortunately, these storms were too erratic and powerful to ensure a safe haven for your purposes, so we had to immediately disqualify Bawna from our Evaluations.

Surveyor Garron proposed the possibility that these storms could be caused or influenced by a newly identified species of avian whose cries seem to incite electrical storms. This may sound ridiculous, but nonetheless, I have ordered a full scientific survey of the planet and the avian creatures, just in case something of value could be weaponized for the Hegemony.

Then, upon traveling to Taloos of the Manchas system, the third planet on our list, we regrettably discovered Taloos had been strip-mined by scavengers in the not-too-distant past. Be assured that we all share in the Hegemony's horror over this atrocity. We were glad, however, for the fortuitous luck that we'd discovered such villainy so quickly after the crimes had been committed. I have sent two ships from my fleet to track down the fleeing vermin who've destroyed the previously pristine Taloos. I have also ordered a full scientific survey to determine whether the planet might yet be restored to some semblance of its former glory via current terraforming technology. You can expect their report within one cycle.

By Hegemonic law, I have attached documents to place under protection all species previously known and cataloged on Taloos. Hopefully, this will avoid a total loss of the genetic history on Taloos. Happily, I have located some specimens in my own personal lab that will be set aside for this very purpose.

I have also included documentation to start the sentencing process on the scavenging thieves, including all necessary documentation currently available. I can only hope the Hegemony will take swift and public action on this matter, with punishments that might give future aspiring raiders due pause.

On a more positive note, we are now in transit to the next planet on the list, Az'Unda of the Pleos system. After three unacceptable Evaluations, I am looking forward to a new planet to sink my scanners into. I am confident your perfect Selection will be established in short order. Be assured that my next report will yield more real candidates.

I have attached my updated schedule so you can remain informed on my progress. You will note that the unfortunate condition of the last few planets has sped up the timeline for Evaluating new planets. As always, I eagerly await any questions you might have.

Eternally indebted to be in your divine service,

Selector Brague

Upon returning to camp, Rai had gone to bed for the night, as she wanted some time to herself to process all of the new information she's learned from Guardian Graeber. She'd laid there alone in the dark of

Laan's wagon for what seemed like hours, listening to the Durmah men's voices around the campfire.

The worst part was that, after trying for months to feel at home with the Durmah Sept, Rai no longer felt like she was one of them. Rai accepted that the daunting reality of her past was something she had to keep hidden from them. Knowing there was a death sentence on her head was sobering, and she feared for the safety of Jesse and Ponar and the other Durmah, should they ever discover her secret.

Unable to sleep, Rai fished out a packet of faown, the animal sedative Jesse had given her, and listened to the forest trees eerily creak and moan as she drifted off to sleep. Predictably, a double-dose of the faown swept her away into a dreamless sleep.

Rai woke the following morning feeling more confused than she had the night before. Her head felt filled with pillow batting. Would anyone notice if she just laid there and slept the day away?

Knock, knock knock. Apparently, they would.

"Hey Rai, you awake yet?" Laan's voice came from the other side of the door, at a much more piercing volume than Rai remembered it usually being.

"Uh, yeah," Rai answered. "Just give me a second to finish dressing." Rai pushed back the bedcovers and realized that she hadn't even changed into her night-clothes last night. At least she hadn't slept in her boots.

"Sure, but the Guardian wants us to get rolling right away. We let you sleep through breakfast, saved you some even, but I'm afraid there's no more time to spare," Laan explained.

"That was sweet of you," Rai replied, pulling on a fresh tunic and pair of pants. "How far out are we from Resounding Cliffs?"

"Two, three days, depending on the weather. The Guardian says the entire eastern coastline is about to get hit hard."

"That should make Ponar happy," Rai replied as she pulled on her boots. "Perhaps those shawls of his will fetch a better price with the poor weather." Rai ran her fingers through her curls, hoping her hair didn't look too wild. Rai grabbed her travel cloak and then unlocked and opened the door. The diffuse morning sunlight shone down in a patchwork through the forest trees, still bright enough to give Rai an immediate headache.

"Are you feeling okay?" Laan asked, lending her an arm down the three-step staircase off the back of his wagon.

"Yeah, yeah," Rai replied. Evidently, the faown had some side effects Jesse had forgotten to mention, like feeling disconnected and emotionally flat. "I'm just exhausted today for some reason."

Laan gave her a critical look. "Ponar filled Meik and me in last night while you were gone. Were you able to find anything before the Guardian caught up with you?"

Rai had to stifle a groan. "No," she lied. "I looked around, but there wasn't anything there."

"I'm sorry to hear that," Laan replied, placing a friendly hand on her shoulder. "I know that had to be a huge disappointment for you."

Rai shrugged. "I think those dreams are messing with my head. I need to just forget about them and move on, you know?"

Laan nodded. "Well, do let me know if there's anything I can do to help."

Rai nodded.

"But right now I've got to get the horses hitched if we're to get moving," he continued.

"Of course," Rai replied. "Would you like some help?"

"I'll be okay. Why don't you go and eat some breakfast before we have to leave?" Laan said and then got to work readying the wagon for their daily journey.

Rai sauntered over to Ponar's wagon, noting that both his and Meik's horses were hitched and ready to go. Rai felt guilty, knowing she'd held them up.

Meik walked over from his wagon, carrying a plate laden with food. "Here's your breakfast, sleepyhead," he said, offering her the plate.

"Thanks," Rai replied, gratefully accepting the plate. She could barely smell the food due to taking faown the night before. However, she realized that she'd skipped dinner the previous evening and so must have an empty stomach.

"Not a problem," he replied. "Say, how did things go last night?"

For a moment Rai couldn't figure out what he was referring to. "Uh, fine," she replied, taking a bite of scrambled egg. "I was just tired and so decided to hit the sack early."

Meik looked confused but kept smiling. "You know, while you were asleep last night Ponar filled Laan and I in on some things," he confided. "And you must know how eager we all are to hear about what you found."

Rai felt her stomach clench. How much of the story had Ponar confided with his Uncle and cousin? It wasn't a good sign that the first thing each one of them had brought up with her was the search for clues by the lake.

"Then I'm sure you'll understand how disappointed I was to find nothing," Rai said, lying for the second time that day.

"I'm sorry to hear that, Rai. I take it that the Guardian wasn't able to confirm anything for you either?" he pressed.

Now, why would Meik, who would do almost anything to avoid talking to a Guardian himself, ask her that?

"No, we didn't even talk, if you exclude him barking orders at me to hurry up. Honestly, that guy creeps me out," Rai added.

Although her head was still foggy from the faown, and Rai now realized her enhanced senses were also a bit muted--no doubt from it as well, she sensed Meik didn't believe her. But why would he doubt her?

Meik shifted uneasily, rubbing his chin with his hand. "Yeah, he gets on my nerves too." He paused and then got a somber look on his face. "He hasn't threatened you, has he?" Meik asked quietly.

Could he have witnessed part of her interaction with Graeber? Certainly not ...

"No, no, of course not," Rai replied. "He's an absolute ass, but I doubt that's personal." Meik laughed, but Rai knew she was missing something.

As if on cue, Guardian Graeber chose that exact moment to walk around the front of Ponar's wagon. A hint of a smile at the corner of his mouth belied his otherwise stern glare.

"Oh good, you're finally awake," he said to Rai. Without waiting for a response, he turned to Meik. "I trust we're ready to go now?"

Meik nodded. "Laan should have his wagon ready to roll."

"And Ponar?"

"He's filling the last of the water bottles at the stream. It shouldn't be much longer," Meik explained.

"We can't dally any longer. Go and get Ponar. Now." the Guardian informed him.

"But we need the water. Most of our supply is exhausted," Meik replied.

"There isn't time for it. We have a long trip ahead of us today if we're to make it to the next protected camp by nightfall. You can refill your bottles when we stop to rest the horses at lunchtime."

Meik shrugged in defeat. "Fine, whatever you say. I'll go help him get the water loaded."

"Would you like me to help?" Rai offered.

"You finish eating. I'll be right back," Meik replied and then walked off towards the stream.

Guardian Graeber stayed, scrutinizing her carefully. "Is there a problem?" he asked.

Rai took the last bite of her eggs. "No, everything's fine. Why wouldn't it be?" she replied cheerily, shaking the last bits of food off of her plate for the forest creatures to feast upon.

"You skipped dinner and then slept late. Are you ill?"

"Don't be an ass," Rai replied and then walked off towards the stream to wash her plate. She suspected her response wasn't appropriately deferential to the average Guardian, but irritation wasn't a rational creature.

CHAPTER 7

THEY WERE WELL INTO MIDDAY BEFORE PONAR
dared break the silence. "So?"

Rai had been riding alongside him for miles, still
trying to work out what her encounter with the
Guardian all meant. The road had been curvy and the
pace swift, making it seem like the forest was flashing
by in a series of picture scenes to some grander story,
except Rai couldn't decipher the meaning. Although
they'd left the shelter of the massive trees in the grove
far behind, vast, dense forest yet surrounded them.

"You can't just say nothing, Rai."

He was not going to just drop it, was he?

"Like I already explained to all of you, there is
nothing to say."

"I don't believe you."

Rai sighed. "And why not?"

"Because you've been sitting there with a confused

look on your face for hours, and whatever is rattling around in that head of yours doesn't seem to be getting any easier for you. Admit it, I know you well enough to know when you're struggling with something. Why don't you open up about it and let me help?"

Rai met his earnest gaze and the temptation to be honest was undeniable. And then she remembered Graeber's warnings. Anyone who knew the truth would also be in danger. She broke eye contact, unable to ruminate further what risks she could bring to the Durmah.

"Things aren't that simple, Ponar." She stared ahead at Meik's wagon in the lead.

"Then explain it to me." He smiled, his relaxed posture an open invitation.

What could she share that would stop him from asking questions? "My water flask is empty. Can I have some from yours?"

"Sure," he answered, deftly fishing his flask out from behind his seat and passing it over to her. "You've been drinking a lot of water this morning."

Rai nodded. "I took some the faown Jesse gave me last night when I couldn't sleep, and I guess it kind of walloped me." Rai gulped down the water, downing nearly the entire contents.

"How much did you take?"

"Just one of the packets. And do I ever feel fuzzy and mellow right now. I swear, a Terror could come barreling down on us right now, and I'm not sure I would even care."

He shivered at the image, casting at her a concerned frown. "Well, no wonder you seem so out of it! You're only supposed to take a spoonful, not the entire thing! Didn't Jesse explain the dosing?"

"I'm sure she did, that doesn't mean I remembered it, as distracted as I've been. Overdoing it explains why my head hurts so badly today."

"*And* why you overslept. And possibly also why you're so confused."

Rai felt the weight of his regard settle upon her like stone pavers, and her breath caught in her throat.

"That must be it," Rai coughed, breathless.

"Could be," Ponar shrugged, evidently not buying the faown was to blame. "I'd still feel better about it if you'd share with me what happened back there at the lake."

"Fine, fine. If it'll make you happy." Rai ran fingers through her hair, catching them in the knotted curls.

Just then Guardian Graeber rode up to them, his horse covered with a thin sheet of sweat. "We'll be stopping at the crest of the next hill. Rest the horses for one hour, then we will resume our pace." Without waiting for a reply, he shook the reins, a single, slight motion, and his mount spun off towards Laan's wagon behind them.

"He's chatty today," Rai said. "How about I tell you

everything after lunch, so I'm not worried he's listening in?"

"Of course." Ponar refocused on the road ahead, affording Rai a brief respite.

Her commitment to discuss the details of yesterday appeared to satisfy his curiosity, at least for the moment. They traveled up the next hill to the designated stopping point in silence.

Ponar pulled his wagon alongside Meik's as there was plenty of room. Meik was already prepping feed bags for his horses. Rai marveled at the view from this rise, which stretched for miles over the dense forest. She watched Laan pull his wagon up close behind Meik and Ponar's wagons.

"I spied a stream down the hill a bit," Ponar said as he climbed down from his perch to the ground. "You interested in helping me fill these water bottles?"

"Sure, it'd be nice to move around a bit." Rai climbed down the wagon and joined Ponar.

"Hey Meik," Ponar asked, "Could you and Laan get my horses fed and watered while Rai and I go and fill the last of the water jugs?"

"We'll do that. I'm quite happy to let someone else help you lug those around," Meik replied.

As Ponar dug out the last four water jugs that still needed filling, Rai watched Guardian Graeber, who hadn't yet dismounted, sit and fiddle with one of his devices. As they set out towards the stream, he met her gaze.

"Don't go far, you two."

"Is something wrong?" Ponar asked.

"I don't think so. My scanner was working fine just a few minutes ago, but now it's behaving inconsistently."

"Huh?" Ponar prompted.

"The topology of the area reports per usual, but no life signs, not even ours, are registering ..." Guardian Graeber shrugged it off and placed the scanner back into one of his vest pockets. "I'm going to patrol the perimeter and make sure there's nothing out of the ordinary out there. Be prepared to leave within the hour." He leaned forward into the stirrups and his horse surged forward as if responding to his urgency.

"That's what happens when you rely too much on technology," Meik called after the Guardian, who paid no heed as he disappeared into the tree line. "At least now he's doing his job proper."

Rai moved closer to Ponar. "Let's get moving," Rai whispered, not wanting to listen to another of Meik's rants.

Ponar dipped his head in agreement. "We'll be back," he called out to Laan and Meik. Rai followed him down the hill towards the stream.

The sunny day held not a cloud in the sky, the crystalline horizon a rare, but breathtaking sight in the distance. "It's sure beautiful out here in the northern forests, so different from the foggy coastlines. You can see all the way to the horizon," Rai said.

"I'd have to agree with you on that one. For instance, from this vantage, I can see even more clearly how good you are at dodging questions and avoiding talking about what's on your mind," Ponar replied.

Anxiety gripped her abdomen, churning her stomach contents. "What, I can't admire the scenery?"

"Sure you can," he replied. "But now we're alone, so I figured you could get back to telling me all about what happened at the lake yesterday."

"All right, I will. Let's see, I'll start from where you left when the Guardian led you back to the camp yesterday. Naturally, I bathed first."

They reached the stream. "It's too shallow here to fill the jugs. Let's walk down the bank a little way and see if we can find a better spot," Ponar said.

"Are you sure that's wise?" Rai asked, looking back up the hill towards the Durmah wagons. "We've already gone so far I can't see the wagons."

"The Guardian said the area was safe, and we can't fill them here. It's just too shallow. I'm sure we won't have to go much farther."

"Okay," Rai replied.

Ponar led the way downstream. "Every so often as the stream hits obstacles in the terrain it tends to form small but deep pools. See, right up there, you can see how the stream widens slightly before cascading over those rocks?" he pointed.

"Yes, I can."

"Well, it's also deepest at those locations," he explained.

"I didn't realize you were so well-versed in forestry," Rai said.

"When you're on the road all the time, you have to be. Actually, if you pay attention you can pick up on a lot of useful information from the Guardians," Ponar replied. They arrived at the spot he'd pointed to a minute ago. "Here we go, see how much deeper it is here?"

He didn't know how right he was regarding the Guardians, Rai thought to herself. "Yes, it seems obvious now that you've pointed it out, I just never thought of it that way."

Ponar crouched at the side of the stream and submerged the first of his jugs. "What happened after you cleaned up at the lake?"

Rai followed his lead with her containers. The ice-cold water made holding the jug opening underwater difficult. "Well, I searched the area of the mound, and didn't find anything out of the ordinary," she lied. "The Guardian returned while I was digging around in the dirt. When he asked, I told him I'd seen something shiny under there. I don't think he believed me. All the way back to camp he lectured me on the dangers of sticking my nose into places it didn't belong." That was what, the third lie she'd told today so far?

Ponar hefted the full container from the stream

and closed the lid tightly before sliding the next one under the water to fill. "That's all that happened?"

"Yeah," Rai replied. "I guess I was just so disappointed over not finding anything that I haven't felt like talking about it."

Ponar's brow furrowed. "So how come I don't believe you?"

Rai finished filling her first container and started on the second one, her numb fingers aching. "What else can I say?"

Ponar finished filling his second jug and tightened the lid shut. He carried both jugs away from the stream, setting them down on the loamy earth. Ponar wiped his hands dry on his tunic, watching Rai as she finished filling her containers and then carried them over, setting them down next to his.

"I don't believe you," he murmured. "You're not telling me everything."

"How can I convince you?" Rai asked. She too wiped her hands dry on her trousers and then rubbed them together for warmth.

"It's not what you're saying, it's how you're acting. Something just isn't ringing true to me, but I can't quite put my finger on it," Ponar replied. "Here, give me your hands." He held out his hands to take hers.

"No," Rai said, remembering what Guardian Graeber had said about not touching others. She took a step backward.

"Let me warm them up," he insisted, a confused look on his face. "I don't bite."

Rai sensed her reaction had offended him and heightened his suspicions of her story. She didn't want to risk alienating her friend and ally. She didn't have enough of those to spare right now.

And then Rai had a thought. Graeber had said that physical touch intensified what she could sense from others, but he hadn't stated that it was only one-way. What if she could push an emotion or thought to Ponar through that same contact, to reassure him that indeed nothing happened at the lake?

She held out her hands to him. "Sorry, I guess I just remembered Jesse asking us to keep our distance, and I don't want to disappoint her."

"I doubt Jesse would disapprove of me warming up your hands. Besides, it's not like there's anyone around watching us right now," he replied.

Ponar stepped forward and took her hands in his, rubbing them gently. Rai felt the warmth of his hands as the shades of his emotions washed over her. His concern for her was palpable, intertwined with his disbelief. Sifting through the layers, Rai recognized that he was still attracted to her but worked to hide it every time they were together. She felt guilty and began to withdraw, knowing her intrusion into his thoughts for the violation it was.

"There!" he exclaimed. "You keep looking almost, what? Guilty? Yes, that's it! Every time you say nothing happened at the lake you get this guilty look on your face."

Rai took a deep breath. "It's just that I'm so disappointed. And I do feel guilty for making you think that we'd find something out there that could answer why I keep having these nightmares." Rai focused on an image of her sitting by the lake, disappointed and pouting because she hadn't found anything. And then she gently pushed the image towards him.

Rai watched his eyes glaze over for a moment. When his eyes refocused, Rai realized she'd made a huge mistake. "What in the world was that?" he demanded, now gripping her hands tightly.

Rai mentally kicked herself for her botched attempt. Graeber was right. She had no idea what she was doing with her abilities, and she had been a fool to expose herself in this way to Ponar. "I don't know," Rai lied again. She could just imagine how angry Graeber would be when he inevitably found out about this. "Shouldn't we be getting back now?" She tried to pull her hands away, but Ponar wouldn't let go.

"Who is Graeber, and what does he want you to keep secret?" Ponar demanded.

Panicking, Rai yanked her hands away, desperately hoping it would break the mental connection she'd opened. Guardian Graeber was not going to be amused.

"What just happened?" Ponar asked, rubbing his forehead with his hands, his expression pained.

"You started spouting some crazy talk," Rai replied. "Why don't you explain to *me* what happened?"

"No, no, I'm NOT crazy," Ponar asserted. "I can't explain how that just happened, but I know it was something real. Someone called Graeber warned you to keep quiet, am I right? Wait a moment! The Guardian's name is Graeber, isn't it?" Waves of anger radiated from him.

Crap, crap, crap! Rai had no idea how to dig herself out from this one. In trying to reassure Ponar, she'd instead managed to open up a two-way conduit between their thoughts. At least it seemed breaking physical contact had broken their connection.

"You can't even answer me, can you?" he asked. Rai stared up at him, at a total loss for words.

"You must be so scared of him," Ponar continued. Waves of sympathy overrode his anger. "And I don't blame you for that. But you don't have to be afraid of him or allow him to threaten you into silence. You have to know that your family will protect you, even from him."

Rai shook her head, eyes watering. "That's just it: you can't. No one can." Rai felt a hot tear break free and run down her cheek. She turned and picked up her water containers by the handles, one in each hand. "You see, it's not Guardian Graeber who's the problem. It's me. It's who I am, and who I've been. And as much as I try and work it out in my head, I can't figure out a way to stop being me!" Rai replied, her voice building to a crescendo. It felt good to express how she felt, Graeber's warnings be damned.

"You don't have to do it alone. I'm here for you. Jesse's here for you. The entire Durmah Sept stands with you," he replied softly.

"But you won't be," Rai replied, a sad, resigned smile reinforced her argument. Rai then brushed past him and headed back towards the wagons. Back to her life of lies.

She heard him hurry to catch up with her. "You don't know that, Rai. Durmah will stand by you, regardless of who you were before you were adopted."

"You say that now," Rai muttered, walking even faster.

"Hey, slow down!" he called. "We need to talk about this!"

Rai stopped and rounded on him, ready to begin a new tirade.

That's when she saw *it*, across the stream from them. The hair on the back of her neck stood on end as she took in the shiny, black, hulking carapace poised motionless. It was no more than, what? Five meters away from them? Less?

Rai felt the water jug from her left-hand land on her foot as she reflexively reached for the dart gun she generally kept hidden in her pants pocket. She felt the color drain from her face as she realized that the weapon was still in Laan's wagon. She'd been too sleepy this morning to remember to take it with her.

Not that it would have mattered, the thing was undoubtedly impervious to such a small-caliber weapon. Wait, what was she thinking? It's not like she could attack a Juggernaut, lest the Hegemony decide to eliminate their colony in retaliation.

Ponar stopped, facing her. "What's wrong?"

Rai didn't dare take her eyes off of it. "Juggernaut," she whispered, not a doubt in her mind.

Ponar stared at her in disbelief, shaking his head. "But that's impossible. Where ... ?" he asked. Rai pointed, and he turned around until his eyes fixed on the alien creature. "It's not moving," he whispered, his face white as a bleached sheet. "Are you sure...?"

Surely it saw them, she reasoned. At this distance, it also heard everything they'd said. Yet it sat there motionless, all two arms, four legs, and three hulking segments encased in a glossy, black, spiny exoskeleton. She couldn't detect any movement in the eyes, which were like large, multifaceted black gems. It reminded her vaguely of a beetle. A very, very large beetle. The wind kicked up, and Rai watched the highest branches brush the shoulder and back of the creature. Rai estimated the trees stood at least twenty-five feet tall.

"Yes. I recommend we move away, slowly," Rai whispered.

Moving with deliberate caution, Rai picked up her water bottles and started walking back up the stream. Ponar followed, matching her pace. Neither one took their eyes off of the black behemoth. Every step seemed to take forever. What was it doing? Thinking? After they'd doubled their distance to the creature, Rai hoped they might even escape. Perhaps it hadn't noticed them, after all? Maybe it slept?

Stop / Cease retreat / I am ... curious.

Rai froze, taking a yet closer look at the Juggernaut. Nothing had changed, and yet Rai felt the undeniable, itchy presence of the Juggernaut lurking in her mind. The images and feelings came all at once from the hulk, but the meaning was clear to Rai. For some reason, it found her fascinating.

Ponar looked at her in confusion, and then back at the Juggernaut, and then back at her. "What is it?" he whispered.

"Keep going, and get the others on the road. I'll catch up in a minute," Rai replied, dropping the whisper.

"That's out of the question. I'm not leaving you here with *that*. Besides, it could be asleep," Ponar whispered back.

Rai met his gaze. "It's not asleep. It wants to talk."

"That's ridiculous. For all we know it could have been dead for a hundred years now," Ponar replied. "We might be staring at a mummified corpse."

Rai felt the Juggernaut pushing, nudging her again. *"No,"* she pushed back, suddenly reminded of Graeber reading her yesterday. *"Whatever you want to know, you come out and ask nicely."* She said this out loud and clearly within her mind to the alien.

Ponar looked at her like she'd lost her mind. Maybe I have, Rai considered. The surreal nature of the past day had continued to slip into dream time potential.

A loud exhalation, which Rai interpreted as irritation, was the first definitive sign of life from the Juggernaut. Abruptly the creature moved towards them, with what seemed an impossible speed for such a mass carried upon its four hind legs. As it crossed the stream with no seeming effort, water splashed everywhere, and Rai could have sworn a few fish leaped out of its path. Ponar fled backward, recoiling from the unspoken might of the creature, falling back over a large rock. Rai did her best to hold her ground, guessing that if it wanted her dead, there wasn't a damned thing she could do about it.

The Juggernaut came to a stop a few feet from them, half in and half out of the water. Rai guessed they were within easy reach of its long arms. If it took any notice of Ponar, she couldn't tell.

Do not challenge the might of the Hegemony, worthless primate child! / I will ask as I deem fit / You will fulfill my curiosity.

Rai was amazed that the images and words could be so clear and yet happen all at once. "How do you do that?" she asked out loud. The ideas *all at once* and *without speech* were woven into her meaning.

The Juggernaut lowered his head even with hers, bringing them face to face. Curiosity had gotten the better of them both. From this angle, Rai could see a brilliant sigil in orange and purple tones which was somehow imprinted into the spike-rimmed carapace behind its head. Whether it pulsed in time with its heart or temper, Rai could not tell.

Without speech? The appalling ethnocentric universe-view of your species never ceases to amaze! / Sufficient intellects, unlike yours, are not limited to single lines of communication / There is a larger question / I have observed you here with the other / Fulfill my curiosity.

The length and intensity of his message left Rai feeling a tad nauseated. She suspected allowing a Juggernaut to watch her clumsily attempt to use her enhanced abilities was also on Graeber's list of what not to do? "What are you even asking?" she yelled into its face.

I had examined many specimens of your species / Never before was this talent found / You will explain to me how it is that you are unique in this way?

His question drove home all of her frustrations. It was unfortunate enough not to know who she was, and to know she had bizarre untapped abilities she wasn't supposed to be using, but to have this alien Juggernaut demand an explanation was the last straw.

If sanity was a thing one could feel snap, would this brittle wildness be how it felt?

"How the fuck should I know? You're my superior in every way, so why don't *you* tell *me*? And besides, why in the entire universe would you ever stoop to asking for *my* lowly assistance?" Rai screamed.

How terribly amusing / You don't know, do you? / Quite insecure about it too / Possibly ridiculed--tormented--shunned by your own kind, yes? / So curious.

"And you apparently love to be right all of the time. Can our analysis end here?" Rai shouted at the alien, who stood motionless.

She sensed the Juggernaut grin.

No / Curiosity must be resolved for the greater good of the Hegemony / Further research is indicated / Cause or causes for the abnormality shall be identified and isolated.

Rai caught an image from him of corridor upon corridor lined with containment cells: his private laboratory of specimens.

Rai recoiled in horror. "Thanks for the offer, but I'll pass."

At that moment an explosion went off in the distance, downhill from their location. Debris flew through the air, plinking audibly off of trees, the Juggernaut's exoskeleton and into the stream. Smoke poured into the air all around them. Rai heard an alarm sound and then saw a small orange light begin flashing on the Juggernaut's left forearm.

"Aw, that's a shame. Looks like you have more important things to take care of right now," Rai continued.

The Juggernaut depressed a series of keys on a touchpad that was integrated into his right forearm. Rai wondered if the embedding of such hardware was painful or time-consuming.

Both, but well worth the time and energy, I assure you / I will investigate the explosion / Then return to collect you / Await my return / Curiosity will be satisfied.

"Yeah, okay. I'll wait right here like the good little inferior species I am."

Go ahead, run / Wherever you go, I will find you / This world is small / Won't even be a challenge.

With that final thought, the Juggernaut pivoted and crashed off in the direction of the explosion.

Great, Rai thought to herself. Not only does the *Core* want me dead, now a *Juggernaut* wants me in his personal petting and gutting zoo. Could today get any better?

Standing up from behind the rock he'd fallen behind earlier, Ponar walked over to her. "Do you think it's gone for good?" he asked.

"I doubt that," Rai picked up her water containers.

"Then we should leave before he returns," Ponar replied.

"I couldn't agree more," Rai replied.

They ran as fast as they could, considering that they were both carrying full water jugs uphill. They arrived back at the wagons covered in sweat and gasping for air.

Instead of finding the others eating lunch, Meik, Laan and Guardian Graeber were all standing there awaiting their return. Meik and Laan took the water bottles from them and loaded them into the wagons.

"You two all right?" Guardian Graeber asked.

They both nodded. "There was ... Juggernaut," Rai gasped between breaths.

"Yes, we know," Guardian Graeber replied. "I came upon them during my patrol and sabotaged one of their transport craft so they'd hopefully be too busy fixing it to notice us moving through the area."

"Why didn't you pick them up on your ... whatever that thing is," Meik asked.

"They must be using a dampening field of some sort," Guardian Graeber explained. "I assume they didn't want to be observed doing ... whatever it is they're doing."

"Too late," Rai replied, coughing.

"We ran into one. It spoke to us, to Rai actually," Ponar explained.

"Spoke?" Guardian Graeber asked. She nodded. "It had a translator?"

"I spoke just like this. And I don't know what it was doing, but I heard it," Rai said. Guardian Graeber looked at her in disbelief. "Look, I can't explain it, but that thing said it was coming back for me, so I'd like to go now!"

"Yes. If we push hard we might be able to reach

Resounding Cliffs late tonight," Guardian Graeber replied.

"Won't the city gates be closed for curfew by then?" Meik asked.

"I'll see that they make a special exception for us when we arrive," Guardian Graeber replied. "Let's get rolling. Push your teams as hard as you dare."

The Durmah climbed aboard their wagons and were off. Meik was at the lead, and Ponar's wagon brought up the rear.

Guardian Graeber brought his stallion up along-side at a fast trot, matching their pace. "Tell me the truth. I guess you pissed off the Juggernaut?" he asked Rai.

She shrugged. "I don't think so. The creature was curious about me. It thought I was unique. But he didn't seem angry, per se."

"Wonderful," he replied sarcastically. "But were you rude to him?"

Rai shook her head, frowning.

"You *did* yell at him, Rai," Ponar reminded her. "A couple of times."

"Well sure, but I really don't think that offended him," Rai replied. "My volume was a total non-issue."

Guardian Graeber scrubbed his face with his hand. "You remember that Juggernauts hate humans, right? And they're just looking for excuses to wipe out our colonies?"

"But he wouldn't destroy the entire colony because

I yelled at him, would he?" Rai asked, horrified. "Would he?!?"

Guardian Graeber shrugged as if to say, how was he to know the whims of the Juggernauts? "Nah, after all, he's *curious* about you now. And I've got to congratulate you on that. You're keeping out of trouble, just as I directed."

Although his sarcasm stung, she supposed she'd earned it. "So what should I do now?"

"Run away, like we're doing. Except you might have to go a lot farther than the rest of us," Guardian Graeber replied. He then kneed his horse into a gallop and rode forward to the front of the line.

"And you wonder why I thought something was going on between you two?" Ponar asked, shaking his head in frustration. "You ready to fill me in yet?"

"I'll make you a deal," Rai replied. "We all make it safe to Resounding Cliffs without the Juggernauts blasting us off the road or dragging me off to some lab zoo, and I'll tell you everything I know that makes any sense at all."

"It's always later with you, isn't it?" Ponar rolled his eyes. "But sure, I'll take you up on that."

Rai turned around, watching the sky and road for any sign of the Juggernaut returning, wondering to herself just how far could be far enough to outrun her past and the Juggernaut combined.

CHAPTER 8

#BEGIN TRANSMISSION#
#ROUTING CODE: ALL CORE IDS, VARIOUS
COM LOCATIONS#
#ENCRYPTION: HIGH#
#PRIORITY: HIGH#

General Alert to the Core,

I'm afraid I am the bearer of dark tidings. The Juggernaut are on Az'Unda.

While escorting a group of merchants along the Northern Road, we encountered a group of Juggernaut near mile marker 117, which is about a day's travel from Resounding Cliffs. They were undetected by my scanner due to the probable use of a dampening field. I am currently en route to Resounding Cliffs with said merchants and expect to arrive late tonight, barring further encounters with the Juggernaut.

Although it's possible that the Juggernaut or other Hegemony forces have visited us in this manner before, I'm sure you all agree with my concerns that this sighting does not bode well.

From what I observed, they were taking flora and fauna samples and running diagnostic tests on our soil and water. I hope whatever they're looking for, they don't find it, and soon lose interest in our world.

However, not knowing what they are looking for, it's impossible to predict their behavior. I can assume that any formal communications from their envoys would have been forwarded to all members of the Core, correct? That no such messages have arrived, and that the Hegemony doesn't even consider us important enough to open a dialogue with before violating the terms of our colony charter, well ...

I think we should meet, as a group and in person, to decide how we should best deal with this new threat.

Suggestions?

Graeber

#END TRANSMISSION#

#BEGIN TRANSMISSION#
#ROUTING CODE: ALL COM LOCATIONS#
#PRIORITY: HIGH#

Fellow Az'Un,

Hegemony Juggernauts have been sighted on our planet. We do not yet know the intent of their visit, but please take heart that your Matriarchs are working to establish a dialogue even as I write this.

As a protective measure to our people, I am declaring martial law, effective immediately. All persons are to stay within city limits at all times and within their Sept halls from dusk to dawn. Travel between cities and towns will be limited to emergency situations. Those Septs who work outside city walls are to remain indoors, restricting all exposure outside except to care for livestock.

In the unlikely event that you encounter Juggernaut representatives in your area, do not draw attention to yourselves. Avoid eye contact and do not speak to them unless spoken to. It is imperative that we show them all due respect as leaders of the Hegemony. Historically, even slight irritations have been met with overwhelming brute force.

Please post these warnings in your Sept halls and community meeting areas. Be sure that all citizens, both young and old, understand the risks involved.

Stay vigilant,

Chieftess Raza of the Guardian Sept

#END TRANSMISSION#

THE DURMAH TRAVELED UNTIL LATE THAT NIGHT. They finally reached the massive, closed city gates of Resounding Cliffs in the wee hours of the morning. Guardian Graeber had a brief discussion with the city guards and somehow was able to convince them to allow the Durmah entry despite the late---or should that be early? ---hour. The gates swung open, and they were met by a small contingent of armed Guardians who escorted them into the city. Ever watchful of potential dangers lurking outside the city walls, the Guardian's eyes and scanners fixated on penetrating the surrounding darkness. It wasn't until she heard the gates shut behind them that Rai allowed herself to believe that they'd actually, at least for the moment, avoided being scooped up by the Juggernaut.

Rai let out a breath she hadn't realized she'd been holding, pulling her cloak tightly around her shoulders. Between being afraid of being captured by the Juggernaut and the long trip, Rai was bone tired.

"Yeah, I didn't think we'd make it either," Ponar said. "I kept looking up, expecting to see one of their ships bearing down on us."

"I doubt they've forgotten about us if that's what you're getting at," Rai replied.

A Guardian motioned to Ponar to stop the wagon. He did as requested, pulling over to the side of the road. Rai looked back and saw Laan and Meik following behind.

Ponar tied off the reins and clambered down to the ground. "Well, it's not like we even know what they're doing here. They'll be too busy doing whatever it is Juggernaut do to bother seeking you out."

Rai climbed the three steps down from the wagon, relieved to feel the firm cobblestones of the city street under her feet. If only her fate could feel so secure. She watched one of the Guardians inspect the outside of Ponar's wagon, shining a bright lantern over every crevice. Rai wondered what exactly the Guardian was looking for.

"Well, that's something you don't see every day!" Meik exclaimed as he and Laan joined Rai and Ponar. "I thought Guardians were forbidden to open city gates at night. Not that I'm not grateful, mind you. Better off behind city walls any night, if you ask me."

Not like anyone asked you, Rai thought to herself. "But now that we are in, what're our odds of finding nice warm beds at this hour?" Rai asked, her yawn sneaking up on her and distorting her words.

"Superb," Laan replied. Rai noted the dark circles under his eyes. "Cheote Waystation is one of the larger ones and not far from here. We're regulars, so they shouldn't mind us showing up at this late hour."

"Yup, we just have to wait until the Guardians finish their inspections and we'll be on our way," Meik said.

Rai looked around and saw Guardian Graeber in a

heated discussion with one of the other Guardians. Finally, the city Guardian shrugged and shook his head, and then walked back into the Guardian's Sept house looking none too happy. Guardian Graeber walked back over to the Durmah.

"I have to get clearance for our trip back to Raven's Call, but plan to leave tomorrow," he informed them.

Rai wished she could talk to him and find out what was going on. Did the city Guardians have news on the Juggernauts' movements? She imagined them swooping down from the sky in one of their big ships, and shivered.

"Clearance?" Meik asked. "What do you mean?"

"Because of the Juggernaut presence, the Guardian Chieftess declared martial law. All travel is being strictly regulated," Guardian Graeber explained.

Laan shrugged. "We can always stay here a few days. There's really no rush for us to get back to the Sept house in Raven's Call."

Guardian Graeber crossed his arms, his face in strict school teacher mode. "That's where you're wrong. We don't know why the Juggernaut are here, or for how long. It could be days, or it could be years--we have no way of knowing. I believe it's in the best interest of you and your Sept to reunite you with them. Besides, I have other business to attend to near Raven's Call, so it's on my way."

"But won't it be dangerous to travel with the Juggernaut out there?" Rai asked. She also wondered if his 'other' business could have anything to do with her, but certainly wasn't going to ask that in front of the other Durmah.

"To a degree, yes, which is why I feel you should return home as quickly as possible. Staying here won't guarantee your safety from the Juggernaut either," Graeber replied, looking right at Rai. She tried to sense something, anything, from Graeber, but he was quiet as a rock.

Rai wanted to ask him outright where exactly would be safe but knew this wasn't the time.

"Where will you be staying tonight?" Guardian Graeber asked.

"Cheote Waystation," Meik replied.

"Good. Try to get some sleep, and we'll leave tomorrow once you and the horses are rested," Guardian Graeber responded.

His eyes met hers for a mere moment. *"Say nothing, to anyone,"* Rai felt the unvoiced words imprint into her mind and linger as if somehow the thought alone could bind her tongue. He then turned and stomped off towards the Guardian Sept Hall.

As Rai watched him disappear through the front doors, she felt oddly alone, stripped of his irascible yet secure presence.

The other Guardians followed him to the Hall, having finished their inspection of the Durmah wagons. A male Guardian approached them. He wore a long, hooded cloak, and Rai couldn't make out his face in the darkness.

"Durmah, you are free to go now," was all he said. He turned and followed the others back inside without awaiting a response.

"'Bout time," Meik replied, not waiting for the Guardian to get out of earshot. "I don't know about all of you, but I can't ever manage to fall asleep once the sun rises. Let's hurry up and hope we can get settled at the Waystation before then."

They mounted the wagons and traveled down the main street of the city. The road was broad and paved with smooth river rocks interspersed with the cobblestones. This street also had separate walkways on each side that were lit with regularly spaced lampposts. The smoky flames from the lamps were almost hypnotic, especially to Rai's tired mind.

"What's that sound?" Rai asked. "It's like a quiet, dull roar."

"That's the ocean," Ponar explained. "Resounding Cliffs is named for the nearby crags that overlook the sea. This main street leads to the Temple, which sits at the edge of those same cliffs."

"It sounds beautiful," Rai replied.

"It is. Hopefully, we'll get a chance to show you before we have to leave tomorrow. This city dates back to the first days of humans on this planet. In daylight, you can see most of the city and the range of settlement structures dating back to the early colony days."

About ten minutes down the street they reached the Cheote Waystation. Laan went inside and returned a few moments later with what appeared to be the night innkeeper, who unlocked the doors to the courtyard and motioned them inside. They were greeted by a sleepy-eyed stable master who was so tired he didn't even bother with greeting them but instead went straight to work caring for the also exhausted horses.

"Our horses are going to need more than one night to recover from this last push," Laan advised.

"I agree, but we'll see if that Guardian will listen to us. He seems determined to get us home," Ponar replied.

Rai opened her mouth to say something witty and rude about Graeber and found that the words wouldn't come. *Say nothing?* Had he somehow influenced her behavior? Rai resolved to find out, right after she slapped him at the next convenient opportunity.

The innkeeper motioned them inside. "I'm afraid the kitchen is shut down for the night. I can offer some beer, wine, and fresh bread or sweet rolls if you'd like." As they walked through the tavern section of the building, Rai was surprised to see that this Waystation was designed much the same way as the Durmah one in Kiya's Grace.

"No thanks, ma'am, although that's very kind of you," Meik answered. "I think all we'd like to do is sleep."

"Let me grab your room keys then," she replied, pausing at the main bar. "As we weren't expecting you I'm not sure we have enough rooms free. Do you mind sharing?"

"No, no, of course not," Meik replied. "We've been sleeping in wagons for weeks now. I'm sure whatever you've got available will feel luxurious in comparison." Rai rolled her eyes. Had he'd intended that as a compliment?

"Then wait here just one moment, please," she replied, forcing a smile. They did as requested and the innkeeper disappeared into the kitchen.

"Well, isn't this a nice coincidence!" came an all too familiar voice from behind them. *Fantastic!* And here she'd thought her day couldn't get any worse.

"Somnu!" Meik and Laan exclaimed and turned to greet him. Rai watched these old friends exchange hugs, and wondered what it was that made her distrust the Tinker so entirely.

Ponar dropped his bag and shook their old friend's hand. "Imagine, running into you again so soon!"

"Yes, what luck!" Tinker Somnu replied. "Why don't you all have a seat here with me," he motioned to a nearby table covered with maps, "and tell me what you're doing rolling into town at this hour?"

"We'd love to," Meik began, "but only for a moment. Hey, what are you doing with all of these maps?"

"Oh, just a bit of research," Somnu replied. "If you're not up for it right now, why don't you get some rest and we can catch up over breakfast--or lunch if you'd rather. It's not like there's any rush."

"It'll be lunch for me," Ponar replied. "And let me tell you, you are not going to believe what we went through to get here!"

Rai shifted nervously, realizing that the Durmah were likely to recount everything to their good friend and confidant Tinker Somnu. Rai wondered if she could talk Ponar into keeping her interchange with the Juggernaut secret. Only he and Guardian Graeber knew about that, as there hadn't been time or opportunity to discuss it with Meik or Laan. Rai hoped Guardian Graeber would wake them all up early with orders to leave immediately just so she could avoid talking to Somnu.

The innkeeper emerged from the kitchen and walked over. "You're in luck. We have two rooms available at the moment. Each is set up for two singles. Will that be a problem?" she asked, looking at Rai.

"If you prefer, Rai, Ponar could stay with me," Somnu offered. "I have a bed I'm not using anyway."

And leave you alone to grill him? Not a chance! "We'll be okay, won't we, Ponar? Besides, we're likely to sleep away most of the day, and I'm sure you don't want to be tiptoeing around your room all morning to keep from waking him up," Rai replied, smiling sleepily.

Rai felt an odd prickling sensation run up her back and neck, causing her hair to stand on end. She recognized it at once: someone was trying to invade her feelings, her thoughts. Rai looked at the innkeeper, who appeared exhausted and bored. Not a likely candidate for the Core, Rai thought. She looked around the room but didn't see anyone else lurking in the corners. That just left one other option besides the Durmah: their old friend Tinker Somnu.

Ponar shot her a puzzled look but wasn't about to protest out loud. Rai smiled back, thinking of how tired she felt. Somnu raised an eyebrow, looking both surprised and a bit put-off by her reply. "You're sure? It wouldn't be any bother," Somnu replied.

Ponar picked his bag up off the floor and slung it back over his shoulder. "Thanks for the offer, but she's got a good point. I wouldn't sleep as well wondering if I was keeping you from something."

"If you insist. Just remember that I'm in room fourteen--in case Rai kicks you out for snoring too loudly!" Somnu replied, inciting weak smiles out of everyone but Rai and the innkeeper.

Fear gripped her, slithering like a snake through her belly. Rai knew she'd better do her best not to think or say anything, so she avoided looking at Somnu and instead busied herself adjusting her weighty cloak. If she was to believe Graeber, the entire Core shared this ability along with their mutual hatred of her.

"We're ready to head up now. Is the room ready?" Rai asked the innkeeper, anxious to end the conversation.

"It is, Mistress Durmah. If you'd like to follow me?" she asked.

"We'll be up for a little while," Meik said. "Laan and I will give Somnu the short story tonight, and let you two fill him in on the rest tomorrow."

"You bet," Ponar replied.

"See you in a few hours!" Rai said to Meik, Laan and Somnu. She felt the fluttering touch in her mind again and thought of the first cheery and meaningless thing that came to her mind; cleaning the sclern gore from their wagons after fleeing the hordes along the Northern Pass.

They followed the innkeeper to upstairs in the back of the room and down a hall to a room with a number five chiseled into the door. The innkeeper unlocked and opened the door, and then handed Rai the key. "Sleep well. I'll make sure the staff knows to not disturb you."

Rai walked into the room, noting that it was a bit less pleasant than the guest rooms back at the Durmah Waystation in Kiya's Grace. The room was small, with the two single beds pressed up against opposite walls, and a small window at the far end, with a table and chair arranged beneath. There were no decorations on the walls unless you counted coat pegs, and the blankets on the beds were dark blue heavy woolens. A single, unlit candle graced the table.

"Thank you, ma'am," Ponar replied. "I hope your night passes well." He shut the door behind them.

Rai dropped her knapsack onto the floor beside the table and hung up her cloak. She reached up and drew the curtains closed, blocking the diffuse, glowing light from the street lanterns below. The quiet darkness of the small space offered an illusion of safety Rai desperately craved.

Ponar lit a match, surprising Rai and causing her to jump. "Sorry about that," he said, leaning forward to light the candle, brushing his arm against hers in the cramped quarters. "You seem a bit on edge. Do you want to talk about it?"

Say nothing, to anyone. Graeber's words echoed again in her mind. "I don't even know where to start," Rai replied, collapsing down onto the closer bed. "I'm sure with a good night's rest I'll feel better in the morning--wait, afternoon. *Whatever.*" Rai rolled back against the wall, anxieties about the Juggernaut, Tinker Somnu, Guardian Graeber, and the Core fighting for dominance in her mind. She rubbed her fingers against her temples, desperate to calm down.

"I'm certain you will," Ponar replied, hanging up his cloak and travel bag on two of the pegs. "I know I will." He sat down on the opposite bed and removed his boots, vigorously wriggling his freed toes. "You want to explain why you were so adamant with Somnu that I stay with you?"

Rai held her tongue, not sure of what to say. She'd grown to trust Ponar and had almost managed to see past their mutual, if silent and unexpressed, attraction to each other. Almost.

"Well, I somehow doubt it's because of my charming wit and good looks," Ponar continued. Rai chuckled and wondered if Ponar noticed the panicked edge to her mood. "Look, you know you can trust me, don't you?" he asked, leaning forward, elbows perched on his knees.

"Of course I do," Rai replied. "It's just, besides that Guardian, only you and I know what happened back there with the Juggernaut. Until I can understand it a bit more, I'd rather not discuss it with anyone else. Does that make sense?"

"But don't you think talking about it might help?" Ponar replied.

Rai shook her head. "I need some time to think it over on my own, that's all." She ran her hand along the blanket, trying to flatten a puckered crease.

"Why do I get the impression you're waiting to talk about this with that Guardian first?"

Rai met his gaze, realizing she should have expected this question. "Why would you say that? I told everyone that nothing happened back at the lake." Rai rolled to her side on the bed, hoping to avoid further questions.

"You can't go to sleep wearing your boots. Let me help you with those." Ponar knelt next to her bed and pulled off her boots one at a time. "I can't speak for my uncle or cousin, but I didn't believe you then, and I don't believe you now. I guess the Guardian caught up with you and threatened you. Am I right?" he asked.

"No, no, he didn't threaten me," Rai replied. Well, not *exactly*.

"But he did catch you snooping around the mound?" Ponar pulled off her other boot and placed it next to the other one at the foot of her bed.

"I didn't say that, Ponar. You're twisting my words around!"

Ponar reached up and brushed a lock of hair away from her face, and then rested his hand on hers. This contact opened a conduit between them, sending a shiver down Rai's spine. His concern for her washed over her like a series of waves, pushing and pulling her deeper into his thoughts.

"Meik and Laan might buy this act, but I don't, and I'm not going to, especially after how the Guardian talked to you after we ran into the Juggernaut out there. I'm worried about you, Rai. And I think you're worried too."

Rai couldn't argue with him but was at a loss for words on how to explain things without putting herself at greater risk. She also knew she should pull away and break the physical connection. However, she remained in contact, worried he might misinterpret any discon-nection as her shutting him out even further. Their friendship demanded she treat Ponar better.

"You're right, I am worried. No, it's more than that. I'm terrified. I am in way over my head in something I don't understand, and I don't even know where or how to begin explaining all of it."

"You open your mouth and words come out, one at a time until you're done. I can help you, Rai," he pleaded. "As can Meik, Laan and Somnu ... "

"NO!" Rai yelled.

Ponar pulled away, startled at her response. "But ..."

Rai reached out and grasped his hand with both of hers, face flushing with the strength of her emotion. "Promise me that you won't say anything to Somnu, Ponar. Nothing of your suspicions or what happened with the Juggernaut."

"But, why? He's a good guy." Confusion filled Ponar, and Rai felt his palpable resistance to her request.

A tear rolled down her cheek and onto the pillow below. She *had* to convince him. Her very life could depend on it. "Please Ponar, I beg of you, don't tell him what you know," she asked with every fiber of her being.

Rai felt Ponar concede to her wish, although he didn't understand her reasons. "I'll do as you ask for now. But you need to tell me what's going on, all right?"

Rai nodded. "I will, but not right now. I'm too exhausted to think straight." She could worry later about how to keep that promise. Always later.

"Well, that we can agree on," Ponar replied, smiling down at her. He released her hands and picked up a blanket at the end of her bed and laid it over her, tucking it over her shoulder and under her chin. "Get some sleep. We'll have plenty of time to figure this out when we're both well rested."

Rai tried to force a smile, but it wouldn't come. Instead, she closed her eyes and shut out the world, if only for a brief time.

CHAPTER 9

"Do you have any idea what you're asking from me?" Chieftess Raza's icy glare conveyed her mood perfectly despite the grainy quality of the video transmitter. "And it's the middle of the night!"

"I know full well what I'm asking," Graeber replied, wishing he could lower the speaker volume without Raza noticing. "Once the girl is safely back in Raven's Call ..." he began.

"Again with the chaperoning?" Raza rolled her eyes. "And then what?"

"And then I'll go help Bauleel with this Zebio situation before it gets out of hand," he replied.

"Out of hand?" Raza yelled. "Honey, it's been out of control for weeks now while you've been wasting your time on this little personal mission of yours." Graeber held his tongue and steeled himself for his sister's impending rant.

"And that's not all!" Raza continued. "While you've been oh so busy Terem has been running around killing dozens of Technicians and Guardians. Who knows who else is at risk? We also have the medicinal contamination of plague anti-infective issue on our hands, as well as the matter of the Juggernaut arrival. How, exactly, do you expect me to keep covering for you to the Core?"

"I thought you were going to tell them I was investigating the medicinal contamination? We were able to locate the source at the Stime Sept's farms and begin cleanup procedures," Graeber replied evenly. "This demonstrates how I've been working towards the Core's goals."

"*We?* Are you even listening to yourself? You're lucky the girl didn't blow your cover with the Guardians on site. And yes, it's wonderful that we know where the contamination started, but who did it? For that matter, we don't even know if only one site is involved for certain. I've had a few queries as to your investigation, but then you take off across the Northern Road with the Durmah in tow as if you didn't have a care in the world."

"I gave explicit instructions to the Guardians in charge of the cleanup before I left. They were to test all of the farmland throughout Barrow's Grove and report any additional findings. For the record, I was able to locate supplementary information on my trip across the Northern Road," he explained.

Raza was not appeased. He could hear her foot tapping with impatience. "I'm waiting."

"I inspected the storehouses at Harper's Sorrow," he said. "There were a total of six missing and unaccounted for aqueous dispersal units."

"At least you had a reasonable excuse for taking off like you did, then," Raza replied. "You're confident of that count?"

"Very. Those storehouses haven't been used since the settlement days. Precise records tracked the usage and location of all terraforming equipment. In fact, most of those devices have transponders which allow for simplified tracking. It would appear that those six missing units have either had their transponders removed or disabled because the database lists them as missing."

"Do you have any idea what you're implying?" Raza asked, her voice a mere whisper.

Graeber nodded. "Only members of the Core have access to those storehouses. Plus, one must assume a certain level of knowledge and skill to set up and manipulate the dispersal units. Therefore, the poisoner must be one of our own."

Raza frowned. "That's gonna go over like a ton of bricks. But, at the least that helps explain what you were doing up there...conveniently in time to run into the Juggernaut. Oh, that reminds me, have you checked your transmittals lately?" Raza asked with a raised eyebrow and pursed lips.

"Not since I alerted you to the Juggernaut yesterday," Graeber answered. "We traveled straight through to Resounding Cliffs, and I came up here to call you as soon as I arrived."

"In response to your alert to the Core," Raza sighed, "Matriarch Natre has called a conclave."

Graeber could barely control his anger. "Who's next on her hit list?"

"It's not like that, brother," Raza replied. "It's been your choice, and right, to not attend the conclaves these past few years. But you need to understand that the Core hasn't *executed* anyone since then. Those were exceptional circumstances, which you need to accept."

"You, of all people, should know better than to ask me that," Graeber growled.

Raza held his gaze for a moment and then shrugged. "You *have* to attend this meeting. I can't stress it enough, Graeber. If you don't, there will be fallout you won't be able to avoid."

"What more can they do to me?" he demanded.

"Uh, plenty!" Raza replied. "No one's *actually* dead yet, remember? If anyone takes a closer look at your activities, they might just guess what you pulled off."

Graeber rubbed his fingers against his temples. "I'm not sure that'd be the worst case scenario anymore."

"What's this I hear? Could my brother have made a mistake?"

"That's not what I said, Raza!" he roared.

Raza's brows narrowed. "Of course not. Then what,

you just changed your mind? Or has there been a problem I should know about?"

Graeber sighed, defeated. "Rai's too capable. Too smart. Bauleel's modifications left Rai crippled, and yet she keeps managing to do things her mind and body shouldn't remember how to do," he admitted, against his better judgment. "I don't think there's a damned thing I can do to convince her to stop trying, and it's wretched to watch her keep searching for someone she can no longer be."

"I take it you've had some frank discussions with her?" Raza asked.

He nodded. "Rai had gotten too close to the truth. I had to warn her and convince her to stop trying to figure out her history," Graeber explained.

"You couldn't convince her to keep hidden to protect her own hide?"

Graeber shrugged. "Since when could I convince that woman of anything unless she'd already decided it for herself?"

Raza smiled weakly, compassion evident in her gaze. "What will you do next?"

"Just as I proposed. With your official permission, I'd like to take her back to Raven's Call, and then go and join Bauleel in her hunt. If I have to attend the Core's conclave along the way, then so be it."

"Are you sure you can trust the girl to behave in your absence?" Raza asked.

"I've tried to impress upon her the seriousness of

the situation. If she won't listen, then it doesn't matter whether or not I'm around to protect her." He raked a hand through his hair. "Where is this conclave, anyway?"

"It hasn't been decided yet, but I'll push for Raven's Call. It's a central location, and it'll look like I'm catering to Natre's whims. Plus, it'll help to justify your trip there with the Durmah," Raza conceded.

"I appreciate that," Graeber replied.

"You better. Do me a favor though?"

"Name it."

"Show up and explain your activities, well, the *legitimate* ones anyway, to the Core. I can't keep doing it for you. At the very least they will want to understand every detail relating to your findings on the luna berry poisoning at the Stime Sept farmlands. They have the right to hear such a grave accusation of a potential saboteur within the Amenoi ranks from your lips," she argued.

"Yeah, that'll be fun," he growled, still enraged by the charges that had called for the execution of Kilawren. Would his accusations fuel the fire to the next such hunt?

"No, it won't. But look on the bright side," Raza said. "The Juggernaut may wipe us all off of the face of the planet tomorrow, and then all of these other worries will be just a memory."

"That's a cheerful thought," Graeber growled at her, knowing that, for the Juggernaut, such behavior wasn't at all beyond the realm of possibility. "I'll see you soon, Sis."

"That's Chieftess Raza to you, brother dear. Stay out of trouble, will you? Well, no more insanity than you already generate daily by breathing." Raza flashed him a sarcastic smile and terminated the video link before he had a chance to defend himself.

Graeber departed immediately for the Cheote Waystation. If he was lucky, he might get a few hours sleep before they set off for Raven's Call in the morning.

"I THINK THAT GUARDIAN OF YOURS IS A BIT addled in the head, thinking he can get special dispensation to travel during the Guardian Chieftess' lockdown!" Somnu laughed, shaking his head over the apparent improbability.

"I'm sure you're right, Somnu," Meik drawled. "And after these last few days, I could use some time to sit around and not worry about anything."

"I doubt any of us will be going anywhere anytime soon, which suits me just fine! I've been running all over too, and it'd be a nice change of pace to spend some quality time with friends."

Laan leaned in, concern evident in his furrowed brow. "I can't stop worrying why the Juggernaut are here. Knowing they're nearby, well, if we do get some sort of special privileges then I for one would jump at the chance to get back home."

Somnu shook his head. "I *still* can't believe your story! The fact that you came across the Northern Pass, right when they happened to be in that area, well, it's just an amazing coincidence."

Guardian Graeber stepped up to the table, startling all three of them. "Are you implying the Durmah intended to cross paths with the Juggernaut?"

"Oh no, of course not. Don't be ridiculous," Somnu replied. His eyes met Graeber's. Although they'd known each other since Colonization days, Graeber and Somnu had never been close.

"Then please accept the coincidence and have some sympathy for the plight your friends find themselves in, and my efforts to help ease their discomfort. We can't know what the Juggernaut are doing or how long they've been doing it. Perhaps if the Matriarchs are able to initiate a dialog with the Juggernaut envoy, we will learn more. Until then, it's best to continue on with things as normal and reserve idle speculation for things like marriages, births, and crop harvests," Graeber stated authoritatively.

"Yes, yes, the Guardian is right," Somnu replied. "Surely it's just the shock of the news that has us all on such poor behavior. Such a visit hasn't occurred in the life of our colony, so folks are just trying to make sense of it." Meik and Laan nodded in agreement, neither willing to speak up to the Guardian. "So, tell us, were you able to get special permission to continue your trip to Raven's Call and return the Durmah to their home?"

"Indeed I was," Graeber replied. "We'll leave once everyone has had a chance to get some sleep," he said, looking right at Meik and Laan.

"Good, good," Meik said, swigging down the last of his beer. "Laan and I will just be heading up to our room then. Night to both of you." Laan followed close on Meik's heels, disappearing up the stairs towards their room.

"Sleep well you two," Somnu called after them. He turned to the Guardian. "Well, you know how to clean out a room."

"They need their sleep," Graeber replied, his voice devoid of all emotion.

"I'm sure they do," Somnu agreed. "Would you like to take a seat?"

"No, thanks," Graeber replied. "I won't be staying long."

Somnu shrugged. "Tell me, do you have any reason for taking them along the Northern Pass? Or, for that matter, why are you bothering to take the Durmah back home during a colony-wide lock down?"

Graeber held Somnu's gaze unflinchingly. "You can wait to hear all about that side trip at the meeting like everyone else. I'm escorting the Durmah back home because it's convenient for me and on my way to the meeting."

Somnu smiled and poured himself the remainder

of his beer. "Ahh, you're going to grace us with your presence this time? What's the occasion?"

"I have something useful to share. A few things, actually," Graeber stated. "I guess I've just been a bit busy lately."

"Haven't we all?" Somnu smiled, his lack of his sincerity evident in his disinterested gaze. "Say, since you're on your way to the meeting I don't suppose you'd mind if I tagged along?"

What a phenomenally bad idea, Graeber considered, but how could he deny Somnu's request without stirring suspicions from the Durmah? Obviously, Somnu was up to something, and Graeber was determined to find out what. "That'd be okay," he replied, gritting his teeth. "Now, if you don't mind, I'd like to get a little sleep myself."

"Sure, sure," Somnu smiled broadly. "Have a good night!" he replied altogether too cheerfully, toasting Graeber.

Graeber wanted to knock Somnu squarely upon his self-righteous ass, his confident attitude needed to be knocked down a few pegs. Graeber walked back to the Guardian Sept house and an available bed, wondering how he was going to manage this new twist to his plans.

A few hours later he awoke, refreshed but the solution still eluded him. He returned to the Cheote Waystation's guest quarters and, with the direction of the innkeeper, knocked on the door to Rai's room.

She answered, still bleary-eyed from the late night. "Can I come in?" he asked.

Rai motioned for him to enter. "When do we leave?" She pulled a comb through her wet hair, her fluid movements the same as they were before ... all of this happened.

"As soon as your uncle and cousin awaken, but I have to warn you about something first."

"What, that Tinker Somnu is one of your Core buddies?" Rai asked.

Graeber stared at her. "How did you know?"

She shrugged. "Somnu's given me the creeps from day one, even though he's supposedly this long-time friend of the Sept. And last night he tried to read me."

"What did you do?" Graeber asked.

"I thought about cleaning sclern guts off the wagons and left the room," she replied. "You know if you'd taught me how to shield against such things I would have been better prepared."

"Well, I'm afraid there isn't the time or the opportunity right now," Graeber replied. "He's coming back to Raven's Call with us."

The color drained out of Rai's face. "What!"

"He asked, and I didn't want to raise the Durmah's suspicions. Besides, I want to keep an eye on him and find out what he's got planned, which will be easier if he's within dart range."

"Then we'll be within his sights too! Fantastic! So, what do we do now?" she asked.

"You play the role you were supposed to be playing all along. Do your best not to make Somnu take further interest in you, and keep well away from me. Don't try and talk to me for any reason, understand?" Rai nodded. "I'll do my best to keep him busy and away from you. We'll be traveling as fast as possible, so the likelihood for long conversations is minimal."

"I understand," Rai replied. At that moment Ponar walked in the door, having just returned from the bathroom. Graeber then noted how both beds had their sheets wrinkled. He couldn't help but wonder at Rai's choice of roommates.

"Uh, hey," Ponar said, running a hand through his still wet hair. "What's up?"

"The Guardian was just saying we need to be ready to leave as soon as possible," Rai replied.

"Yeah, that's the impression I got. Would you two like another few moments alone?" Ponar offered.

"That won't be necessary. I've said all that needs saying," Graeber replied, putting his hand on the doorknob. "I'll be waiting downstairs when you're ready to go."

"We'll be right down. Thanks," Rai said, her eyes pleading with Graeber to understand.

"Make it quick," Graeber replied. He closed the door and walked out to the street.

As he waited and pondered the situation, the way out became apparent. At this point, there was only one option left.

Removing her memories hadn't worked. Hiding her was not going to work for much longer. The only option left, if they could manage it, was getting her off Az'Unda. It was an extreme solution, but at this point, Graeber had to consider all of the options available if he was going to keep from losing his Kilawren forever.

CHAPTER 10

"Do you want to talk about it?" Ponar asked, watching Rai finish throwing her dirty clothes into her backpack.

"No," she replied. "Look, I need to pick something up, so I'll meet you downstairs."

Rai walked out the door, and Ponar was left wondering what the Guardian had said to her. She'd seemed to be in a better mood this morning, and he'd hoped for an opportunity to talk about her fear of the Tinker. But, predictably, the Guardian had spoken to her and shut Rai up, yet again. Ponar knew Rai trusted this Guardian, but the more he watched the effect the man had on Rai, he'd grown more and more suspicious of Graeber's motives.

Ponar met up with the rest of the Durmah and Somnu at lunch, or was it breakfast? Rai was conspicuously missing, but he didn't dare ask in case he was supposed to somehow cover for where she was and didn't know it. Everyone ate quietly, exhaustion dampening their interest in small talk.

The Guardian arrived, looking about as sour-faced as usual. "Everyone ready to go?"

"We're just waiting for Rai," Meik replied.

"Well, there's no time to waste. It looks like we'll hit some rough weather by tonight. We'd best get the wagon's ready to go," the Guardian said.

Ponar, Meik, and Laan all rose and headed towards the stables. Somnu followed, walking alongside the Guardian.

"I'm looking forward to this trip," Somnu said, smiling broadly.

"Good for you," the Guardian replied, a grim expression pulling down the corners of his mouth.

If Ponar didn't know any better, he'd swear those two knew each other. Nothing else was said, but the tension this morning was palpable. He was aware that Meik would never outright say he was scared to travel with the Juggernaut roaming around the planet, doing who knows what, but just because you won't admit to something doesn't mean no else one notices.

Rai returned right as they were leading the wagons out of the Cheote Waystation's courtyard and onto the street. Without a word, she clambered up onto the seat next to Ponar and stowed her backpack under the seat.

"You got back just in time," Ponar said. Rai stared off into the distance, not meeting his eyes. "Where did you run off to?"

Rai shrugged. "There was something I had to pick up."

Ponar waited for more explanation, but she sat quietly, face unreadable. Better to give her some time, he reasoned.

A few hours south of Resounding Cliffs, the rain began rolling in off of the ocean and pouring down upon the wagons. The small canopy above their seat provided little protection, and Ponar was glad he wasn't riding on horseback like the Guardian. The roads here were well constructed and high above the marshlands, so the horses and wagons were able to keep a steady pace without being bogged down in the muck.

Ponar looked over at Rai whose expression was still one of mild disinterest. "You know if you want to talk I doubt anyone else could hear us over this racket."

"There's nothing to say," Rai replied, her voice flat.

Ponar had to bite his tongue to keep his frustration from boiling over. Rai had always been so open with him in the past. He *knew* this silence couldn't be of her choosing; surely the Guardian was behind it. That's how the Guardians and Temples worked: no one could talk about what went on inside those hallowed walls, just like Rai wouldn't talk now. It's why he never knew what had happened to his mother, Kait, and why she was so sickly now.

"He never has to know what we've talked about. I'll keep secret anything you confide in me. For your own sake you need to get it off your chest," he said.

Finally, Rai looked at him. "I can't," Rai replied, her words slurring together. "He'll kill me."

"The Guardian threatened to kill you?"

Rai shook her head violently. "No, no. The Tinker, if he finds out about me ..." Tears welled at the corners of her eyes.

"The Tinker?" Ponar asked, scoffing at the ludicrous idea. "That doesn't make any sense, Rai. I can assure you, Somnu is our friend."

Rai looked at him, finally meeting his gaze. "He's one of them ... us ... whatever. The point is, I know what he is, and soon he'll figure out what I am. Whatever it is I am? Well, he'll know I know. And then he'll want me dead. It's inevitable. Don't you see?" Despite her disoriented state, Rai's undeniable anxiety assailed him.

Ponar couldn't make sense of her rant but did notice how dilated her eyes were and the worsening slurring of her speech. "What did you take?"

Rai shrugged. "Just a little faown."

"A little!" Ponar exclaimed. "Dammit, I wish Jessie had never introduced you to that crap! How much?"

"Two packets," she replied.

No wonder she was gibbering like a fool. Ponar was amazed she was still awake. "Give me the rest." He held out his hand, but Rai made no move to comply. "Now!" he ordered.

Rai frowned, but even in her drugged state, she seemed to understand that his demand wasn't negotiable. She pulled out her bag and handed over about a dozen more packets, which Ponar threw down onto the drenched road.

"I'm sorry," Rai replied. "I didn't know what else to do. Once he knows who I am, he'll kill me, and I don't even know why. At least on the faown, I can barely feel anything, so hopefully, he won't either. Right?" She hid her face in her hands and sobbed.

Ponar drew her to him, encouraging Rai to cry on his shoulder. He didn't understand what she was talking about, but he suspected it had a lot to do with the faown messing with her mind. He'd heard that in excessive doses the general calming effects could instead cause agitation or even paranoia. There was no way Somnu would hurt Rai; Ponar had known him practically his whole life, and he was a decent guy. She must have meant the Guardian...that had to be it. He *must* be the one threatening Rai. But why? Ponar resolved to confront the Guardian directly and find out what was going on. Rai was family, and he wasn't going to let either the Guardian or the Tinker hurt her.

He'd wanted to share the conversation he'd had

with Meik before they left Resounding Cliffs this morning with Rai, but he decided it would be best to wait until the faown had worked its way out of her system. Meik remained determined to confront Rai on the Harper's Sorrow incident and the conversation he'd seen Rai have with the Guardian. Meik was convinced Rai was keeping something from her Sept, and Ponar worried Meik was not going to let it go. Ponar had argued that it'd be best if they gave Rai time to reveal the truth herself, but Meik had held his ground, claiming she'd had plenty of time.

Eventually, Rai's tears stopped and then her body grew limp as the faown overtook her. Ponar laid her head in his lap, hoping that when the faown had worn off and she woke, things would be clearer for both of them.

IT WAS DARK AND STILL RAINING WHEN THEY pulled into the small outpost known as Jeweled Cove. This time Ponar wasn't surprised to watch the ease with which the Guardian secured their entrance into the high-walled compound. There were a few Guardians' stationed here, and they proceeded to inspect the wagons and cargo for anything unusual. Happily, the Durmah had been able to scour the sclern parts off the wagons and ensure no living beasts had hidden away within any nooks or crannies. If any of the live vermin had made it into town, the effects could be disastrous, as they had voracious appetites.

Ponar had spent the night here a few times while he was first learning the merchant's art from Meik, back before he'd been given his own route along the western coastline. From what he could see of the city through the dim torchlight, not much had changed.

The three-story fort was built of massive rectangular blocks in the old style; much like the other Guardian outposts that he'd seen in his travels. The structure stood right at the cliff's edge, its single distinguishing feature a tall tower reaching up into the darkness. Ponar imagined you could watch for pirates, like in the childhood folktales of old, except there were no pirates on Az'Unda. From the maps, he'd seen there weren't any islands or continents besides the one they were on now, so there should be nothing out there to look at. The mystery of why the Az'Un ancestors had built such a high tower, overlooking nothing, never failed to stir his imagination.

Ponar waited until the Guardian's inspection was completed before rousing the still-sleeping Rai. She awoke, rubbing her eyes. Her features drooped, the lingering effect of her sedative overdose.

"Where are we?" Rai asked. Her voice was hoarse and dry, so Ponar offered her his water bottle. "It looks familiar somehow."

"This is the Guardian's outpost at Jeweled Cove," he replied, climbing down and securing his horse's reins.

"Jeweled Cove?" Rai asked, looking alarmed. She slowly climbed down the wagon steps to the ground, appearing not altogether steady on her feet.

"Yes, is there a problem?" Ponar asked.

"It's just ... this is that place I remembered, where I dreamed of being down on the beach." She shivered and drew her cape tighter around her body.

Ponar could only hope the faown wasn't making Rai overly paranoid. "Oh yeah, I remember you mentioning it. Did you ever remember more, besides the nightmare?"

Rai sighed and shook her head, but said nothing. She had a resigned look in her eyes that worried Ponar. He had to find out what the Guardian had said to her.

"Perhaps being here will jog your memory, if we're lucky," he said. Ponar saw Laan and the Guardian go inside the outpost's door, no doubt to arrange their accommodations for the evening.

Rai looked around, her eyes fixing upon Meik and Somnu talking at the other end of the courtyard. "Now that would be phenomenally bad timing."

Ponar didn't want to argue with Rai, especially when he knew her mood must still be altered by the faown. "Why don't we head inside and get some dinner?

She nodded and walked into the outpost with him.

Perhaps after eating she'd be clearheaded enough that they could discuss Meik's comments from this morning and how best to handle his continuing curiosity. Hopefully, Meik would heed his request to wait until Ponar had a chance to speak with her on the subject.

CHAPTER 11

"You getting cold feet?" Somnu asked as he walked up to Meik.

Meik shifted uneasily. "Who wouldn't in weather like this?" He laughed, and his friend Somnu smiled broadly, showing his appreciation for Meik's sense of humor. Meik appreciated how Somnu seemed to always understand him, which spoke volumes to the depth of their friendship.

"Well, you've had some time to think about the plan today. Did you come up with a better idea?" Somnu asked.

Meik shook his head. "No, she needs to know we're serious, and that we Durmah don't keep secrets from each other." Rai's lack of honesty was like a kick in his gut. "It's like you said, up till now she'd been behaving like honesty is optional. We need to show her we're not taking no for an answer."

"And you're prepared to be firm with her if need be?" Somnu asked.

"I don't want it to come to that, but yeah, sure, if that's what it takes."

"Your elder brother Stoi would be proud of you, taking charge like this," Somnu replied, clapping Meik on the shoulder. "I bet you can get this whole matter cleared up today. Then when we get to Raven's Call, you can advise the entire Sept on the next step to helping Rai."

"When do you think we should try this?" Meik asked.

"After dinner. I'll do my best to keep the Guardian occupied while you, Laan, and Ponar talk with Rai," Somnu said.

"I sure appreciate your help," Meik replied. "It means a lot to us that we can count on your help."

"Anytime!" Somnu said. "Hey, you sure it was a good idea to tell Ponar about the plan? Those two look pretty thick." He motioned towards the outpost.

Meik looked up and saw Rai and Ponar enter the building. "That's why I told him. I figured as they're good friends, he'd be motivated to get the truth from her. And if that fails, then we follow through with our plan."

"That's quick thinking on your part, Meik," Somnu replied. "Why don't we go and see what he found out?"

When they entered the outpost, Laan, Rai, and Ponar were already sitting around a circular table in the dining hall eating. Their Guardian escort was, predictably, nowhere in sight, although a half-dozen Guardians sat at the table next to the Durmah, quietly eating.

"Is that stew?" Meik asked as they approached.

"Sure is," Laan replied.

"Ahh, my favorite!" Meik said, pulling up a seat and claiming one of the other bowls Laan had ordered. Somnu sat down next to him and did the same.

"Everyone manage to keep warm on the way here?" Somnu asked.

Meik watched Rai, but she didn't even look up or say anything. Somnu was right, she needed their help.

"We did," Ponar replied. "My clothes are feeling a bit damp though."

Their eyes met for a moment, and Ponar shook his head and frowned. Meik nodded his understanding and took a bite of stew. Rai, her eyes locked onto her bowl of stew, didn't appear to have noticed this silent exchange. But from the looks on their faces, neither Laan nor Somnu had missed it.

"If I remember the timing right and the clouds break, we might be able to watch a meteor shower before going to bed," Somnu said.

"That'd be a pleasant treat," Laan replied, playing along.

"I'm certainly not tired enough to sleep yet," Meik said. "Count me in. How about you two?" he asked Ponar and Rai.

"Well, I need to check on one of my horses first," Ponar replied. "I think my mare has a loose shoe, but that won't take me long, and then I can join you."

Meik wondered what Ponar was playing at; if his mare had needed a shoe checked or replaced he'd have done it on the road, lest she damage her hoof along the way.

"I'm feeling a little tired, myself," Rai replied. "Perhaps next time."

"Oh, I think some time on the roof would do you good. Help to clear your head," Ponar replied. "Besides, you napped most of the day, so it's likely you wouldn't be able to get to sleep again so soon."

Rai looked confused but didn't seem to have the energy to fight with Ponar. "You're right. It'll be fun to see meteors too, I suppose."

"Ahh, that settles it then; we'll all go!" Somnu replied. "Trust me, my dear, you'll never forget the view."

Rai seemed to force a smile but said nothing in reply. Poor girl, she almost looked scared. Despite this ruse, Meik was sure his sister Kait would be proud of how well he'd dealt with the situation once they got home and knew just how the Guardian had been interfering with their Sept.

CHAPTER 12

Brague paced back and forth in front of his research terminal interface, awaiting the results of his queries to the Hegemonic archives.

The human female had escaped his initial capture, but that wouldn't last long. No one could hide from the Hegemony for long.

To distract himself from his overwhelming curiosity, Brague reviewed all completed Evaluation results on Az'Unda, chittering loudly, gloating over his abilities as a Selector. The tests on Az'Unda's biometrics were yielding results well within all desired metrics so far. In fact, if the subsequent round of tests also yielded positive results, he might go so far as to invite Princess Qwell's emissaries to come and visit the planet while he was completing the final rounds of testing.

The world's surface was covered by 86% water, well within Princess Qwell's requirements. The planetary size and core density translated to a gravity quotient eight percent less than optimal for Juggernaut physiology. The air, soil, and water of Az'Unda contained none of the contaminants which might interfere with developing Juggernaut pupae. Instead, the earth and water were rich in all of the desired nutrients, and the atmosphere's chemical makeup lent it a faint, sweet smell. Even the harmful spectrum of sunlight, which could cause defects in the undeveloped protective pupae shells, was filtered out by the planet's unusually dense cloud cover in the lower regions along the coastlines. He made a note in the world's file to investigate the cause of this cloud cover, with particular attention to if it had shifted in density over time.

There were yet more tests to be run: compiling mappings of climate shifts over the planet's history, preparing statistical probabilities of planetary impacts based on historic sites and levels of space debris in the galactic vicinity, and calculating fuel and time lag from Az'Unda to the heart of Hegemonic space. Counting all of that, Brague knew he could still be within mere weeks of completing this assignment. A successful match this soon in the process would certainly add an impressive entry in his dossier.

The interior highlands were not as well suited for pupae farms, but perhaps Princess Qwell could use these areas for other more typical Juggernaut structures. Brague could already envision vast palatial estates for her Highness, libraries, and universities to educate young Juggernaut minds, farms to grow delicacies to remind her Highness of her homeland, and of course, no settlement could be complete without a Temple of Observance in honor of the Progenitors.

But Brague suspected he knew what would please Princess Qwell the most. He pulled up a geologic scan of the largest continent, no--let's instead call them islands, Brague decided. The scan revealed an extensive network of caves extending well inland from the coast of each island, perfect for the Princess' needs. Brague could already envision those caves filled with millions upon millions of incubating and hatching Juggernaut pupae, overseen by an army of servitors and caretakers. What an incredible sight that would be!

This planet also met his personal criteria, and although this didn't supersede the Princess's needs, it added to his pleasure with the task. The primate colony amounted to fifty thousand, two hundred, and fourteen inhabitants. From what he could tell, their birth rates weren't anywhere near optimal to stabilize the population. Most pathetically, the primates had not adapted to a pathogen the Hegemony had long ago classified a minimally contagious agent. Hadn't Brague been infected with it as a larva, with no long term effects? Why these primates were unable to adapt to such a simple disease escaped him. It would be *almost* compassionate of him to free them from such a wretched existence. *Almost*, Brague thought, running his forelegs down this antennae quickly.

This invigorating thought was brought to an abrupt stop as his research terminal flashed a 'Query completed' message upon the screen. He pulled up the results and had to read the message twice.

Archive search completed. No instances of 'Homo sapiens' or 'primate' paired with 'multi-dimensional speech capability' found.

Brague stared in disbelief. Surely he couldn't have been the first researcher to catalog this combination?

And yet ...

Brague knew what to do. Protocol dictated that new and unusual traits of existing species be inventoried and reported with all due haste, to maintain the Hegemonic database and ensure that the information not be lost. After all, the Hegemony was nothing without their history.

Hours later, Brague submitted his updates to the Hegemonic Archives appropriately indexed and cataloged, including all pertinent details. He also drafted a message to Princess Qwell, updating her on their progress to find her the perfect breeding grounds, and included all of his relevant new findings. He aimed his wording to be circumspect, as was proper for one of his stature.

The communiqué's finished and sent, Brague refocused his attentions on recent survey findings on Az'Unda, but he'd already reviewed all completed reports two, three times before.

He needed something to distract him, and luckily he knew just the thing.

Brague retrieved his bio-scans of the amusingly irate primates once again, enlarging the images until they dominated the terminal's screen. He pored over the minutia of every detail captured by his scan, looking for the key which made this female different from the rest of her kind. There was something else about this specimen, and it was a puzzle he was determined to solve. Most likely she wasn't the only one on the planet gifted with multidimensional speech, but he also couldn't count on that.

Because if there was one thing which had always been true for Brague, it was this: one way or the other, he'd always managed to satisfy his curiosity. Always.

———

BRAGUE WAITED IN FRONT OF THE FULL-WALL terminal on his research vessel. Knowing the call would come in momentarily, he resisted the urge to perform any last minute checks on the perfect sheen of his carapace. After a few seconds, the interface prompted him to accept a call from the Hegemonic Senate building on the Juggernaut home world. He keyed in his access code and then bowed deeply before the screen as the real-time connection activated.

"Greetings on this Perith Prime-Latne of the Dark

Trine, Selector Brague. You may rise," intoned a rich, deep voice.

Brague rose and was surprised to see Queen Klimitzi in all her glory. He'd only previously seen pictures and statues of her before this moment. Gratefully, the accuracy of those dedicated artisans served to inform him with such accuracy that he had no doubt, at this time, to who he now genuflected.

When the transmission had arrived advising him to expect a call from the home world, he'd assumed Princess Qwell or one of her emissaries would be contacting him concerning his efforts. Seeing the Queen herself, much less having a direct conversation with her, was an unexpected joy he'd never expected to experience.

"Your Eminence, I am honored beyond measure to meet you. How may I be of service to the Hegemony today?"

"I hear that your Evaluation of planets for our Princess Qwell is proceeding far ahead of schedule. You are to be commended for your exhaustive efforts," she replied.

"I am merely a humble servant of the Hegemony, working as best suits my capabilities," he said with a small bow. He was immensely flattered that the Queen herself was reviewing his progress. Surely this spoke well of his future.

"I have also reviewed your report on multidimensional speech capability in association with a primate specimen," the Queen replied. "Are all of the details accurate?"

So, *this* must be how he came to her attention. But why would she care about a report on a primate? "I can assure you they are exact. I witnessed the specimen, and I will be collecting it to run further tests once my duties to my assignment are fulfilled."

"Based on your history, I assumed the report could be taken at face value. This presents another problem, however, which I hope you will be able to help me resolve." The Queen angled her head slightly, inferring query.

Without hesitation, Brague mirrored her posture. "I am happy to assist in any way the Hegemony deems appropriate."

"Are you aware of the nature of the speech phenomenon you observed in this creature?" the Queen asked.

"I'm afraid I am not so enlightened to understand what that implies, my Queen," Brague replied. "I have rarely noted this speech phenomenon outside of Juggernaut physiology, and never have I encountered an instance of this ability within the primate species. Thus, it stood out, and I knew it warranted further investigation."

"It's that exact curiosity which I wish to reward," she said. "Effective now, your security clearance is elevated to white."

White was the highest clearance that existed, and

two full steps above his current standing. "My Queen, thank you for this honor." His antennae quivered. With white clearance, he now had access to the entire research database, including the restricted areas.

"What I'm about to tell you must not be repeated, as it is known to only those of us at white level."

"I will honor this confidence with my life," he replied.

"Yes, you will. You see, the multidimensional speech capability we Juggernaut all share is not an entirely genetic trait. Our base DNA has the basic building blocks necessary, but it's a virus that transforms these blocks into a cohesive, functional ability. An ability we Juggernaut take great pride in, and in fact consider to be one of our species defining superior qualities," Queen Klimitzi explained.

"A simple virus is responsible?" Brague asked.

"Not so simple, as it turns out. We believe the virus was designed by the Progenitors to help our people, to shape us. Think of it as their technology, passed to us through our DNA."

"They bestowed an amazing gift upon us, and are to be praised," Brague replied.

"Indeed they are. The problem is we don't have any solid proof for this theory. Occasionally, we encounter other species who share our susceptibility to the virus. It is our sincere hope that by investigating these other species, we might discover more of the Progenitors' intentions. And why they have allowed other beings to share elements of the Juggernaut supreme perfection."

"A prudent course. Your Grace's direction is unerring."

"I need your help in this," she said.

"I am delighted to assist you in any way, my Queen," he replied.

"I'm happy to hear you feel that way. To investigate this newest discovery of Progenitor viral DNA-infiltrating a primate colony, I hereby elevate you to the position of Assessor to the Queen and Arbiter of Sentience. Your first assignment is to study the impact of the Progenitors on Az'Unda, including determining the method of exposure if at all possible," the Queen pronounced.

Assessor? Brague? Too bad he'd always hated Assessors ... "I am, again, honored, your excellence, by your generosity. I will begin interrogating the populace at once. I assume I am no longer in charge of Princess Qwell's assignment?"

"Selector Rinneau will be handling the Selection process for the Princess. He is en route and will arrive within days to assume command of that operation," the Queen replied. "You will retain command of your personal fleet, with the added authority of Assessor."

"Selector Rinneau's record shows a two percent less efficient process than mine," Brague said. He regretted the jealous words immediately, wondering if the Queen would think him unappreciative of her gifts.

Queen Klimitzi's slight nuances of motion stilled, her form rising; the slight elongation of her height a deliberate reminder of her superior rank. "Do not concern yourself with this. He has been instructed to follow the exact methodology you set forward, and all will know that his assured successes will be due to your diligence," she replied.

Brague turned his head, symbolically exposing the vulnerable folds of his neck to her. "My thanks, again, your Grace. I will attend to this new assignment at once."

"There is one last thing, Assessor Brague." Brague straightened his posture, sensing she wished his complete attention. "Under the Hegemonic law, all beings who have been elevated by the Progenitors' gifts must be treated as our brethren. Because primates, at least on this world, may have been so honored, you must accord them all due respect. Therefore there can be no 'interrogations,' nor aggressive tactics. Use of force is specifically disallowed. Do you understand these constraints?"

Disgust burned in his belly as he considered her words. Treat that scum as equals? How could she be serious? "I understand, my Queen. But what if I find no evidence of this gift? What if this individual's abilities are unique to her alone?"

"If that is the case, then feel free to keep her for your personal collection as a souvenir, and raze the planet to meet Princess Qwell's needs--or your own. As you are the Assessor, you make the decision. Just make sure it's the right one. We wouldn't want to offend the Progenitors, now would we?"

"Never, my Queen, never." Brague bowed again so that his antennae brushed on the floor.

"Send me regular reports, and contact me via ansible should you find anything particularly interesting," Queen Klimitzi said. "Happy hunting, Assessor Brague." He heard the connection drop before he saw it, and so drew himself to his full height.

He'd gotten the honor he sought by decades of hard work through a chance occurrence, and this left a bitter taste in his mouth. Luck wasn't the method he was used to winning by. He should instead have won honor through the perfection of his abilities. And yet with his latest promotion, he was guaranteed the breeding rights he desired. No doubt the Queens had already picked the time, not that he'd be informed until it was about to happen. It was a personal victory, slightly bittersweet, but a triumph to be celebrated nonetheless.

Brague had his orders, and although he didn't have to like them, he'd be lying to himself if he didn't admit that he'd already made up his mind. But first, he had to visit his colorist so that all could know his new status.

Communiqué

From: Assessor Brague, Arbiter of Sentience
To: The Matriarch Council of Az'Unda
Latne: Perith Prime-Latne of the Dark Trine

Greetings to the Matriarchs of Az'Unda:

Agents of the Hegemony are conducting research in the Northern Highlands of your largest continent. During a recent visit to this area, I met one of your colonists who I now wish to question at greater length. Attached is a graphic of the female and the male who was accompanying her, along with the exact planetary coordinates at the time of our meeting.

I would appreciate that your Council deliver the female to me. To expedite the process, I am willing to retrieve the subject from her current location, wherever planet-side that may be. Your compliance or lack thereof will affect the research results presented to the Hegemony's Acceptance of Sentience Oversight Committee.

I look forward to hearing your reply within the next three Az'Un solar days.

Regards,

Assessor Brague

CHAPTER 13

"Any updates?" Tinker Somnu asked, closing the door to the outpost's communications room behind himself.

Guardian Graeber didn't look up and continued to review messages circulating the global network. "Nothing from the Juggernaut, despite numerous requests from the Matriarchy." He sensed nothing from Somnu, but then he didn't expect to. Both of them had long ago learned to suppress their thoughts around other Core members.

"I'm not surprised," Somnu replied. "If the history of the Hegemony has taught us anything, we'll know their intentions once they take whatever it is they came here for. Assuming they don't kill us all to harvest some obscure mineral they've decided is essential for the future growth of their empire."

"That's what I've always liked about you, Somnu.

Your optimism. But are you really convinced the Juggernaut are here to raze the planet?" Graeber asked.

Somnu shrugged. "I don't know why they're here, but I do know they don't consider humans a sentient species. And with this plague ... well, I doubt they would see our presence here as something of benefit to the Hegemony."

Graeber didn't want to admit that Somnu was right. "Until they make a move, we can't know their intent. I prefer not to waste my time with useless speculations." He hated to admit it to himself, but if he couldn't keep Kilawren safe, he didn't much care what happened to the rest of Az'Unda.

"True, true," Somnu replied. "Perhaps instead you can shed some light on another subject for me?"

Graeber felt a familiar tingle at the base of his neck. "You think that's going to work on *me?*" he laughed. "Why don't you just ask your question and be done with it?" He shut off the communications terminal and turned to face Somnu.

"I'm wondering if you can help me work something out?" he asked.

"If I can," Graeber replied.

"I've noticed some interesting things about the Durmah's new adoptee, and I'm wondering if you might have picked up on it yourself?" Somnu asked.

Graeber didn't know if Somnu knew something, or just suspected. "She seems to get herself into trouble on a regular basis, but perhaps that's just her youthful spirit."

"Oh, I think it's more than her simply being a free spirit. You're familiar with her condition? Her supposed amnesia?" Somnu asked.

"I've overheard the family discussing it," Graeber replied.

"I'm sure you have. You seem to have been around the Durmah often, which is why I'm even bothering to bring this up with you first."

"First?" Graeber asked. "I'm beginning to get the impression that you have taken up the grand Durmah quest to discover the cause of little Rai's amnesia?" He guffawed. "Please, tell me you don't have anything better to do?"

Somnu frowned. "As you said, there's not much we can do about the Juggernaut, and I'm no scientist or Technician, so it's not like I can do anything about the plague either."

"It's a good thing you have the Core to fall back on then, isn't it?"

"I also have my research. My past as a librarian offers me endless sources of amusement. You know, I looked up Rai's original birth family. I was just visiting them, actually. They live in Resounding Cliffs. Friendly people. Very sincere and talkative to a Tinker who can help fix their aging and ailing equipment."

Graeber tried to sound nonchalant. "You know it

would be a bad idea to reveal their identities to the Durmah? That information is sealed, after all."

"Sealed by the Matriarchy, yes. But never to the Core, which you know," Somnu replied. "And there's no reason to disclose my findings to the Durmah, as Rai is not the daughter of the family the records claim her to be. I saw a family portrait of the Sept, the likeness of their daughter was similar, but not the girl."

An icy chill ran down Graeber's spine, such that he had to exert firm mental control, lest Somnu detect he'd hit a nerve. "A clerical error, perhaps?"

"Perhaps, but I think not. Bauleel arranged the paperwork, and I can't believe she would be so neglectful. I fear there may be another motive at play," Somnu said.

"And what might that be?" Graeber asked, sighing audibly.

Somnu took a step forward, speaking in a whisper. "I'm afraid Bauleel is attempting to pass off this girl, Rai, as an average Az'Un, but I think there is evidence of her sister's handiwork upon her."

"Explain yourself!" Graeber growled. Could Somnu have been shrewd enough to guess? And if he had, how far would he have to go to cover up their deeds this time?

"I'm sorry, old friend," Somnu replied, moving to place a friendly hand on Graeber's shoulder, which he shrugged off. "I don't want to bring up painful memories for you of Kilawren. However, this girl has displayed certain traits, the like of which have only before been witnessed by those of us in the Core. By those of us who survived the Ordeal."

Graeber sensed echoes of heartache in the air. Somnu had lost his wife and children during the initial plague outbreak during colonization. It had truly been an Ordeal for all who lived through it.

"I have seen none of this evidenced in her," Graeber replied. It was a bold-faced lie, but Somnu didn't mistake the genuine nature of his anger.

"I have taken the necessary time to observe her, while I suspect you have not had the time," Somnu replied. "She is not one of the Core masquerading as a mere citizen; we would have recognized her. Therefore I'm afraid there is only one possible explanation remaining. And I intend to confront Bauleel with my suspicions at the Core meeting in Raven's Call, but I wanted to get your opinion on the matter. You are close to Bauleel, and perhaps could help me talk to her in private, before the meeting."

Graeber imagined dozens of ways to end Somnu's life, but covering up his death would take more than an excuse. "What do you intend to accuse Bauleel of?" Graeber asked. The real irony is that Bauleel, although a willing participant in this colossal charade, was not the instigator. If anyone were to bear the brunt of an accusation, it would be himself.

"I think the girl is one of Kilawren's ... test subjects. I believe that, after her sister's death, Bauleel needed something to hold on to. That she couldn't let her sister's lifetime of work go to waste. That Bauleel intends to prove her theories through keeping this poor girl alive and hidden as long as she can. And I think in this endeavor, she is blind to the danger inherent in Kilawren's tests."

Somnu had it so wrong, and yet so spot on. Graeber needed time to consider how best to handle this new development, and Somnu had provided the perfect out. Whatever Somnu did, Graeber had to remain calm and do what he could to protect Bauleel.

"I have not witnessed anything to raise my concerns on the girl, but if you'd like, we can speak to Bauleel together. Perhaps through the rest of this journey, I may also witness these traits you've spoken of. Or it may be a simple matter of misplaced or misfiled paperwork."

"That is a distinct possibility. Still, I am heartened to hear you say you will join me in talking with Bauleel. It will make the task easier," Somnu replied, smiling jovially.

"Now if you'll excuse me, the Commander here has asked for a word with me. I'd rather not keep him waiting any longer," Graeber replied.

Frustrated, Graeber headed towards the room Rai had been assigned for the night. They were low on options, and getting shorter on time by the day.

Guardian Graeber knocked softly on Rai's door.

"She's not there," Ponar said, emerging from his room across the hallway. "Didn't you tell her not to speak with you anymore?"

"That's true," Graeber answered. Graeber knew Ponar hadn't overheard that part of their conversation this morning, so Rai must have shared information with Ponar on the trip here, despite his warnings. He wondered how much more of her confidence Ponar had gained, and it galled him that this utter stranger had somehow earned her trust. She was much too trusting of all the Durmah, this one in particular.

In the lifetimes he'd lived Graeber had hardened his heart against trusting others, allowing only his sister Raza, Rai, and her sister Bauleel, into his confidence. Knowing Ponar knew Rai's secrets, which could threaten all of them, caused the peculiar sensation of panic to burn through his chest. Or, perhaps was it jealousy?

He'd need to interrogate Ponar to learn all that Rai had disclosed, but this was not the time. It would have to wait.

"Do you know where she is now?" Graeber asked, forcing a passive expression onto his face.

Ponar smiled. "Sure, but why would I tell you? From what I've seen, you've already harassed her enough today. No wait, I take that back. Plenty enough for this entire trip."

"That is not my intent," Graeber replied. "If you don't mind, I'll leave you here to stew in your irritation while I continue my search."

"Oh, I do mind," Ponar replied. "Why don't you come in here for a moment so we can speak in private. Candidly. There are things you should know."

Graeber sensed Ponar's concern for and desire to protect Rai, and if Ponar had been at all up to the task, Graeber might even have taken him seriously. Instead, Graeber got the impression Ponar wanted to rant at him, which he would usually avoid but he thought might be useful in this situation. Ponar might reveal what other parts of their conversation Rai had shared with him, and what he had in turn shared with his Sept-mates. Graeber shook off his emotional reaction, determined to understand Ponar's awareness of Rai's situation. "Only for a moment. My time is short."

The room was small, containing a narrow cot, a three drawer dresser and a table pressed up against the wall with two chairs. Graeber sat across from Ponar at the table and waited for him to speak.

"You're going to drive her crazy. Do you know that?" Ponar asked.

"What makes you think I am the cause? She seems to be getting herself into plenty of trouble all on her own." Graeber smiled, as if unconcerned by Ponar's accusation.

"I know you've threatened her to keep quiet, so she doesn't tell us what she knows. I know something happened back at the lake. And I watched Rai *talk* to that Juggernaut, if you can call it that, and I saw how you reacted when you found out she'd spoken to it. I've walked in on the two of you, how many times now, in private conversation?"

Ponar's face was red and his expression full of vehemence as he spat out the words. Graeber resisted the urge to answer what he understood to be rhetoric questions as he felt Ponar's wrath build to a crescendo. If Graeber were a different man, he'd have felt physically threatened. But instead, Graeber suppressed a grin, allowing Ponar's rant to continue rolling.

"I've come up with a theory. Well, Meik and Laan and Stoi and Jesse came up with part of it, to be honest. But I've embellished it a bit based on what I've witnessed over the last week or so. You interested in hearing it?" Ponar asked.

"Sure," Graeber replied.

"We Durmah are convinced that Rai used to be a Guardian, and was cast out. Her memory was wiped or damaged in some way, and she was placed with the Durmah for some reason. Whether to help us or later report back to the Guardian Sept on us, we don't know."

"You think she's a spy?" Graeber asked, laughing.

"I don't think she's a willing tool, but some in my family have doubts. Some even think she might be dangerous. I do believe she's being controlled by you. From what I've witnessed, that much is obvious. Every time she's about to remember something, it seems you show up and interrupt the process. At the Stime Sept's swamps, you turn up right after she discovers that her dreams of that poison's smell are real. At Harper's Sorrow, Meik saw the two of you have an extended conversation on the way back to camp, but when we ask her about it, she says you didn't even talk. Then when you find out she communicated, or whatever you want to call it, to that Juggernaut, your reaction wasn't surprise or shock like I had when I witnessed that feat."

"There's not much that shocks me," Graeber replied. He didn't know Meik had seen his conversation with Rai at Harper's Sorrow. How could he have missed noticing Meik? Moreover, Ponar's recounting of events read like a litany of Rai's inability to keep her past a secret from her Sept-mates. If her secrets became common knowledge within the Sept, then it was only a matter of time before the Core learned everything.

Graeber's options to salvage the situation continued to dwindle, leaving off-world a comparably favorable outcome, despite the risks.

"That may be," Ponar continued. "But since then I keep walking in on the two of you talking. And you know how it looks to me?"

"Enlighten me."

"I believe my family is right now. Rai *was* a Guardian. And more than that, I personally think you knew her and cared deeply for her. Otherwise, why would you be hanging around, pestering her, and keeping her from moving on with her life?" Ponar asked. "You've managed to poison her against the Durmah and our trusted friends."

Graeber couldn't believe he'd been so transparent, but Ponar *had* seen the two of them together, heard parts of their conversations.

"An intriguing, although baseless, conclusion."

Ponar laughed at him, shaking his head. "It'll take more than that to convince me otherwise, *Graeber*. You're going to tell me right here, right now, why you keep interfering with her, and the Durmah's lives."

Ponar's break in protocol wasn't lost on him. "Well, *Ponar*, I don't owe you any explanations for my behavior. I've done everything I can to keep your entire family out of danger on this trip, and now you act like an ungrateful little wretch. It's pathetic."

"That's not true, you know. You're putting one particular member of my family through a great deal of unneeded stress," Ponar replied. "And it needs to stop."

Graeber wished he could comply with Ponar's request, but the stress was a better option than death. "I've only done what I had to do to protect your family."

"Protect?" Ponar asked. "Do you have any idea what this is doing to her? How lost and confused she is?"

"I live to protect all the Az'Un," Graeber answered. "And I will get back to doing my job now." He stood and walked toward the door.

Ponar followed him. "Do you know she slept most of the way here after taking enough faown to knock out a horse? Frankly, I'm amazed she can walk and talk now."

Graeber groaned inwardly. At those quantities, the faown would make it harder for Somnu to read her, but it would also make her more pliable and talkative. He'd had no idea she'd go overboard like that. The Kilawren he'd known never would have, but he had to remind himself, again, that Rai wasn't the woman she used to be. Rai wasn't the Kilawren he'd loved and lived lifetimes alongside. All of those memories and past had been lost to Rai. The possibility that he'd truly lost her, despite his best efforts to save her no matter the cost, loomed darkly in his thoughts. "Where is she at now? I'll go and talk to her, see if I can get her to stop ..."

"No! I don't think that's what she needs, *friend*. Besides, she's with her family, having a little heart to heart right now about the truth and the importance of Sept," Ponar said. "I think that Somnu is even there to help out, being the true family friend he is."

Graeber felt ice pour down his spine. "Where? Now!" he demanded.

"No, I won't let you interfere ..." Ponar began.

"Look, you're right." Graber let loose an exasperated sigh and then ran a hand through his hair. He dropped his usual rigid stance and reached out to Ponar, placing a hand on his arm in a silent request. "I did know her, and I am trying to protect her, especially from people like Somnu. If he finds out the truth about her past, he'll have her put to death," Graeber said. "And I won't be able to prevent it a second time."

The color drained from Ponar's face. "Why? How?"

"We can discuss the details later. If you value Rai's life, then take me to them now," Graeber said. He tried to calculate how long it had been since his discussion with Somnu, and how much time he and the Durmah might have been questioning Rai. Drugged as she was, it was already too long.

Ponar nodded and led the way, confusion etching a mask of fear across his face. Graeber knew he'd scared Ponar, but he had no other choice. He had to stop this family bonding session. Kilawren's, Rai's, life could depend upon it.

CHAPTER 14

"Somnu was right," Rai said. She looked down over the ocean, far beneath the parapet she leaned upon. Patches of moonlight broke through the clouds, spattering shimmery reflections off of the dark water's surface. "The view *is* amazing from up here."

Meik leaned on the wall next to her, sharing her admiration of the view. "It's a rare sight to see. Between the height of the cliffs and the shape of the cove, it feels almost like a gigantic theater."

"That's almost poetic, cousin," Laan replied from behind them. "You're not about to break into song, are you?"

Meik and Rai both laughed. "Nah. After all, I don't have a beer," Meik said, and then they all laughed.

It felt good to laugh with them. Although Rai's head was still stuffed with the cotton of faown despite not having any since Ponar took away her stash. If Rai didn't think about it, she could forget about her unusual talents, the Core, the Juggernaut, even her amnesia. On second thought, forgetting wasn't even a possibility.

"You know Rai, I've meant to share something with you, but things have been so crazy lately it seems I never find the time," Meik said.

"We're just us Durmah up here," Rai replied. Speaking of Durmah, where was Ponar? "Share away."

"I think I can speak for the entire family when I say how happy we are to have you as a part of our Sept. You've been such a great help to Jesse these past few months. You also helped us out with finding the cause of the tainted luna berries so that Durmah wouldn't have to worry about being held responsible."

"Thanks, Meik," Rai replied. At least someone saw her as help, and not just a source of trouble.

"You're welcome," Meik put a hand on her shoulder. "You know, you've been such a great little helper, my only concern is that perhaps we aren't there for you as you need us to be."

Rai was glad of the insulating layers between them and the fuzziness in her head; she didn't want to get caught up in Meik's emotional share-fest. No, she couldn't.

"Oh, I think it's just because we haven't spent all that much time together yet. Jesse and Ponar have been a great help to me in adjusting," Rai replied.

"We're very grateful to them for that," Meik said, removing his hand. "However, I know Kait, Stoi, Laan and myself have some concerns with how things have been going and that you're getting the help you need."

"Don't bother beating around the bush," Rai replied. Was that too blunt? She couldn't tell through the haze of faown. It was just her luck Meik would pick today for a heart-to-heart. "Go ahead and ask."

Rai heard footsteps and looked back to see Tinker Somnu walking up to stand beside Laan. They shared a brief smile, the kind of look that co-conspirators often share. Rai looked back out over the ocean, sure now that this was a deliberate setup.

"Well, Laan and I think that your memory has returned, but that the Guardian, our escort, has threatened you. You know, so you don't reveal what you've figured out" Meik said.

"Threatened?" Rai asked. "Where would you get that idea?"

"When we were at Harper's Sorrow after we all got cleaned up at the lake, I saw you and the Guardian talking," Meik explained.

"You were spying on me?" Rai asked.

"No. I just happened to be in the right place at the right time," Meik replied. His smug smile said this hadn't been an unhappy coincidence. "And I'm glad I was. When I asked you about it the next day, you said nothing had happened."

"Nothing did," Rai replied. Knowing Somnu was

standing behind her right now made her skin crawl. Would Meik reveal something that could put either herself or Graeber in danger?

"That's what we're talking about," Laan chimed in. "Meik has told us that it appeared the Guardian threatened you, and yet you refuse to talk about it. I don't know what's keeping Ponar at the moment, but I can tell you he shares our concerns. He has said that he's seen the Guardian speaking to you threateningly, on more than one occasion. If this is true, we need to know."

Rai forced herself to not look at Somnu, but she imagined this wasn't the first time he'd heard these stories from the Durmah. Graeber had been a fool to think their conversations wouldn't be remarked upon. And she had been a fool to trust Ponar. Rai crossed her arms, gripping her sides in her fists, willing her rising panic to subside. She wanted to run away and escape their questions. But how could she flee from family, when they were supposed to be her safe harbor?

"That man is threatening to everyone. It's like he thinks it is his job or something," Rai said. "I don't get the impression that it's anything personal."

"Guardians are bound by a strict code of conduct with their charges," Somnu replied. Both she and Meik turned to face Laan and Somnu. Rai remained leaning against the wall, for support in her befuddled state, while Meik took a few steps away. "And from what I've heard, this goes beyond rudeness or flippancy. I think we all have concerns that this particular Guardian is attempting to influence your behavior."

"Exactly," Meik said. "And if that happens, you need to know that the Durmah are here for you. Tell us what's going on so we can help you out. That's what it means to be a part of a family. We support each other in all things."

Rai's mind wasn't clear enough to formulate a cover story. She felt too betrayed and exposed to even try. "But I don't know what he wants. How can I tell you what I don't know?"

Meik frowned. "If he's harassing you, we can always report his behavior to the Matriarchy and the Guardian Chieftess. We'll push for a formal reprimand."

"No. You can't do that," Rai replied, remembering Graeber's warnings that exposure might bring too much attention to them.

Somnu, Meik, and Laan all shared furtive glances, shifting uncomfortably. "Rai," Laan said. "Can't you see that it's precisely this type of reaction which makes us think he's threatening you?"

"I suppose," Rai replied. A tear ran down her cheek, which she hastily wiped away.

"Tell us what he's said to you," Laan asked. "We're your family. We can help you work this out. You don't have to do it alone."

The door to the stairwell opened noisily. An apprehensive-looking Ponar emerged, followed by a stony-faced Guardian Graeber. From the depths of her subconscious mind, Rai recognized his expression and knew that this was how Graeber wore his fear. This look reminded her of when he'd found her inside her old house at Harper's Sorrow and had her pinned to the wall, demanding answers. Remembering Graeber's cavalier bravado in the face of the sclern, or his total lack of concern the night he'd faced off with the Terror at the park, or so many other instances--Rai had repeatedly witnessed his unwavering self-confidence. He never showed fear, not to anyone. She suspected he was simply too egotistical.

But at that moment, somewhere deep inside, Rai knew they'd lost their gambit to keep herself, Kilawren, alive. Whether it took a minute or a month, the inevitable fall had begun.

"Thanks for joining us, you two," Somnu said. "We'd only expected Ponar, but I can't say your arrival is at all surprising, *Guardian.*"

"Sorry to interrupt your family meeting," Graeber replied. "I asked Ponar to bring me here so I could give you an update on our itinerary."

"And that would be?" Meik asked.

"From the weather reports, it appears we won't be traveling in the morning. The rain is expected to return with a vengeance. I feel it's a better option to wait a day and hope the conditions improve," he explained.

"Whatever you feel is best," Laan replied. "Now, if there's nothing else, we'd like to continue our conversation. In private."

"Of course," Graeber said. "Your family has been through quite a bit these last few days, and you certainly have my sympathy for it. Before I leave, could I make just one suggestion?"

"Sure, what?" Meik asked.

"All of you have pushed very hard during this trip on little sleep. As such, everyone is stressed and exhausted. As we're going to be here for another day, why not get some rest and resume this conversation tomorrow?" Graeber replied.

Rai had never heard the Guardian speak so evenly, or respectfully. He must be terrified to be so nice, and this realization shook Rai to her core. Dread flooded her senses, a cold sweat broke out across her skin. Their eyes met. *"You need to get out of here before they make you reveal what you know,"* Graeber's thoughts urged. *"You're more vulnerable right now because of the faown."*

"What, so you have yet another opportunity to corner Rai and keep her from telling us the truth?" Meik asked. He walked toward Graeber, pointing a finger in his face. "I don't think so! We've had enough of you. When we're done up here, I'm going to demand a new escort to finish this trip with us."

"You're welcome to do whatever you feel is best for your family," Graeber replied. "I'll go process your request for a new guide now if you'd like. I just don't want to see you bicker because you're too tired to think straight."

"Don't you dare imply we're confused and imagining the affront you've delivered to our Sept!" Meik yelled, spittle flying. "We are no fools!" Meik raised his arm as if to strike the Guardian, and both Laan and Ponar stepped in to hold him back. Somnu took a step backward towards the door, eyes fixed on Graeber and Meik.

Graeber never even tensed. "Take care, Durmah, lest you start something you can't win."

"Enough!" Rai shrieked. "Stop it!" Her voice startled them, at once deflating the peaking tempers. "I can't live by your rules," Rai said to Meik. "Nor can I live by yours," she said to Graeber. "There's no way through this maze. It's your maze, not mine. And you know what? I'm done puzzling out the way." Rai placed her hands flat on the rock wall she was leaning on. The cold, damp surface of the smoothly polished stone chilled her to the bone.

"It's been a long day, Rai," Ponar replied. "You're just tired. Let me walk you back to your room, okay?"

"Yes, it's been a long day for all of us," Laan said. "I'm sure things will be easier to talk out in the morning, when we're all well-rested, as the Guardian suggested."

There was a hysterical edge to her laughter as it

echoed off the outpost's parapets. "I don't even know what direction I'm supposed to be headed!" she screamed. Once again tears filled her eyes, mercifully blurring the demanding expressions of the Durmah, Tinker Somnu, and Guardian Graeber.

"Everything will look better in the morning," Graeber said. Although Rai couldn't make out his expression through her blurred vision, his anguished tone spoke volumes.

"You can't believe that," Rai whispered.

"*I do*," Graeber replied without words. "*We can run farther. Much farther. It doesn't have to be like this anymore. We can leave Az'Unda.*"

"It will, child," Somnu piped up, apparently oblivious to Graeber's message. "There will be more time to talk in the light of a brand new day. All of this confusion can be sorted out, and whatever help you need your family will get you."

"We'll do whatever we can, Rai," Meik said.

"All of us will," Ponar said. "You're not alone."

"That's where you're wrong. I am alone. And nothing any of you can do will ever change that fact."

Rai turned and looked out to the horizon, blurred by darkness, clouds, waves, and tears. In a fluid movement, she pulled herself up onto the wall and then jumped out into the night. For a brief moment, Rai heard footsteps and screams. But those sounds were quickly whipped away by the wind, as she fell like a rock down the sheer cliff face. As the seconds passed, Rai extended her arms and legs wide as she prepared to embrace the ocean's cold, quiet depths as they rushed up to meet her.

CHAPTER 15

"Are you sure you want to stay?" Graeber asked. "I can't guarantee you'll be able to get another escort before this situation with the Juggernaut passes."

Ponar rested his hands on the rock wall Rai jumped from the night before, looking out into the calm ocean waters. "If anything washes ashore ..."

"I understand," Graeber replied. The Guardians stationed at the Outpost had been searching the area for Rai's body, yet had found nothing. "You need to know: they might never recover her body. The ocean current along this shoreline runs south-south-east, directly away from the Cove."

"I know, but I can't leave yet," Ponar replied.

"I wouldn't be leaving either, but there's a time-sensitive situation to which I've committed my assistance." Graeber ran a hand through his hair.

"The Juggernaut?" Ponar asked. It wasn't appropriate to question a Guardian this way, but Rai's death had left him feeling raw and brazen.

"No, actually. I trust the Matriarchs will do whatever can be done to manage the Juggernaut. I have to catch up with an old friend and help her eliminate a particularly dangerous Terror." By all accounts, the Terror known as Terem had ground a wide swath of destruction through the Guardian Sept and showed no signs of slowing down.

"Aren't they *all* vicious? I mean, I can't imagine a Terror would scare you?"

"Oh, I'm not scared of the Terror," Graeber explained. "I'm concerned for my friend. She almost died the last time her path crossed with the Terror, and I'm afraid she's taking this kill a bit too personally because of it." Plus, when he shared with Bauleel the events of last night, well, hearing about her sister's death wouldn't improve her mood.

There was a pause as they both stared off into the ocean, each lost in their own grief.

"I still want to know the truth," Ponar admitted. Graeber turned and met his gaze. "I know it won't bring her back, but I loved her and can't help but wonder what she discovered from her past which drove her over the edge."

Silence hung in the air as Graeber considered his request. For a moment Ponar thought he'd give in and explain it all, but then Graeber shook his head.

"I'm sorry, Ponar, there's not much more I can tell you."

"I can tell you my mother, Chieftess Durmah, isn't going to give up on finding out about Rai's past."

Graeber took a deep breath. "Write to your mother. Tell her Rai was driven to deep depression over fears of her past and started using large quantities of faown. Her addiction caused her irrational behavior and drove her to suicide."

"She won't buy it," Ponar replied. "I know I don't."

"She'll have to. I don't have any other explanation for you."

"Just not one you're willing to give."

Graeber looked back out at the ocean, expression grim. "Rai was dead before you ever met her. She tried to hold on--to become someone new and leave her past behind--but she couldn't let go of who she used to be."

"Neither could you," Ponar spat back.

"No, I suppose I couldn't." Graeber turned and walked away without another word.

"Yeah, I can't seem to either."

CHAPTER 16

"What's the plan?" Rilte asked.

"We wait, and watch," Bauleel answered.

Both lay on their bellies in the tall grass under the shade of a large frond tree. Bauleel studied the Jonquin's Sept's farm with military precision. She'd noted all access points to the facility's outer wall and inner compound, done a headcount of the staff, and mentally logged visible weapons. Not that Terem would need them, but she'd be a fool to ignore them.

Rilte sighed. "We haven't moved for hours. You sure he's here?"

"Positive." She'd managed to track Terem's scent here, a mere four days after discovering his handiwork back at the outpost. It was unmistakable; this was the place.

"But everyone's acting normally. And the Sept members are alive," Rilte said.

"That's true. Remember what Captain Tiine said?"

"He claimed Terem wanted a quiet life on the farm, right?"

"That's correct," Bauleel replied. "And it looks like this is the farm of his dreams. Too bad for the Jonquin Sept."

"Yeah, and I'm not sure we're much safer," Rilte said. "You sure he won't be able to see us?"

"He might, but we're well hidden. As long as he's not wandering around outside the compound walls ..."

Rilte spun around, checking behind them anxiously. There was no one there. Bauleel once again regretted allowing him to join her on this trek. Unlike her, Rilte had no way of protecting himself against Terem and was certainly of no use fighting him.

"When are you going to alert Chieftess Raza?" he asked, settling back down.

"As soon as--well, now," Bauleel replied, pointing. "Look there, coming out of the stables."

Terem Zebio walked out of the stable and stretched his arms into the air, a broad smile on his face. A young boy who'd been playing in the yard walked up to him, and they talked. They seemed fast friends.

"He looks, uh, good?" Rilte said. "How long can he maintain like this?"

It was a rhetorical question; Rilte's training as a Technician meant he knew as much or more than she did on the matter. "He's got a stable mutation, remember? That's why they're called stable," Bauleel replied.

"You're not thinking of granting him his wish, are you? Letting him live here and not interfere?"

Bauleel pulled her roaming comm from her pocket. "Oh, never. Sure he can have a pleasant conversation on a sunny afternoon, and possibly maintain most of the time. It's the inevitable exceptions that make this farce completely unacceptable. We've both seen what he's capable of. That's a line you can't uncross."

She keyed in the GPS location, added a note that Terem was in a stable phase, and sent the short message to both Raza and Graeber. Although she saw some high-priority messages flashing in her queue, she slid the comm back into her pocket and her attention back to Terem's behavior. If he lost control, she'd have to intervene without any assistance. Hopefully, Graeber would respond and join her sooner than later. Terem wasn't going to be an easy kill.

"I've sent word," Bauleel explained. "Backup should arrive within a day or two."

"And in the meantime?"

"We watch and wait. I don't want to confront Terem and risk him turning on the Jonquin." Hopefully, when backup arrived, she would also be able to remove Rilte from the situation. The possibility Terem would recognize Rilte and then use him as a hostage had been haunting both her dreams and mental scenarios of the fateful encounter.

Repaying Rilte's kindness with such a death wasn't in her game plan. Somehow along this journey, she'd transitioned from admiring Rilte for his mental acumen and his upbeat personality to relying on him and caring for him. Not that she was altogether clear what her initial game plan with Rilte had consisted of, but now it included a depth of feeling she hadn't accounted for in her plans.

"I like the sound of that. Better to leave the matter to professionals anyway," Rilte replied.

Bauleel didn't take her eyes off Terem. "Don't worry. I'll get you away from here before things get messy."

She felt his level of anxiety rise. Rilte had grown protective of her, and oddly enough Bauleel didn't mind that.

"You're planning on fighting him alongside the Guardians, aren't you?" he asked.

"They'll be assisting me."

"You can't be serious?"

Bauleel watched Terem toss a ball back and forth with the boy he'd been talking with. "He and I had some conversations before his escape. I'd like to think I'll be able to use that rapport to distract him long enough to get him out of the Jonquin Sept's compound."

"We're back to negotiation with a Terror now? And what if that doesn't work? What if, once he recognizes you, he attacks you in the compound, putting everyone inside at risk, including you?"

"He has to be stopped," Bauleel said. "If I'd done

my job back at the Temple, stopped him then, then no one at the Outpost would have been killed by his madness."

"No one holds you responsible for that," Rilte replied. "Despite these clothes, you're not a trained Guardian and can't be expected to fight off a Terror."

Bauleel's frustration got the better of her. "I have extensive training in all aspects of the Guardian Sept's arts. I can assure you I've killed more Terrors than you could count without your stupid calculator."

Immediately Bauleel regretted her outburst. Rilte's distress was palpable. "I'm sorry, that was rude of me. I'm just so angry with myself. If I hadn't been so out of practice, fewer people would be dead now."

"I understand your frustration, but I'm sure even the best, well-trained Guardian gets caught off guard," Rilte murmured. "All of those who died at the Outpost were trained extensively, yes? Yet they were also caught off their guard. I'd also like to point out that you're not healed, and despite those Methuselah treatments you're not immortal."

She knew he was gently reminding her of her promise to explain those treatments. It was one of his motivations for following her on this journey. That and his admiration which, due to her gifts, she knew continued to grow.

"Thanks to you I'm feeling almost myself again." Bauleel smiled, but he was right--she was still well below her enhanced physical abilities.

"That's wonderful. But you've been Matriarch Bauleel for as long as I've been at the Guild. How long has it been since you've used your Guardian training to kill a Terror?" Rilte asked.

Bauleel had to consider that for a moment, it was long before her time spent serving as Matriarch for Raven's Call, wasn't it? "38 years, give or take a few months."

"Most Az'Un don't live past 60, you know? What with the plague and the side effects of the treatments." Bauleel didn't reply. "Anyway, I'd say that 38 years might just qualify for being a wee bit out of practice. Don't you think?" Rilte asked.

"Perhaps," Bauleel conceded.

"Yes, and *maybe* you shouldn't be so hard on your-self for missing Terem's transformation? It's not like you've had to deal directly with Terrors for some time."

"It's no excuse. I took an oath to protect all Az'Un from all forces threatening our existence. I failed." Terem finished playing ball and walked back into the stable, oblivious to their presence. Bauleel breathed a sigh of relief.

"That's a solemn duty. How long ago did you take the oath?" Rilte asked.

Bauleel pulled her eyes away from the Jonquin compound. Now she was faced with either honoring her promise to Rilte or, again, breaking her word. In all of her years, Bauleel hadn't bonded with anyone outside of her immediate family. Instead, she'd maintained a predetermined emotional distance from those around her. Somehow, after the trauma of Terem's attack and Rilte's subsequent aid, Bauleel had let him in past her walls.

"Remind me, how long ago did humans settle Az'Unda?" Bauleel asked.

Rilte's brow furrowed. "Six hundred and thirty some odd years?"

"And the trip we took from the United Federated Territories? Do you remember how long that took?" Bauleel felt his disbelief mounting, seemingly in accord with her own anxiety.

"The history books record it at two hundred and twenty-six years if I remember correctly."

"You do," Bauleel confirmed. Beyond other members of the Core, she'd never discussed her past with anyone. Just add it to all of the other Core's rules she's broken over the previous two years. Considering aiding Kilawren's escape, this indiscretion would just be a footnote to the long list of transgressions they could hold over her head.

"I'm not sure I'm following you," Rilte replied. "Because I'm tempted to think you're implying you took your oath and the Methuselah treatments before getting on the settlement ships, but that can't be ..."

"Yeah, I know," Bauleel laughed. "That would make me, what, over eight hundred and fifty years old?"

"Exactly, that's ridiculous," Rilte replied. "Especially since the Hegemony lists Methuselah drugs as banned substances. If they found out human settlers were using them ... they might go so far as to prohibit passage to our ships through their territories."

"They might also decline our petition to be recognized as a sentient species," Bauleel continued.

"Which is why the risk would be too great," Rilte said.

Bauleel shrugged. "There are many risks in settling a new world. The risk in selecting a good crew to safeguard transport of tens of thousands of settlers in cold sleep. The risk of extended flight times due to hardships finding a suitable settlement location."

"Those are known hazards," Rilte replied.

"Yes, but imagine how difficult it would be to train a new crew mid-stream, and how much easier and safer it would be to maintain the same staff throughout the long journey."

"That's a tremendous risk to take, assuming the Hegemony would never find out," Rilte said.

"Granted, but the failure rate of Earth-built colonial settlement ships is historically about thirty percent. The Hegemony views our inability to expand successfully beyond our starting galaxy just one of humanity's many failures, and each ship lost is calculated in our overall success score. It's a simple risk/gain formula," Bauleel explained. "If Az'Unda cannot thrive, we fail, and if they find out humanity bent the rules to succeed, we also fail."

"And I thought discussing Terem was depressing," Rilte said.

Bauleel laughed mirthlessly. "You wanted to know where I got my Methuselah treatments. I got them off-world before boarding the original colonial ship bound for this sector."

Rilte remained amazingly calm, given the revelation. "How many of the crew received these treatments?"

"All one hundred and fifty," Bauleel replied. "But most of us died during the initial outbreak of the plague," Bauleel explained.

"I remember from the history books, only a few of the crew survived, but all of the colonists revived up to that point perished. And you were there--you witnessed the tragedy first-hand."

Bauleel nodded. "For some reason, those of us who'd used the Methuselah treatments were *resistant* to the plague. We got it, but it didn't have the same effects as it did on the colonists. Our bodies kept fighting it, and we reached a point of balance." Balance; yeah that's the word for it. Explaining the nuances of the gifts the plague had left the crew wasn't something she was willing to divulge. "But the colonists were not so lucky. They went mad, becoming Terrors. They killed each other and killed many of the crew. Then they died from the illness, and those of us left began researching ways to control the virus."

"Wouldn't it have been easier to pick another location?" he asked.

"It wasn't an option. We'd already repurposed critical ship components for structures on the surface. Remember, we'd been here for nearly eight years when the plague hit. Moving on would have meant losing those resources and leaving behind a significant portion of the colonists who were still in stasis, waiting to be awakened when food production levels could support them. We had to find a way to make it work."

"What are the rest of the crew doing now?" Rilte asked.

"What we've been doing since we got here; helping build a human society while seeking a way to overcome the plague. We formed the Technician's Guild and sent all of the best and brightest to study there, in hopes that a cure could be found."

"All in secret," Rilte said. "From the Az'Un and the Hegemony."

"It had to be that way."

"How many of the original crew are left?" Rilte asked.

"Just over two dozen, I'm afraid. Some were killed facing Terrors, some in tragic accidents. Like you said, we aren't immortal--we just don't age at the normal human rate," Bauleel explained.

Rilte rolled over onto his back, looking up at the sun filtered through the tree's leaves. "I kept trying to come up with a way some colonists or the Matriarchs might be allowed off-world access for the Methuselah treatments, but with the quarantine, that explanation didn't make sense. But this ... I never imagined."

"No one has. The history books record how a few colonists survived and started over, but their names aren't listed."

"It's quite the tale," Rilte said, gazing at her awestruck.

"It's a story you can't ever repeat." Why did she entrust this knowledge with him? Perhaps because he'd saved her life at great risk to his own, but she suspected that had only opened the door to deepening the emotions between them.

"I won't. You have my word on it." He paused, his expression unguarded, his eyes intently holding her gaze, and she believed him with absolute certainty. "I'm amazed you shared this with me. I'm pretty sure the rest of your crewmates won't like what you've done."

"I seem to be taking a lot of risks lately," she said. "Especially when it comes to my crewmates."

"After all this time, why now?" His unspoken 'why me' begged to be answered.

"I guess I lost the faith. We're no closer to a cure for the plague. We find a new treatment that kills it and then it mutates into something even more deadly, like Terem. It's a battle we're bound to lose."

"Are you the only one who feels this way?" he asked, expression incredulous.

"Everyone is frustrated," she explained, more surprised than Rilte over her confession.

"That's to be expected, isn't it?" His curiosity, evident in the tension of his body, the pitch of his voice, and the sharp scent of his emotions, reminded Bauleel of how much she'd revealed in the conversation.

"Yes, indeed." Bauleel wanted to explain about Kilawren, and how her faith in the Core's mission had eroded steadily since they'd sentenced her sister to death, but she'd revealed enough already without putting her sister at further potential risk.

"It feels like there's more on your mind?" Rilte asked.

Bauleel smiled. "There is. I can't tell you how nice it is to have someone new to talk to after all these years."

"I'm glad you trust me," he replied. "And I'll keep listening all day. It'll keep us busy while we wait, after all."

"Thanks, but I'd better not say too much more about my crewmates. I'd be in big trouble if they found out I'd told you all of this."

"I told you, I'll keep your secret," Rilte replied.

"I know you will, but they have ways."

"Fair enough," he said. Rilte laughed and shook his head.

"What?" she asked.

"I can't get over how good you look, considering you're an old lady."

Bauleel frowned. "Yeah, and this old lady can still kick your ass."

Rilte laughed again. "I'm sorry, Bauleel, you don't scare me."

Bauleel forced a smile, profoundly touched over his surprising yet genuine sentiment. "Yeah, that's what I like about you." Her attraction to Rilte blossomed every time he displayed his trust and utter lack of fear. Rilte smiled back, and the authentic warmth of his reaction disarmed Bauleel, who had lived for years surviving on the fear of others.

CHAPTER 17

A THOUSAND ICY BLADES DROVE INTO RAI'S FLESH as her body smashed into the cold, dark ocean. She'd expected her existence to blackout on impact with the water, but death refused to live up to her expectations. Consciousness lingered by a thread as she plunged downward, the inky depths obliterating all remnants of moonlight and starlight. Surrounded by darkness, Rai breathed in salt water, then coughed, expelling all air from her lungs.

Through the crushing pressure of suffocation Rai feebly fought to breathe, which only served to flush more cold water through her body. If only I had gills like a fish--she thought to herself--then I wouldn't have to drown like this. Suddenly fresh pain cut through both sides of her neck like a knife. Although Rai couldn't see what caused the gashes with her eyes, her hands discovered identical semi-circular flaps of flesh which hung slightly separate from the skin. With her right hand, she explored the depth of the cut, bringing on a new coughing fit. The pressure forced water through the openings in her neck--bringing an instant sense of relief.

Gills? Rai breathed in more water, and then again and again and was rewarded with the oxygen she could now pull from the water. The process was harder than breathing, but it beat drowning. No longer suffocating, Rai noticed she wasn't moving upwards or downwards, but instead floating with neutral buoyancy along an underwater current. She also noticed that the effects of the faown had faded--either from the shock of the impact, being exposed to the chilly water, or breathing the water, she didn't know--but her thoughts were once again clear.

How did I do that? She touched her neck again, feeling the salt water forced out through the gills. Was this yet another unusual ability which had always been there but, because of her amnesia, she couldn't remember? If only Graeber hadn't been so stubborn, she would know!

Then Rai remembered the looks of horror on the faces of the Durmah and Graeber--Somnu, however, had looked smug--when she leaped over the parapet wall. Most likely they all thought her dead, and although Rai regretted the pain this would cause Ponar, she didn't regret being free from all of them. Dying had brought her the one thing Rai wanted, freedom. She hadn't expected to survive but was glad of the opportunity it provided.

But where would she go now? Perhaps she could return to the underground home she'd discovered in Harper's Sorrow, the one Graeber said she'd lived at for a while. Surely she'd find more evidence of her past, especially as she wouldn't have Graeber there to prevent her from finding out.

Assuming, of course, that he also believed her dead. Rai thought he not only knew of her secret talents but also shared them. He'd have to at least suspect that she might still be alive. She'd witnessed his tracking skills, and if Graeber wanted to find her Rai had no doubt he'd be able to do so. Would he seek to keep her from her past now that the Durmah thought she was dead? She had no way of knowing.

An odd fuzzy sensation had been slowly growing through Rai, and it was beginning to make the back of her head and neck itch. Could it be a side-effect of using the gills or the remains of the faown still in her system? It didn't feel like the drowsy medicinal but instead made her feel focused and aware. Rai began to notice--no, *feel*--fish and other sea creatures swimming around her despite the enveloping darkness. She remembered hazily reading books filled with stories of sea monsters and warnings not to venture too far from shore. But Rai was fearless, feeling connected to the ocean itself as if it was merely an extension of her own being.

Come.

Rai felt the command and couldn't help but respond. She began swimming downward, out of the current she was traveling in and into deeper waters. Her skin tingled as a state of blissful peace permeated her mind.

Come.

The command came again, louder this time. Rai willed webbing to grow between her fingers and toes and then swam faster. The voice reminded her of the way the Juggernaut had spoken with her, except this was compelling. A blue glow became visible across the landscape, faint at first, but ever more luminous as she approached. The shape reminded her of the lake in Harper's Sorrow, but here it was bordered by limestone cliffs and coral walls.

Here.

Rai's eyes were drawn to a dark spot near the center of the shimmering azure lake. A single black stone column only a few feet wide ran from the depths of the ocean floor to a point high above the lake, gleaming eerily in the reflected light. Rai swam to it, keeping well above the churning waters below. The surface of the column looked almost fluid, but Rai couldn't tell if that was an optical illusion from the bioluminescent light below.

Join.

Panic pounded through her veins as her hands involuntarily reached out and touched the column.

The surface was hard, smooth, and unexpectedly warm. White and blue pinpoint lights began flashing up and down its entire length. Rai was terrified, yet mesmerized under its blissful spell. What had she discovered?

An electrifying current coursed through her body as visions of her past flashed through her mind. Muscular seizures wracked her frame as she relived every moment since she'd awakened in the crèche in Raven's Call, yet her hands remained fixed to the column. The process finished with Rai reliving her fall from the outpost at Jeweled Cove into the ocean.

Incomplete archival.

"It's called amnesia," Rai replied in her mind.

The glowing miasma below began to roll and move upward like an amoeba. Rai pulled violently in a futile attempt to release her hands. The waves of pleasure subsided, replaced by the sensation that every molecule within her was being examined.

Non-native species / Alive / Not of Vidaaquar / Provide origin point.

"That's right. I'm a human colonist, one of many here. We came in a ship from Calypso VII a long time ago." Rai had no idea if that would make sense, yet felt compelled to answer the question.

Provide origin point.

"Oh, you mean like where my species originated? That'd be Earth."

No / Provide a point of origin on Vidaaq.

"Oh! You mean where the human colonists landed on this planet?" Rai asked. There was no response, so she continued. "It was somewhere up north, but the city was destroyed in the first plague outbreak. No one even lives up there anymore. Eventually, we built towns in the lowlands along the shore."

Need location of the point of origin.

"I don't know," Rai replied.

More images flashed through her mind, remnants of memories before her awakening in Raven's Call. Pictures of abandoned buildings lining dust-covered streets. Images of Graeber and a woman, both looking upset and distraught as they all flew in the air on some sort of craft Rai didn't recognize. They stood on the shore at Jeweled Cove, Graeber bidding the woman good luck. 'Don't forget to keep her drugged, and she won't remember a thing. I'll return this to Sebaiya for safe keeping...'

Sebaiya. The word rung like a bell in her mind as images of the town cycled like a picture book. Both Rai and the device knew its location and layout, pulled from the reconstructed memories.

Sebaiya / Origin point of the invading species. Rai detected a note of satisfaction in its tone.

"We're colonists, not invaders. We are the human stewards of Az'Unda, working to develop a balance with life on this planet."

I am the only steward of Vidaaq / I am Vidaaquar / Constituents in your bloodstream deny my full steward-

ship / Species which do not conform to the designated guidelines must be destroyed for the health of Vidaaq.

"Wait! You control the plague? The Terrors? But humans aren't a threat to Az'Unda! We're protecting ourselves from getting sick!"

Arguing with the device was useless. The blue glow flowed up and enveloped Rai, obliterating all thought in madness.

Blocking constituents will be cleansed / You will be remade a suitable vessel of Vidaaq / Seek the origin point of contamination / Destroy.

Rai screamed as millions of tiny organisms passed through her skin and into her muscles and organs, intent on transforming her, cell by cell, into the being known as Vidaaquar.

CHAPTER 18

Matriarch Natre pressed her hand to the keypad marked 'Storeroom #12' and then waited while the device displayed her full name and flashed green. The door lock cycled slowly, creaking from neglect. It wasn't often anyone came down into the bowels of the Temple's old supply corridors.

Planned population growth hadn't happened, so the storerooms built to hold surplus goods had been emptied long ago and were never refilled. Storeroom #12 was different--it housed some electronic devices salvaged from the colony ship, including additional comm systems. Between the little traffic, door lock, and comms, it was the perfect secluded spot for the Core to congregate in Raven's Call.

The door swung open, and Natre stepped inside, closing it behind herself. Natre threaded her way between stacks of equipment towards the voices near the back of the cavernous room. From the scent in the air, Natre could tell the conversation had already heated up. When she emerged into the central space, Natre saw the vid comm screen was already active, displaying the faces of members who hadn't been able to attend in person.

"I see you all began without me," Natre said, interrupting the conversation. "What's left to discuss?"

"We're all peers here, *Matriarch*," Somnu replied. He was covered in dirt and stank of horses. "Or have you forgotten?" He pointed at her veil.

Natre removed the veil covering her face, tucking it into her belt. What use was a veil in the Core, where everyone could quickly pick up on your emotions without even looking at your face? "Excuse me. I'm afraid I don't even notice that thing anymore. Sorry I'm late. It's taken me longer than expected to come up to speed on Temple affairs."

"Do let Aleta or myself know if we can be of assistance, Natre," offered Taessen. She was the Matriarch of Barrow's Grove, and Aleta was Matriarch of Resounding Cliffs.

"Thanks, Taessen, I'll take you up on that," Natre replied.

"Aleta, how soon do you think we might transition some of your Technicians to our facility?" Natre asked. "It's been cleaned up and restocked, so now all we're missing are the scientists."

"I've finished reviewing the rosters, and I have

selected suitable candidates to rebuild your crew. The entire Guild at Resounding Cliffs wants to help, and I can tell you safety protocols have been the main focus, from specimen handling all the way through test subjects. We'll need to wait until the Hegemony ships leave, but once they do let's get your guild halls re-staffed," Aleta said.

"Speaking of the Hegemony," Natre said.

"Let's get back on topic, shall we?" Elder Rebea said. She must be the moderator-elect for this meeting, Natre reasoned. "Raza, you were about to give us an update on the Terem Zebio situation?"

Raza nodded. Flecks of mud stuck to her leather boots and cape, evidence of her hurried arrival. "For the past two days, Bauleel has been monitoring Terem at the Jonquin Sept farm. The situation sounds stable for the moment. Terem's destruction of the Northern Outpost near Raven's Call forced me to send reinforcements from the Eastern and Southern Outposts of Barrow's Grove. I expect they will arrive within two more days, depending on the roads after all the rain we've had."

"How many are you sending?" Natre asked.

"I've pulled four dozen from their regular duties, so enough to re-staff an entire outpost if needed. If Terem manages to infect others before he's taken down, then there should be sufficient personnel to handle the collateral damage. Any survivors will then help rebuild the Northern Outpost once the area is secured," Raza replied.

"Four dozen?" Rebea asked. "Is the situation that dangerous?"

"I believe so. In fact, after this meeting I'm planning to head north myself, and join with Bauleel to defeat Terem," Raza replied.

"Don't you think you're overreacting?" said Cerry, one of their more elderly-appearing Core members. His grave features reminded Natre of a hawk.

Natre reflected on the composition of the Core and how traveling here as the crew had brought them together. However, surviving the first plague had further cemented their relationships at an entirely deeper level. Protecting the colonists had transitioned from a long-term mission into an interminable calling. They'd lost members over the years to accidents and plague-related deaths, but the dedication of the Core crew meant no one would quit the task until the plague was cured.

In other words, effectively never.

"No," Raza replied with a frown. "I suppose every-one's forgotten the last stable mutation that got away? I know it's been close to three hundred years, but I seem to remember that's the reason Three Moons, that little fishing village south of Jeweled Cove, got wiped off the map."

"No one's forgotten that tragedy," Taessen replied. "Nor have we forgotten how bloodthirsty the plague's victim's become. I can only imagine how deranged Terem is, considering how long he's survived the mutation. I took part in the early studies, and I'm appalled the Technicians were allowed to maintain the experiment. The rare mutations that led to a stable presentation inevitably manifested the most violent behaviors. That said, do you require our assistance?"

Raza shrugged. "If you have Guardian training and you're not otherwise occupied, then I'd love the help. Hopefully, this situation will be resolved within another three days, one way or the other."

"Where's Graeber?" Cerry asked gruffly. "He's the best fighter we've got."

"He and I arrived in town this morning," Somnu replied. "He said he didn't want to waste time chatting with us when there was something to kill." Cerry nodded in stoic agreement.

Raza laughed mirthlessly. "That sounds like my brother. Funny, he hasn't sent me any messages saying he's heading up there." Raza pulled out her roaming comm unit, activated it and checked, then frowned and shook her head as she put the device back into her pocket.

"I'm not surprised. Graeber seemed pretty angry when we parted," Somnu replied.

Raza didn't say a thing, nor could Natre read a thing off of her. Raza must be shielding, but why?

"Who cares?" Cerry replied. "He's helping out as best he can, that's all that matters. Now, it seems to me we've talked the Terem situation to death, and I'd like to report on my progress."

"Of course," Rebea replied. "How goes your investigation into the thallium poisoning in the luna berry farms?"

"During an audit of the storehouses, I identified eight total missing aqueous dispersal units. I was able to modify a sensor unit and track down the other seven units, which had been placed in various swamps throughout the Barrow's Grove farmlands. I'm transmitting the list of locations now, along with the products grown at each," Cerry said.

Rebea brought the list up on the screen for everyone to read.

"Wait a minute, those are the exact ingredients contained in the plague medicinal," Taessen said. "Someone's trying to destroy our ability to fight the plague!"

Natre wasn't the only one who was visibly shocked by this revelation.

"Could you identify who removed the units from the storehouses?" Aleta asked.

"No, those log entries were erased. In my opinion, this was a direct attack, not just against the survival of Az'Un society, but against the Core itself," Cerry explained.

"Who would do such a thing?" Natre asked.

"I think the bigger question is: who *would want to destroy everything we've worked for?*" Somnu asked.

"What are you implying?" Rebea asked.

"Think about it. Who would have the codes to access the storehouses? Who would know how to operate the aqueous dispersal units? Who would know how to modify the access logs to the storehouses? And, who would know which farms to target for maximum destruction to the plague medicinal?" Somnu asked. "I'm telling you, all of you, it's one of us. Only one of the Core could have the means necessary." Cerry, a well-known close friend of Somnu, nodded ruefully in agreement during this exposition.

"That's impossible!" Aleta cried. Many others echoed her sentiment, but Natre held her tongue. Feelings of anger and betrayal flooded her senses.

"No, Somnu is on the mark in his suspicions," Cerry said. "No Az'Un citizen has the knowledge or capability to pull this off."

"Do you have any leads?" Raza asked.

"Of course not, if I had I would have shared my suspicions," Somnu spat out. "But now I believe Kilawren is to blame."

"Kilawren has been dead for some time now, Somnu," Raza replied. "Many years have passed."

"No, it's a possibility," Cerry replied. "The devices had been in place for a while, possibly before her death. She could have planted them there long ago."

"I disagree," Raza replied. "The crimes she committed weren't treasonous in nature--what you're suggesting now is. As misguided as she was, Kilawren claimed to be looking for a cure."

Somnu frowned, holding his hands up. "I didn't mean to imply Kilawren planted the devices. I feel her misdeeds divided us deeply, and I think we need to consider and research all of the options. As we all know, her death sentence caused ill will with notable members of the Core, and perhaps that led to some rash and ill-conceived reactions? However, Cerry has a solid point, Kilawren certainly could have planted the devices years ago. "

Everyone knew whom he meant: Graeber and Bauleel. Natre felt waves of sadness and anger pass through the group; Kilawren's treachery had heralded a loss of trust between them all, and this was still a palpable sensation.

"Choose your words carefully!" Raza said. Her anger flared like a torch. "I won't hear more of your baseless accusations!"

Somnu smirked. "Dear Raza, surely Graeber can defend himself without his big sister's protection?"

"Oh, he doesn't need my help. But you know, I find it a cowardly act to accuse *friends* when they aren't present and able to defend themselves," Raza replied.

"If they weren't both absent..." Somnu began.

"Silence!" Rebea shouted. "I think we've all had enough of your bickering!"

"Indeed, but the concerns raised bear investigation," Cerry replied, predictably rising to the defense of

Somnu's argument. "I'd like to ask for volunteers to assist me with flesh-to-flesh investigations of all Core members, so we can flush out who may or may not be involved in the poisoning."

Natre scanned the crowd, focused on reactions to Cerry's invasive suggestion. Curiously, Raza alone paled slightly. Were Cerry and Somnu on the mark with their suspicions? If so, offering to lead the investigation would have deflected focus away from those in charge. Or was she being paranoid?

"That's a sound course of action, Cerry," Rebea replied. "I'm sure we're all willing to submit to such questioning to find those involved. Who is available to help him?"

Somnu raised his hand, as did Lillien and Kaed. Raza raised her hand after another moment, her jaw clenched.

"Five of us should be enough," Cerry said. "Although I thought you were heading north after this meeting, Raza?"

"I'd like to assist with the interrogation of my brother and Bauleel, to make sure they are treated fairly," Raza replied. Natre recalled how vehemently Raza had defended Kilawren, likely on her brother's behalf, during the trial. Was Raza just being a protective sister at the moment, or did she suspect, or worse know, something was amiss?

Cerry nodded. "Then we'll head to the Jonquin

Sept with you first, and kill two birds with one stone that way."

Natre almost smiled, wondering if he'd meant that as a joke, but then thought better of it.

"With that item resolved, we have one final order of business to attend to. Let me reread the Hegemony's request, so it's fresh in our minds," Rebea said. She pulled up the text of the communiqué on the screen, and then read it in its entirety. She then displayed the image of Rai and Ponar Durmah on the screen.

A contemplative silence followed, into which Natre was happy to take the lead. "There is only one solution with the Hegemony: complete and total compliance with the Juggernaut demands." Natre saw many nods of agreement. "We should give them what they want, as soon as possible. Has anyone been able to identify the girl or her location?"

"I have," Somnu replied. "She's Rai Durmah, and that's her brother Ponar in the background. But her name alone isn't going to satisfy them. She's dead."

"What?" Raza exclaimed.

"Are you absolutely sure?" Natre asked.

"I watched her jump off a cliff, so yeah you could say I'm pretty sure," Somnu replied.

"Was her body ... recovered?" Raza asked.

Somnu shook his head. "No. With the undertow there, I guess the Guardians won't find it either."

"That's a shame," Natre replied. "We could have

turned over Rai's corpse--that would have been something."

"I think this outcome is much preferable to the Juggernaut getting their hands on that girl," Somnu replied.

Cerry chuckled. "Going soft in your old age, Somnu? It may have been a few years since we were stationed together, but you're a big picture man. I'm surprised to hear you concerned over a single citizen."

Somnu clapped Cerry on the shoulder. "For the record, I'm not going soft. I'd been checking into Rai's situation, and from what I'd seen, I'm not surprised the Juggernaut had an interest in her."

"What do you think they're looking for?" Rebea asked.

"The girl was altered, somehow. She's not one of the Core, yet she appeared sensitive to the emotions of others," Somnu explained. "The Juggernaut might have keyed into that, and want to know how it happened."

"Was she perhaps a stable mutation, like Terem?" Lillien asked.

"That's possible, but I don't think so. We know the plague follows two models: quick and sudden devolution or a relatively stable mutation where the victim is able to partially maintain for a short period of time, usually a period of days to weeks but never more than a Latne. Well, at least until Terem's case presented. Still, Graeber spent some time around Rai, and I'm confident he would have eliminated her if she posed any sort of threat. However, his continued interest led me to wonder whether she might be the product of one of Kilawren's illegal experiments."

"All of those subjects were destroyed," Taessen said. "I can vouch for that personally."

"I do not doubt your word, Taessen," Somnu replied. "But I have no other explanation for Rai's gifts. It's also possible that Graeber continued Kilawren's experiments on his own ..."

"Enough!" Raza cried. "I'll not hear any more of your baseless allegations against my brother!"

"Then you are welcome to leave," Rebea spoke quietly, and none dissented.

Raza fumed, and Natre swore she could hear Raza's teeth grinding. "I would like to see some evidence against my brother to accompany Somnu's deluge of innuendo," Raza demanded, her Guardian bearing apparent in the hard lines of her stance.

"I don't have any evidence, but not for lack of trying," Somnu replied. "I could never get close enough to the girl for a DNA sample, so I can't prove genetic tampering. Yet I'm sure she was altered, perhaps even similar to the Methuselah tampering done to all of us within the Core. If she's not somehow transformed, then how else can you explain her ability to read emotions? And I'm glad the Juggernaut won't have her, so they won't discover those few benefits we've gleaned from exposure the plague."

"Raza," Cerry began, "This is something we can

investigate in person with your brother. You will be there and can affirm that the questioning is handled fairly and humanely. Until that time, there is no further need to speculate."

Raza nodded, and by the acrid odor of her mood, Natre surmised she was not appeased. From what Natre knew of Raza, her anger had shifted into slow-banked embers, biding its time for a final eruption. Raza and Somnu had never been close, but after the Kilawren incident neither had been able to see eye to eye on any issue. Natre was glad both she and Somnu would be leaving town soon, so she wouldn't have to endure further quarrels between the two.

"Then it seems we have only one thing which might appease the Juggernaut," Natre said. "And I'm sure no one here will argue the necessity of my solution."

Natre explained her proposal, and true to her prediction, no one dissented.

MATRIARCH NATRE HESITATED BEFORE HITTING the send key, her fingers hovering in midair above the communications terminal. Deliberately choosing to contact a Juggernaut wasn't something she'd ever thought she'd do. After all, what human in their right mind would bring undue attention from a race who could exterminate them on a whim? Then again, choice wasn't an element in this conversation. When the Juggernaut realized the girl they wanted was dead...Natre cringed at the thought.

"Is there a problem?" Journeywoman Camille asked, ever helpful.

"Nothing is wrong with the terminal," Natre replied. She hit the send key, and then took a step back from the screen and waited. Camille stood near the door, poised to record the outcome of this meeting for posterity. Natre fought her nerves, forcing herself to stand still. As the voice apparent for the Az'Un people, she couldn't appear weak. Of course, being draped from head to toe in her white Matriarch's robes didn't hurt, not that her privileged position would impress the Assessor. However, the Juggernaut would hear her voice but wouldn't be able to see her expressions or read her scent, which definitely bolstered her confidence.

Natre heard Camille's sharp intake of breath as the screen came to life, filling the four foot high by three feet wide screen with the visage of a Juggernaut against a pale gray background.

"State your request," the Juggernaut asked, his level voice gravelly and deep-toned.

"I am Matriarch Natre, speaker for the colonists of Az'Unda. I humbly request an audience with your Arbiter of Sentience, Assessor Brague."

"I will inform the *honored* Assessor of your request," he replied. "Stand by."

A few minutes later the screen flickered, now displaying a Juggernaut who, except for the intricate yellow patterns on the carapace behind his head, looked just like the one before. Natre wondered if humans appeared as homogenized as a species to the Juggernaut as well.

"You would be the esteemed Matriarch Natre, I presume?" This male's voice was downright melodic in comparison to the others but just as deep.

Natre nodded assent. "That is correct, honored Assessor Brague."

"I appreciate your timely reply to my request," Brague replied.

"The Az'Un people wish to comply in every way possible with the Hegemonic Emissaries."

After all, what other choice do we have? So far they've managed to evade Juggernaut notice simply by being one of the few human colonies with longevity and the one far from the Hegemony's main shipping lines. From Natre's perspective, this amounted to a combination of luck mixed with Juggernaut disinterest. She knew some of the Core felt emboldened because the colony had been trending towards long-term success, which usually ensured Hegemonic disinterest. Now that the Juggernaut focus had turned their way, Natre was hard pressed to understand how they could avoid whatever consequence the aliens chose to mete out.

"That is wise. Then I trust that the female is prepared for retrieval?" Brague asked.

Natre paused--afraid that this otherwise polite conversation was about to turn deadly. "I'm sorry to report that the day after your encounter with the female we knew as Rai Durmah, she tragically drowned."

The Assessor tilted his head. "That's convenient timing."

"Let me assure you, honored Assessor, we seek no deception. I can provide multiple witnesses' testimony, as well as the exact location of the accident for your review."

"What of the male? Is he also dead?" Brague moved side-to-side, legs and belly scraping against each other creating a cacophony of high-pitched noise.

Natre was taken aback by the Assessors behavior, which she understood as indicative of a typical stress reaction. Was he genuinely concerned? "No, he is alive and well. His name is Ponar Durmah, and he is presently at these coordinates." She stepped forward and entered Ponar's exact location via the comm. "He was a brother to the girl and witnessed her demise, which happened at the outpost he's staying at. Perhaps through interviewing him and the Guardians there you will be assured I speak the truth."

Natre again considered whether to inform the poor man of his fate. Would knowing you were about to be a prisoner of the Hegemony be preferable to finding out when it actually happened? Besides, she couldn't risk him fleeing.

"I will withhold judgment until I have had an opportunity to review the facts for myself, but regardless this finding does significantly hamper my research efforts. I may be required to seek out and interview other similar subjects instead."

Natre had the distinct impression that the Assessor was asking for permission. The entire conversation had so far been downright pleasant. However, instead of alleviating her fears, this only made Natre more suspicious. With the force of the whole Hegemony behind him, why was he so, well, polite?

She had never known a Juggernaut to be polite.

"Perhaps if I knew what you were looking for, I could provide it more quickly to you?" Natre asked, hoping for some insight into the Juggernaut's curiosity with Rai Durmah. If Somnu was right and Rai had been a product of Kilawren's experiments... that might explain his interest.

"I noticed certain genetic variances with the female. Perhaps I could have Rai's remains to examine before your people perform your customary cremation?"

Could he be talking about the plague's genetic effects, she wondered? Or was it something else? Perhaps what Somnu had also noticed ... "Unfortunately we were unable to recover her body, but if you are able to locate it, you are quite welcome to run whatever tests you deem appropriate." Even as Natre uttered the words, she knew it was an empty promise. Deep-sea feeders would surely destroy whatever remained of Rai Durmah's corpse.

And if they were able to somehow, against all likelihood, recover the girl's body? What then? Was it possible there were genetic differences indicative of the Methuselah treatments? Anxiety settled as a hard lump in Natre's stomach as she considered the Juggernaut reaction to the Az'Unda colony if they were to discover such a violation of the Hegemonic law.

"Superior Hegemonic technology may make it possible to locate her," he replied.

"I wish you the best of luck in your efforts. May I be of any further assistance to the Hegemony?" Natre asked.

"I will inform you when your efforts are again needed. Your cooperation has been appreciated."

"I am glad to be of service to the Hegemony," Matriarch Natre replied, bowing.

When she stood up the screen was blank. Natre let out a long sigh and then turned to Camille, who was finishing her notes despite looking pale and scared.

"At least they are appeased for now," Natre said. "That's an enormous relief."

Camille nodded. "Do the Durmah know Ponar is being given to the Juggernaut?"

"Their family returned earlier today from Jeweled Cove, so they are still coping with the death of their adopted daughter. I need you to draft a letter to Chieftess Durmah, dated and to be delivered tomorrow, detailing Ponar's delivery to the Assessor. Note what an incredible service he has performed for the Az'Un people, how the Temple will reimburse any and all costs involved in his impending marriage..."

"He's not coming back?" Camille exclaimed.

"My dear Camille," Natre replied, placing a gentle hand on the other woman's shoulder. "Although the Assessor was polite, I certainly doubt his intentions with either of the Durmah involve them being returned alive or in one piece. Remember: humans aren't yet classified as a sentient species in their definition. We may converse at length, but in the end, they will treat us as we do our lab rats."

"It's just hard to accept we'd willingly hand him over to be tortured," Camille replied. "I can't imagine such a terrifying experience. Surely you can make another choice?" A single tear ran down her cheek.

"I did not act alone, Camille. The Matriarchs are in full agreement. We either cooperate with their demands, or more will die until they are satisfied. We felt this was our best chance to minimize fatalities," she explained.

"If they ask for the entire Durmah Sept next, will you hand them over?"

"I'd prefer not to speculate on what the Juggernaut will want next." Natre's tone made it clearly evident; this conversation was over.

"Yes, Matriarch," Camille replied. "I'll have that letter ready for you to sign within the hour." The Journeywoman turned and left.

Matriarch Natre turned back to the terminal and summarized her conversation with Assessor Brague in a text message, and then sent it along to the Core. She wanted to go with those who were catching up with Graeber and Bauleel, but her duties here called. For a moment, she marveled at how Bauleel had tolerated being cooped up for so many years as Matriarch. Natre wondered which was worse: a quick death via the Juggernaut or interminable frustration of putting out the seemingly daily fires.

CHAPTER 19

Bauleel finished her sweep of the area, finding nothing out of place around the Jonquin farm. Moonlight from both Ence and Bruoh illuminated the night, so it wasn't necessary to rely on her enhanced senses to navigate through the darkness. Over the past two days, they had witnessed Terem leaving the farm in secret and then sneaking back in hours later. There was no evidence of any deviant behavior by Terem, no dead animals, no telltale blood, nothing she could connect to his absences. Perhaps he *was* actually able to maintain in a stable state? Bauleel had seen others endure for a time, but the stable longevity he'd enjoyed was unique to how the plague manifested within him. She again, fruitlessly, wished they'd been able to contain him within the Technician's ward to understand the unique nature of his mutation.

Bauleel approached their camp, and caught a smell on the air, a scent which was all too familiar. *Terem.*

Rilte had been asleep when she'd gone, but even then how could she have left Rilte alone? Bauleel forced control over her emotions and steeled herself for the worst--at least she didn't smell blood. Not yet.

She stepped into the small clearing they used as their sleeping space. Terem sat on a felled log while Rilte was bound and gagged, lying motionless at his feet. This was no chance occurrence, she realized, noting Terem must have brought the rope with him and waited for her to leave Rilte alone. She knew exactly what Terem had been doing during those conspicuous absences from the farm. He'd been monitoring their daily movements.

"I'm glad we finally have the opportunity to talk. Do you mind if I have a seat?" Bauleel asked.

"Be my guest," Terem replied, motioning to a location some ten feet away from him.

Bauleel took a seat, wary but attempting to display a sense of ease. Rilte's eye's flashed wildly, and he struggled against his bonds, but she ignored him.

"I'm sure you received my message at the outpost?"

"We all did," Bauleel replied. "But I felt that, because of our ... history perhaps we could yet speak candidly."

"And Rilte is here because?"

"He saw to my healing, and he refused to leave my side until I was fully recuperated."

"That seems a poor decision, right about now, doesn't it." Terem gave him a swift kick to the ribs, and Rilte grunted through his gag.

"Now Terem, there's no need to punish him for his charity. This is about you, and me, after all."

"True, Matriarch, but he makes a nice bargaining chip."

Bauleel frowned. "I no longer fit that title. You can call me Bauleel now."

Terem shrugged. "But can you still bargain for me?"

"Oh yes. My Matriarchy was never the seat of my power."

"And I'm to believe you're here to bargain? That's why you've been waiting in the woods? It seems more likely you've been awaiting reinforcements for an attack." His hand rested around Rilte's neck. His grip was loose, but the implied threat was clear.

"I was watching your interactions with the Jonquin Sept. Seeing if your statements of seeking a quiet life were, indeed, correct."

"Liar." Bauleel cringed when a trickle of blood ran down Rilte's neck. She'd be better off killing Rilte and Terem both, for the good of all. Wouldn't she?

"Now, Bauleel, tell me how many Guardians are coming, and how soon I can expect them to arrive, or your pet loses an organ. Want to pick which one?"

Bauleel broke out in a cold sweat. She couldn't do this. She couldn't even look at Rilte.

"Four dozen," replied a deep voice from behind her.

"Give or take a few more heavyweights of my and Bauleel's caliber. Count on five dozen in total, just to be safe." Bauleel gasped and spun around to meet Graeber's icy blue stare. The hollow tone in his words resonated with her instantly, and she shot to her feet.

"What's happened?" Bauleel demanded. Sorrow hung from every line in of his body and face.

"We're leaving, now." The statement was unequivocal. His eyes, empty.

"As you can see," Terem rose with Rilte trapped under an arm, sharp-clawed fingers at the ready to shred his neck at the slightest hint of approach. "We were just in the middle of something."

"You were just talking yourselves to death, as I saw it." Graeber spat on the ground in disgust. "Look, have your farm, and best of luck with the coming onslaught of Guardians. Bauleel and I have to leave. Now. You're no longer our concern."

Disbelief shimmered in Terem's eyes. "You'll leave me alone, honestly?"

"Yes, but the others won't. You'll need to fight them or get out of this place."

"But they'll follow me. The Guardians always follow. Then they'll fight. They'll never stop fighting. I...I can't stay here. I'm coming with you," Terem replied with wild eyes but a steady timbre to his voice.

Bauleel stared incredulously. "No, Terem, you're still threatening Rilte!"

"Oh, fine then." Terem dumped Rilte to the ground

and hastily removed his bindings. Rilte scrambled a hasty retreat while rubbing blood flow back into his hands.

Bauleel moved between Rilte and Terem. "Doesn't matter. I'll kill you before I allow you to accompany us anywhere."

"No, we don't have time for this, Bauleel," Graeber said.

"Why am I not going to kill him?" Bauleel asked Graeber, frustration pounding like thunder through her veins.

Graeber drew her aside so they could talk privately. "Because Kilawren jumped from the fort at Jeweled Cove, killing herself. The Juggernaut arrived and are about to declare Az'Unda critical for their use, our colony defunct, and then raze our population. And because Somnu is accusing us of keeping Rai alive as Kilawren's lone surviving test subject, I have no doubt we'll be flesh interrogated by the Core force being sent here. Then they'd know the full truth. When all is revealed, we'll be executed. Thus, your little vengeance with Terem no longer matters in the larger scheme of things."

Bauleel's heart sank, for too many reasons to process in such a short period. Overwhelmed with the sudden news of Kilawren's death, she fought back inevitable tears. "What's the plan?"

"We leave Terem here for the Core to deal with. It will slow them down."

"If we flee, they'll assume our guilt."

Graeber shrugged. "They may also assume our defeat at his hands. Either way, I don't plan to wait around and see."

"Where do we go?"

"Sebaiya. We grab a colony shuttle and hike it off-world. There are plenty to use. If we get lucky, the Juggernaut won't even shoot us down."

Bauleel fumed. "That's it!" she yelled. She cursed. "You know the chances of us surviving a journey off-world are marginal at best. Besides, we'd not be traveling under the protection of a colony charter. We'll likely be killed by Juggernaut, or captured and sold by slavers. Best case, we'll starve or freeze to death when the shuttle suffers some catastrophic failure." She cursed again. "Besides, we can't abandon the people we swore to protect and flee like frightened insects."

Rilte approached, but Graeber held up a hand to stay him. Placing his hands on Bauleel's shoulders, he rubbed gently. "Yes, we go. After eight hundred some years, we've fulfilled our oaths many times over. We transported the colonists safely, established the settlement against all the odds, and have guided these people to a prosperous and stable culture as best we could. The plague was never our fault, and we persevered despite the challenge.

"We have no power over the Juggernaut, either here on Az'Unda or on a rogue shuttle in space. Perhaps the Core can persuade the Juggernaut that our colony is viable. Or maybe they will lose interest for their own reasons. You need to accept there is little, if anything, we can do to change the present course."

"I'm not willing to sit around here and die just to see how this plays out, or to try and win a battle of wills with the Core. At this point, I'd give us even odds between the Core's law and traveling in a potentially derelict shuttle with no jurisdictional protection. Now pick up your things, get your horses, and I'll get mine. It's a long ride."

Tears ran thick down Bauleel's face. "Yeah, okay. But I'm bringing Rilte. I mean if he wants to come." She couldn't see clearly through her blurry vision to make out Rilte's or Graeber's faces.

Strong arms surrounded her, answering her question with more than mere words. "I'm with you. Now, where are we going?"

Bauleel wiped her eyes. "We're leaving Az'Unda, we'll have to figure out our destination if we survive getting off world."

Rilte smiled, but she could see the fear in his eyes. "You sure know how to show a guy a good time."

At least with his Technician's training, Rilte knew more about other worlds than your average citizen. In fact, he might be more up to date with intergalactic affairs than most Core members. He'd spent his entire adult life reviewing disease research from around the galaxy. His team had even corresponded with scientists on other worlds in their search for the cure.

"Thank you, Rilte," Bauleel replied. "I know your knowledge of other species will be invaluable in our journey, wherever we end up."

"Um, excuse me?" Terem called from across the clearing.

"Oh yeah," Bauleel replied. She walked over to him.

"I overheard you say you're leaving. Are you sure I can't come with you? I promise I won't be any trouble."

The earnest look in his eyes almost undid her. Almost. Her willingness to entertain any sympathy for this creature was a direct result of her state of emotional exhaustion.

"You know Terem, how you sensed something special about me?" Bauleel asked. "Something similar to how you are now?"

His eyes lit up. "Yes!"

Bauleel nodded. For Graeber's plan to work, they needed every edge possible, even if it meant trusting the creature before her. "Can I give you something, something that might help you control yourself better?"

He smiled happily. "I'd be ever so grateful. There are times the voices are so difficult to bear."

"But in return, I'll need a favor."

"Yes, of course, anything."

"Don't tell the others you talked to us or saw us, at all. Can you do that?"

"Yes, of course, Bauleel."

"Wonderful. Now, take my hand, and I'll do the rest."

Terem laid his hand on hers, and Bauleel let her skin merge with his. She pushed a small portion of her Methuselah-altered blood and immune factors into him, knowing her body would regenerate as needed. When done, she pulled back and let the wounds close.

The Methuselah treatment had kept her and the other Core members safe from mutations all of this time; perhaps it would lend Terem some strength and stability. She'd prefer Terem dead, but making him into a more potent threat to the Core would slow down whoever was on their trail, perhaps enough to make a difference in their ability to escape.

"That was incredible," Terem said.

"What will the impact be?" Rilte asked, anxiety and curiosity warring across his features.

"He should be more stable, for a time," Bauleel replied. "It's not a permanent fix to the mutation, but it will delay the inevitable."

"My thanks," Terem replied. "I can feel it working. Helping me."

"We need to go. Now. According to Raza, they are only two days behind us," Graeber said.

Once on the horses, they headed north until they came to a less-frequented road, and then picked up the pace.

"What do you think the chances are that he'll follow us?" Rilte asked.

"Fair to middling," Graeber replied with a wry smile. "But with what Bauleel did, at least we'll get a head's up."

CHAPTER 20

PONAR WALKED ALONG THE SURF LINE ALONG THE beach of Jeweled Cove, knowing he was one of the few allowed such access in recent years. The Guardians had included him in their search efforts at Graeber's behest, and he was grateful for something to do other than sitting around mulling over his vociferous parting of ways with his family and the Tinker. He had no idea when he'd get back to Raven's Call under the present travel restrictions, but he was in no hurry to see any of them at this juncture.

And now to be part of a search party for a corpse. How'd they put it? It was literally the least a person could do.

Well no, the least he could do was stay at the Waystation and drink himself into a stupor, but that path held no dignity for himself and gave no honor to the memory of Rai.

The Guardians had said there was little chance anything would wash up, but if it did, currents favored this Cove. And the Juggernaut had asked for a search to be performed, so the Guardians had been over this and other area beaches several times already. The trouble was, you never knew when, or if, something would surface. Or how much. Ponar shuddered to think of the possibilities.

The waves in the cove grew furious, churning white and gray, drawing Ponar's attention. Was some giant sea creature beaching itself? He strode in that direction, seeing pointed black fins and scales breaking through the roiling surf in a shallow pool. As the water receded the creature calmed, and was it just Ponar's imagination, or did the color wash out too? No, soon the flesh took on the color of pale sand, and the crea-ture shrank, although it was hard to make out the particulars under the mask of sea foam. The trunk shrank, and the limbs extended until he knew it to be more human than anything else, and with that shock of auburn hair forming the head, Ponar fell to his knees in disbelief.

Was this a Terror? Rai? Whatever it was, it was living, or close to it, and he was alone to meet it, her, for better or worse.

The form shivered and shook with what Ponar assumed was pain. The surface of her skin was fluid, motion underneath spoke to upheaval and undoubt-edly painful internal remodeling. Yet she laid there, half-covered in foam and seaweed, curled into a ball, unmoving. Yet, with every passing moment, Ponar was more and more convinced this was what had once been his sister Rai. What it was now?

A soft, keening groan emitted from the ball of flesh before him, and his heart went out to her. No, it. The high-pitched noise oddly echoed off the walls of the cove high above.

"Who... who are you?" Ponar asked.

"I'm sorry you had to be the one to find me, Ponar." Her voice was rough, dry. But it was her voice.

"How? Is it you?"

"Don't come any closer, brother. I'm not myself." Rai rolled onto her knees and sat up. Still naked, she pushed herself up onto her feet and shook the water off. The motion sent the moisture rolling down her body as if repelled and unable to stick to her flesh. Her hair was inexplicably longer and darker, and she ran her fingers through the now-dry locks.

Ponar rose to stand with her, still keeping his distance, fighting his animal instinct, which demanded he flee. "That's an impressive trick."

Rai closed her eyes, and sand rose up and sheathed her flesh, transforming the sand into a delicate and supple fabric. As Rai shifted from foot to foot, the fabric flowed gracefully around her slight form. It reminded Ponar of the multicolored garments the Guardians wore, yet this dress had the appearance of being somehow improved, although he couldn't quite put a finger on the difference.

"That, that's better. So, you're not resurrected as a Terror, then? Just to be clear."

A momentary confusion passed across Rai's expression, furrowing her brow. "You assume you could have a conversation with a Terror?"

"Well, no, I suppose not, come to think of it. But whatever you're doing, this..."

"No, you're right, this isn't normal. Something happened to me, Ponar. And to be honest, I think I'm every bit as dangerous, or perhaps even more dangerous, as every Terror on this planet right now."

"You seem fine..." Ponar heard the skepticism in his own voice even as he said the words. Just because he wanted Rai to be alive and well didn't make it so. Whatever had saved her life had also transformed Rai into something distinctly other. Something unnerving and a touch terrifying.

Rai cut him off. "Don't be a fool!" she spat. "Underneath this surface is something I fight every second to retain even a speck of sanity. There is an awareness, an other, within me."

"What happened to you, sister? Do you remember?" Ponar took a step forward, but Rai waved him off.

He took two steps back at her urging. And again fought the urge to run. But this was Rai, he knew her. Well, he used to know her, whatever she'd become had nearly alien overtones.

Rai clutched her chest, panic or shock filling her expression. "Please, stay back. She wants you dead. She wants all humans dead." She took a deep breath, and held her head in her hands as if breathing slowly would somehow control the beast within. "Ponar, when I went under the water, I thought I'd die. But then something found me, called to me, and drew me in. Then she filled me, every molecule of me, with herself. There's nothing left of me."

Ponar watched, full of apprehension as Rai paced, continuing to hold her head.

"You look like Rai. You sound like her." He heard the tremor in his voice. Surely she did too?

"No, I am just a vessel now. She's called Vidaaquar. She's been here, on Az'Unda, forever. She sees humans as an infestation of her bio-system. She won't tolerate our presence. Can you take this message to the Matriarchs, so they can understand what's about to happen? She's the cause of the plague. The Terrors. They were just a weak initial response of her consciousness before she was fully awake."

Ponar drew a hand across his brow. "First the Juggernaut, and now this? Rai, if you're still in there, I weep for you."

Rai gave him a weak smile. "I stopped crying when the pain from the transformation became unbearable. Vidaaquar is not a gentle mistress, and she is limitless. And the Juggernaut, I fear they are another matter entirely."

"Surely Vidaaquar fears the Juggernaut too?" Ponar asked. "We all do."

"*Vidaaquar fears none. We go to the source of this disturbance. Sebaiya.*" The words rang out, monotone yet clanging off the cliff walls. Rai's eyes swirled pearlescent ivory, and Ponar staggered backward, knowing he'd roused the beast from her distractions.

"Noted." He lowered his eyes, unable to look directly at Rai when that voice issued from her mouth. The words had exited Rai's mouth but were clearly not her own. He flicked his gaze back up and watched her eyes roam the crags of the cove, seeking. When they lit upon the caves, recognition hit her face. Then the iridescent sheen cleared from her eyes, returning them to normal.

"It was lovely to see you one last time, Ponar. Tell the Durmah I'm sorry."

"Can I go with you?" Ponar replied.

A brief look of horror flashed across Rai's face. "No, I can barely keep her under control as it is. If we hadn't been close before, been family, you'd be dead and not a messenger instead." Ponar paled at her words, spoken so plainly. "Now go, a Guardian will be here soon. And another. But we must go. Good luck, brother."

Rai turned from him and half-ran, half-flew towards the steep walls of the cove, clothing and cape billowing out behind her. When she reached the rock, she disappeared into a dark cave, and he could see her no more.

The surreal experience was mocked by the waves, rushing up to smooth away her footprints from the sand. Soon enough, as predicted, a Guardian appeared along the upper rim of the cove and Ponar motioned him down, unable to move from where he was standing. When the Guardian arrived, at first all he could manage was to point, gaping at the footprints, which the fellow followed to the cave mouth and back.

"So, you encountered a Terror and lived to tell the tale?" the Guardian said. He was an older man, who gave Ponar the impression that he was not easily swayed or shocked. "I noticed we start off with bare feet here, then booted, and midway the boots widen and shorten into something resembling a horseshoe. No worries, I'll get a team down here to dispatch it."

"You don't understand. It was Rai Durmah, my sister."

The Guardian let out a long whistle. "Ouch, that's a rough one."

"It's worse, she had a message. I need to get it to the Matriarchs."

It was the Guardian's turn to gape. "Terror's aren't articulate. I mean rarely they are, but what they say never makes sense. It's all nonsense."

Ponar shook his head, resolute in every aspect of his being. "She's not a Terror." The Guardian opened his mouth to argue, but Ponar's passionate conviction must have swayed him because the other man didn't speak. "She's something new," Ponar continued. "Something older and altogether more dangerous. C'mon, I fear we don't have any time to waste."

Undeterred, Ponar strode in the direction of the steps which led up and around the cliff wall. He would carry her message as far as needed.

———

PONAR AND THE GUARDIAN RENDEZVOUSED WITH the rest of the squad at the top of the Cove rim after a brisk hike. The Guardian did most of the talking while Ponar drank his water rations greedily. A female Guardian drafted a message to the Guardian Chieftess, per protocol as they explained, who would then pass the information along to the Matriarchs herself. Ponar was allowed to review the message, but not write it himself, which chafed at first, but he didn't begrudge them their protectiveness over the equipment either. Soon the message was off, and a strange sense of ... something washed over him.

He shifted on his feet, not at all comfortable in the present company of Guardians. Shouldn't he feel relieved, now that he'd delivered Rai's message to them? But he didn't. Not at all. Rai was out there, inhabited and tortured by this Vidaaquar. All he wanted to do was chase after her and help her, but how? And where was this 'Sebaiya,' anyway?

He did no one any good standing around.

"Will you be taking me back to the Waystation now?" Ponar asked.

The Guardians didn't meet his gaze, which wasn't at all their regular mode. They'd stare you down until you blinked first and then stare you down some more. Today...this eerie silence. Eventually, the woman at the terminal spoke up. "You're to be held here for a short while."

Guardians avoiding an issue? "What do you mean, held? I can find my way back to the Waystation without difficulty."

"It will become apparent soon enough. We are handing you off to another for transport," she replied, again pointedly not meeting Ponar's eyes.

Another? Another what? And where were they taking him? Perhaps the Matriarchs wanted to speak to him directly after his discussion with Rai? If it could help, he'd do whatever they asked.

At that moment, a thundering boom rang through the air and he jumped, his ears aching from the sudden reverberation. Ponar's gaze was drawn skyward, and he had to shield his eyes from the glare reflected from the underbelly of the descending shuttlecraft. He'd never seen a spacecraft in person before, and the sight was more startling than the preceding sound. This craft was covered with a reflective black shell, and its sleek lines reminded him of the mighty Juggernaut he and Rai had encountered in the forest. It was large; about three stories high by human standards, sporting three engines and exhaust ports with streamlined fins along each one.

Could the Az'Unda colony even afford something of this caliber? Likely not. He'd seen pictures in the history books of the human colony ships, but the Juggernaut craft's design had not been included in those books. These were aliens who didn't just travel through space; they owned it with a finesse that brooked no equal.

The hulk kicked up a bit of dust as it settled down, and when the air cleared a large hatch opened on the side. A retinue of Juggernaut traveled down the extended ramp and approached. Ponar admired the steadfast Guardians, who held their ground, not appearing one bit startled by the Juggernaut's dominant display. They made not a single move to leave or otherwise flee the situation.

The Guardian's earlier statement suddenly slammed home. Surely he wasn't going to be 'handed off' to aliens? Though Ponar was ashamed to admit it, he felt weak in the knees.

Ponar tried to meet the eyes of the Guardians, who he now realized surrounded him. All of them had their gaze trained on the approaching Juggernaut envoy. All but one. The woman who'd sent the message to the Matriarchs met his gaze straight on, but no words were expressed. Her look wasn't filled with tenderness, but instead with quiet resolve. It said one thing: don't make this any harder than it has to be.

Adrenaline flooded his system. Why were they doing this? Yet there was no point trying to run. So he turned to meet the envoy face to...shell? Remember not to flee in terror, right?

The envoy consisted of three of the aliens. Each stood nearly nine feet high when they chose to walk bipedal, which was a change from when Ponar and Rai had met the one in the forest. It had been on all six arms, or was it legs? Scurrying about at the time, and even then it had been over six feet in height due to the length of its limbs.

The Juggernaut came to a stop a few paces away. "Thank you for signaling us with the pickup location. We are pleased with your compliance. The subject comes into our custody for questioning now."

Questioning? Sweat broke out on Ponar's brow, and anxiety sank into his stomach. So this is how the defiant Matriarchs dealt with Hegemonic demands? By giving random citizens into the hands of monsters?

The female Guardian took a few steps forward, undaunted by the hulking alien. "This fulfills the terms of our agreement?"

The lead Juggernaut stepped forward and swung his upper torso around, so he towered over the woman. "For now. Ponar Durmah, you will accompany us back to our cruiser."

"Can I ask why?" Ponar stalled.

"This was not explained to you?" asked the Juggernaut in charge.

Ponar shook his head, beads of sweat running down his temples.

"Your sister, Rai Durmah, is of interest to my people. You are to answer questions as to her whereabouts. Is that a satisfactory explanation?"

He hadn't thought the sinking sensation in his stomach could get and worse, but there it did. How could he answer questions about Rai, when he didn't understand himself what had happened to her? He didn't want to betray Rai to the Juggernaut, even if she was no longer fully herself. "Yes, thank you. Lead on."

Ponar didn't look back at the Guardians. Instead he focused on the Juggernaut, understanding they held his fate in their inexorable grip.

Despite his raw fear, Ponar couldn't help but examine the aliens, his curiosity--at least temporarily--winning out. They were curious creatures, each black carapace identical except for the different imprinted sigils in the ridges behind their heads. There, the color flared and pulsed, perhaps according to their heartbeat, or was it something else? Whatever the mechanism, the effect was stunning.

A sense of finality hit Ponar as he passed over the threshold into their craft. How long would the Juggernaut keep him for questioning? Would this be the last time he set foot on Az'Unda?

Inside the cruiser, the ship was just as sleek and streamlined as it was on the outside. They placed him in a small sling-like chair and otherwise ignored him.

No doubt, they expected Ponar to remain a complacent and willing prisoner. He was not ignorant of the situation or how poorly things might fare for him if he did not comply fully. The Juggernaut were not known for their goodwill, patience, or even temperament.

Ponar tried not to overthink his situation, as he sat and stared at the Juggernaut while they worked at the consoles. His home world drifted away into the distance as the shuttle docked with an alien mothership. Perhaps he should have been making plans, strategies, or well, coming up with a methodology for dealing with the upcoming inquisition? All Ponar knew was that he was out of his depth and utterly without an advocate, having been abandoned by his people. What he knew about Rai, or whatever she'd become, was likely unbelievable to a species as advanced as the Juggernaut.

He was used to a life traveling as a merchant and often being across the planet from his family, but home had never been so far away as it was right now.

After docking, one of the envoys led him down a series of corridors and into a room filled with a menagerie of creatures, some he recognized but many he didn't. A zoo? What sort of aliens traveled with a zoo? None of the creatures appeared or sounded particularly happy, and many were bandaged.

Within this vault, Ponar was led to a cell that looked like a human inhabitance, or more specifically, an Az'Undan bedroom, kitchen, and bath. The front glass panel was opened, and he was ushered inside. Nauseated, Ponar looked out from his cage. Had the Matriarchs known what would happen to him?

"Someone will be with you shortly. Feel free to rest a while." The platitude, spoken without emotion nor inflection but a clear indicator of business as usual, chilled Ponar to the bone.

He'd become yet another attraction, one of the dozens? Hundreds?

Ponar's escort faded into the distance, and he was left alone in the menagerie.

CHAPTER 21

Rai traveled through the underground caves, lost within the substance of Vidaaquar. It had taken so much out of her to sustain herself, her form and cohesiveness while talking to Ponar, and now she'd let go and allowed herself to drift in the sea of overwhelming consciousness she'd become so accustomed to these past few days.

Whatever Vidaaquar was, it was ancient. Rai thought of it as a she, as Vidaaquar had risen from the feminine-natured oceanic expanse. She'd nicknamed her 'Vida,' and thought of her as a colossal organic super computer. Watching and observing Vida had taught her much, but nowhere near enough to stop Vida's plan to wipe out the colony.

Vida knew everything about the planet. With each footfall, each brush of contact against her skin, Vida processed information on the flora, fauna, and geologic makeup and condition of the world. Vida would, at times, stop and modify the actual DNA of the things they passed if she assessed a need for drastic repairs. The few times they came across species the humans had introduced, Vida'd stopped and, with a single touch, commanded their DNA to split and dissolve, turning a once-alive creature into an oily puddle. These actions made Rai's stomach turn.

And yet, Vida had no qualms using Rai, a human, as her host. There was something about Rai that Vida found unique and stable, and therefore useful. 'Useful' meant something not to be destroyed, Rai was learning. If only she could prove the humans 'useful', or at the least, not harmful?

Would she be thrown away when Vida was done? Rai couldn't know, couldn't divine that secret from Vida. It simply wasn't important enough on Vida's eternal agenda. Rai did know the plague was Vida's work. Time and time again, Vida lamented how ineffective it had been. And Vida rejoiced in finding herself a physical host, Rai, to be her avatar of destruction.

"What a fool was I, to jump when I did. I should have trusted in Graeber," Rai thought to herself. Except she wasn't allowed private thoughts anymore.

"If it means that much to you, you can have him back. A prize for your efforts." Vida must be feeling generous today.

"I doubt he'll want what I am now. He's something of a racial purist."

"He gets no choice. No want. What I declare is. Or he dies."

Rai remembered back to those moments in Harper's Sorrow when she and Graeber had almost touched. When she'd almost known him again, but he'd never allowed it. Her heart ached to go back to that moment, to know who he was, who they'd been together. To have all of her questions answered before Vida destroyed everything.

And, of course, Vida was listening. And she understood at levels Rai didn't yet comprehend, but Rai was beginning to integrate. Each memory was synthesized through all her senses, but also Vida picked up on the history around the moment, all of the plant and animal activity in the area, and bio scans of each of them too. Things Rai must have been aware of, on some level, before.

"It's called multi-dimensional awareness. You'll get used to it, as it's a part of us now. And yes, you will have that moment, it is assured."

Rai imagined herself frowning. As she wasn't physically in control of her body, her consciousness was limited to the mental image Rai had of herself. "Why would you do that for me? For Graeber and I?"

"Because, child, you may not see it through my mind's eye yet, but he's just like you were when you came to me. Another perfect vessel. I can see this

through the strength of your memories and the bond you had with him. I need to know before I complete my task, how this came to be. And I need the use of him."

Rai laughed. "He is not one to yield."

"Neither were you."

Rai recalled all too vividly how her will and body had been stripped away. Rai felt chills pass over her consciousness, pocketed within the space she inhabited inside Vida.

"You've said you can see things through your mind's eye. What does that mean?"

"I am aware of all life here, and elsewhere, through my mind's eye. It is how I became aware of the humans. Without a suitable vessel, however, I was not able to bring action to your doorstep."

"And how does it work, this eye?"

"Would you like me to show you? We are one. We are to be of one will. The sooner you understand the true nature of things, the easier for all."

"So, what, using this will change how I think?"

"No, it shows truth purely. Absolutely. Then you are driven to act accordingly, as a creature of conscience would be, yes?"

Was this a trap? Was it mind control, or could Rai use it and then use what she saw to give Vida a human's perspective on the viewings? Would a better understanding of humans impact Vida's planned course?

Rai had no idea, yet her curiosity won out.

"Show me how."

"Willingly, vessel."

Rai's consciousness was drawn out of her protected little pocket, and into the wholeness of Vidaaquar. Again she felt her feet moving upon the ground, the wind rushed past her body, and her hair whipped to and fro. The world rushed past them in a blur, but somehow the effort was insubstantial. It was always that way with Vida, although Rai didn't know why.

Now she was fully back in her body, but she didn't presume to be in charge. Next, her vision shifted, and it reminded her of her previous enhanced night vision, but this was altogether better and more complex. Everything around her gained an extra dimension of intricacy and information, and yet her awareness held a dreamy, disembodied quality. The trees they passed; she knew their ages, exact dimensions, how much water they took in and how much oxygen they put out, and their relationships to each other without even having to ask. The same was true of a family of rodents living in the hollow of one of the trees, which she glimpsed in passing.

But that was only the beginning. Beyond physical eyesight, Vida's mind's eye observed other beings further out and other structures. Some were natural formations like caves, and some were human-made. Rai felt, instead of seeing, where the roads were, and how far away they were. Stretching farther, she felt the cities, the farms, the outposts. She felt the humans, all of them. Rai felt the city, Sebaiya. It would not be long before they reached it.

However, they did near a Guardian outpost, and she knew Vida meant to encounter it. Rai's mind cringed, it would not go well here. It hadn't worked well for the past few farms they'd passed. Rai had protested, begged, and screamed for Vida to stop, but to no avail. Rai had withdrawn into silence after that, willing herself unsuccessfully to not witness her people's piecemeal destruction.

"You saw all of this before? Knew we were here?"

"I merely glimpsed. I knew only of a wrongness. I did not have the focusing lens of this vessel. Together we are stronger."

Glad to be of service, Rai thought to herself.

"But you have been."

"I will show you we are not pests. We have value."

"I have already seen. I already know."

"You use me. I have value."

"Ah, but you are not like them. You who are the vessel. You will be made to understand. I have seen the way to this truth as well. I will make you whole."

Rai pulled back from the mind's eye, stupefied. "You can do that?"

"Oh yes. Nothing is beyond us."

"Thank you, Vidaaquar. Perhaps when I'm whole again, I can do a better job of convincing you to save my people."

"I think when you are whole, you will no longer try."

Rai went silent, and within her mind, wept.

They walked up to the outpost, the walls standing firm, Guardians on alert. Rai began to withdraw, knowing what was next.

"No, *we are one. I will no longer permit this.*"

"I cannot bear it. These are my people."

"*You are no longer of them. You are the all-knowing, all-seeing Vidaaquar. You will not separate.*"

And Vida fixed Rai in place, with a series of mental peg holes, and her mind was draped and affixed in front of Vida's mind's eye. Surely, this will drive me insane. I can only hope sooner than later, I suppose, Rai thought

A Guardian approached them, and asked her business, surprised to find a lone traveler on the road during a state of martial law, when no such travelers should exist.

This time, when Vida touched the Guardian and directed his cells to dissolve into their molecular components. Because she was watching through the mind's eye, Rai understood the mechanism and knew the commands necessary to make it happen. And because she was so intertwined with Vida, this time tears ran down her face as she watched the Guardian disintegrate into a pile of slime. The soft parts like the skin and organs more quickly slimed, the bones and cartilage took longer to break down. After that, even the clothing followed. In the end, the earth swallowed him up.

Alarms blared, but this didn't bother Vida, she cherished the humans knowing that fate was upon them. After all, to her, they'd earned their fate, hadn't they? Soon there were more, and they used every trick they knew, but Vida anticipated it all as if she had the universe itself on her side.

Rai wondered: if there were gods, would Vidaaquar qualify? Could Rai convince this veritable goddess that not all of humanity had earned her ire? How does one bargain with a god? Vida had cultivated and curated this world towards her goals for millennia. Could she be convinced to somehow include humanity within her grand design?

Rai caught a glimpse of energetic waves shooting off through the sky, headed towards the cities in a color of blue she knew to be beyond her human perception. Radio waves? Vida adeptly translated the message, using Rai's awareness of Az'Un language. The electronic message warned of another attack by the unknown beast, most likely the one warned of by Ponar Durmah. Well, at least they had their facts straight.

The Guardians attacked with all their weapons, but Vida had thickened her skin to make it impervious, so nothing penetrated, and she felt no blows. They were used to animals and humans and Terrors. An armored assault by stone was unknown to them. All Vida had to do was touch them to take them down, and she was as fast as lightning. They had no chance.

Rai watched it all. Lived it all, as if it were her own

doing. And with each death, Rai lost the will to resist. Each step, in this new configuration Vida had forged upon their minds, brought Rai from the background and into the present. Vida had begun drawing the ending out, reveling in her triumph over the interlopers, insensitive to Rai's emotional distress. With the final few deaths, Rai herself gave the kill order, not waiting for Vida to act. Disgusted and exhausted from the display of Vida's power, Rai wanted it over. Needed it over, to retain her sanity.

In the end, none escaped. Not even the horses.

"We could have ridden a horse. Horses are very fast."

"We're faster. We never tire. Cease your petty defiance."

"Surely your energy is not boundless? Even stars have limits," Rai goaded.

Vida laughed, and it was full of joy and the room filled with a shimmering light. *"My kind, we imagined the stars before they ever were. We are the bringers of harmony and light."*

"So, why not choose to harmonize with my people, instead of destroying them? Because, if you have a choice, wouldn't the peaceful option be better?"

"Harmony isn't about peace. It's a grievous mistake to assume so. Nothing in your human ways promotes harmony through longevity. In time, your processes would have stripped this planet. This is why my micro-organisms reacted to your kind as an invader. We

sensed the inevitable imbalance which would occur with your continued presence, and your destiny was set."

Rai was dumbfounded. "Resources can be used without ill effect. Rocks are used to build houses, but they aren't destroyed."

"No, but trees are cut without being reseeded! Wild game is killed wholesale in areas! Whole segments of forest were wiped clean for cities, and nothing is done to relocate the animals first! The water was befouled with chemicals from the machines used to remove and cut apart the land!"

Rai sighed, unable to argue Vida's points. "We could have, and should have, done better to steward this land. The Az'Un can be educated to follow your guidelines."

Vida walked away from the outpost, and to emphasize her point, the entire structure flattened to the ground, slowly again becoming wood, rocks, and any natural items that remained inside. All else dissolved. The sound was deafening, at least to ears that weren't Vida-proofed.

Rai couldn't speak to Vida's charges; she didn't remember that time in the colony's history. Rai didn't even remember the teachings from the classrooms. "I'm sure no disrespect was meant. I'm sure the colonists were trying to do things in the most economical, fastest way possible."

"*They cared only for themselves, not for harmony. This is the end result.*"

"They can be made to change. This close to you, I sense you can make a difference, yes?"

Vida was still for a moment. Had Rai pushed her too far? "*I can create new things through change when I find them worthy. You, as a vessel, spoke to me. I found you worthy and necessary for my task. You were already partly reformed, and I finished the process and then joined with you.*"

Rai's curiosity peaked. To have a being so powerful judge her so... Could this entity understand Rai in a way her own kind never did?

"Why do *you* feel I am worthy, Vidaaquar? In my attempts to adapt humanity to Az'Unda, to your plague, I went to extreme lengths. People died because of my choices. Many of my peers judged me undeserving of their forgiveness. How can you find otherwise?"

"*I see into your heart. I see the crimes you do not remember. You tried to create harmony, at a high cost, even when you were forbidden to do so by your colleagues. You tried to understand me, through the plague, and they stopped you. You came the closest to grasping my pure form, and so I have rewarded you by allowing you alone to abide.*"

Suddenly Rai understood, without further detail, when Vida had used her as a vessel that she'd had the option of obliterating her, but hadn't, because of Rai's choices in her life. Funny, the Core wanted her dead for her crimes, and yet Vida had kept her consciousness alive for just the same reason.

"Do you wish I hadn't kept you? Is this all is too much to bear, gentle soul that you are?"

Rai sighed. "I am gentle no more. I fear I never was. But I will not surrender my arguments. It is not in my nature to do so."

"That's what I like about you."

Together in spirit, they ran towards Sebaiya. Rai felt stunned that Vida had not only spared her but had come to like her. Moreover, Rai was beginning to discover, beyond a healthy fear and respect for Vida, an understanding and sympathy for Vida's point of view. Sharing Vida's skin for only a few days had already shifted her perspective. How much farther would Vida be able to push her before Rai broke completely?

CHAPTER 22

Sometime later, Ponar was roused from sleep by bright lights. He sat up and rubbed the sleep from his eyes, and looked out upon a solitary Juggernaut observing outside his cell. This one had a gleaming white sigil, and his body was broader, taller, and bulkier than the others. Feeling every part a prisoner and not wishing to earn any ire at this early juncture from his presumptive captors, Ponar stood and walked to the open door.

"I trust you are well rested?" the Juggernaut asked.

A courteous question, was this how all questionings began? "Yes, I am well rested."

"Good. Let us walk."

Ponar hurried to keep up, but he managed. Soon they exited the zoo and entered a sitting room of sorts. There were large, flat couches in a semi-circle opposite a series of full-wall screens. Flat short tables in the middle held an array of both local and off-world foods and beverages. If not for the addition of technology and the difference in scale and shape of the couches, the room might even feel homey.

The Juggernaut climbed on top of a couch and motioned for Ponar to assume one across from him. Ponar did as directed, growing progressively befuddled.

"I am Assessor Brague of the Hegemony, on special assignment to Queen Klimitzi. You are honored to be in my presence. There are none other who outrank me on this vessel, or in this quadrant."

"I am, so honored, Sir."

"Ponar Durmah, I'm sure you are ill at ease right now, yes?"

"Of course."

"Let me assure you, my interest in you is ancillary to my main investigation. Once my questions are answered, you may return home to your family, or wherever else you wish on Az'Unda."

"That is quite a comfort, Sir."

"As it is meant to be. Feel free to enjoy the refreshments. They are intended to help you relax and to sustain you during our discussion."

Brague accessed integrated circuitry in one of his forearms and the scene from the forest replayed silently on the screens in front of them but from a third person angle. How he'd captured the scene, Ponar had no idea, but the images were perfection. He'd heard in school that the most superior technology was manufactured by the Juggernaut.

"I'm sure you remember this scene well?" Brague prompted.

Seeing his sister set him at ease, calming him more than he'd thought possible. "It's rather etched into my memory." Ponar served himself a glass of water, sipping slowly.

"I'm sure you do. It's not every day a pair of colonists comes face to face with the superiority of the Hegemonic Empire with no warning. And yet, your sister, Rai, that's her name, yes?"

"Yes, Rai Durmah."

"Yes, Rai, met me with no fear at all. She was, if anything, perturbed by my disturbing your personal discussion, wouldn't you say?"

"I do not think she meant to offend you, Sir. Your eminence. Please forgive her," Ponar stuttered.

"No, please, do not use such honorifics. Sir does quite nicely. And you cannot apologize for her. Among my people, although you would not know this and so I will forgive you this once, this is seen as an insult. We all stand alone, on our own merits or without them. She will answer for her transgressions, where any have occurred. You cannot answer for her. You are responsible only for your own faults. And that day, you acted quite honorably towards the Hegemony, Ponar. You deserve no shame."

"Thank you, Sir," Ponar said, oddly pleased at the

Assessor's praise. *A brief wave of shame fluttered through his gut--this Juggernaut was his de facto captor. What value did Brague's approval mean, as seen through that lens?*

"A simple statement. That first time we met within the forest, I noticed there were differences between you and your sister. I take it you are not from the same genetic pool? Explain how this has come to pass."

"Oh, Rai's a recent adoptee to the Durmah Sept, just a few months ago." Brague remained silent, so Ponar continued. "We'd petitioned for another addition to our Sept, for help running our Waystations. We're always expanding and needing more help. Besides waiting for more children to grow up, it's another way to expand our Sept."

"So she's not of your genetic strain?" Brague helped himself to a drink as well, something translucent and blue. "Was she taken from another Sept?"

"No, the other Sept gave her up."

Brague stilled. "Why?"

Ponar shifted uncomfortably; how to best answer so he didn't upset his host? If Brague had been a human, Ponar would have been better able to guess his reactions. As it was, he had no idea if the behemoth was simply curious or enraged.

"She was found barren by the Temples; unable to bear children. It was within the rights of her birth family to shun her and focus their resources on their productive members."

Brague swayed his head, which Ponar took as a sign of agreement. "In a small colony such as yours, an inability to breed would indeed hold a significant social stigma. Every barren member could be viewed as a missed opportunity for the society to grow and prosper. Even so, you must know your colony's efforts do not flourish?"

"I am not privy to the details, Sir." But Ponar wasn't surprised. The cities and schools were not growing and or as full as promised, that much any fool could see.

"Can you name her birth Sept for me?" Brague once again keyed the interface terminal on his forearm, and a small transparent display shimmered into existence above his arm. Ponar had never seen the like of it before. "Her birth Sept?"

"We did not know, and if she had known, it would have been forbidden to speak the name." Ponar put the empty water glass down but was too nervous to claim any food to eat.

Brague grumbled and rearranged himself on his cushions. He made notes on his screen, and then shut it off. "I'm sure the Matriarchs will know. But now, elucidate further."

"Of course, Sir. Rai had lost her memory before joining our family, and we didn't know when this had happened, or who was at fault. She didn't remember her birth family at all." His anger at the Temples flared within him, suddenly fresh and new. The Durmah had suffered so much at the hands of the Temples. Kait's failing health, Stoi's facial scars, and Rai's amnesia. Now, Ponar had been given up by those same Temples to the Juggernaut, never to see home again. How must his mother, Kait, be dealing with his loss? Ponar hoped the grief would not be her undoing.

"That's fascinating, Ponar. And the Durmah suspected the Temples?"

Ponar shot out of his seat, ready to bolt. Brague held up three hands to reassure his guest. "Please, sit down." Ponar sat, unable to do otherwise. "I'm afraid I have you at a disadvantage. My race is highly skilled at reading subtext and nonverbal communication, which your small human minds cannot comprehend. Your sister, however, surpassed my expectations. She was able to talk to me in my native tongue, which should be impossible for a human. It's not a skill you have, for example. So, why her?"

"I don't know, but she did tell me afterward when we fled the forest, that she'd spoken to you." Of course, he'd thought Rai daft at the time.

Brague made a chittering noise, almost akin to purring, as his front mandibles tapped lightly and quickly together. "I'm glad I picked you, for you are most agreeable to work with. What did the Durmah suspect the Temples of doing to Rai?"

Ponar shrugged but damned if he didn't still hate the Temples. "We were never certain, but we suspected they damaged Rai's memory, somehow gave her amnesia during her temple service."

"Explain this 'temple service.'"

"It's forbidden to speak of it."

Brague leaned forward and bared the sharpened teeth behind his large mandibles. "Ponar, you will speak of all things to me. Let things be civilized between us, yes?"

Ponar nodded, thinking of the damaged creatures he'd seen in the menagerie. Brague was willing to do whatever necessary to get the information he needed, and he had all the time in the world. Ponar was also beginning to suspect the Assessor didn't just read nonverbal cues but could trigger them as well. Just another skill in his formidable arsenal, Ponar suspected.

"When a girl becomes a woman, er, fertile, she goes to the Temple to do her term of service," Ponar explained.

"Ah, an institutionalized breeding program. That's not in your colony charter."

Ponar shrugged. "I haven't read it myself."

"I'm certain you haven't, but it would improve the chances of colony success. Continue."

"The woman stays at the Temple and has as many children as possible. When the Temple deems it's no longer safe for her to have more, she's sent back to her Sept. Of course, the children are sent to the Sept when they're weaned and raised there."

"And her life afterward?"

"Well, depending on how fertile she proved, she

will marry high or low, drawing a certain dowry from the man she marries. Sometimes the older children may even be part of the exchange to the man's Sept, it all depends on how close the Septs are."

Brague made a noise much akin to a growl. "And what role do the males play in temple service?"

"We are called to serve, to, um, be with the women. Sometimes once, sometimes many times. It's at the will of the Temples."

Brague stood and paced, and Ponar wondered what to do or say next, but instead kept quiet.

"This also is against your colony charter, but I can deduce why they've done it. No doubt the Temples are breeding every fertile woman with every fertile man for the broadest availability of genetic material and then keeping the traditional colony Sept structure intact. But it's a pure mockery of the charter! All those poor girls treated as breeders. It's a disgrace." He collapsed on the couch, lost in his own thoughts.

Put in those terms, Ponar felt Brague's righteous indignation mirrored his own. "I didn't imagine a Juggernaut could care about mere humans."

The Assessor cast him a grim look. "It's true, I have no fondness for primates. I find your species inferior in virtually all aspects. Additionally, my kind is a matriarchal species. No one treats females as mere chattel. And although this is not my primary concern, it will be dealt with in addition to the other offenses of your people. This I promise you."

Ponar felt sick to his stomach. Did he just manage to make things even worse for Az'Unda?

"Now, back to your sister," Brague continued. "She emerged from her temple service barren, an amnesiac, and in your family's care?"

"Yes. And, before I tell you more, I need to know, what do you plan to do with her when you find her?"

Brague leaned forward, his movement slow and precise. "They told me she'd leaped to her death a few days ago. Did they lie?"

"They did not lie. I watched Rai jump myself." Ponar's breathing was shallow, and he gripped the cushions beneath him like a lifeline.

Brague moved with an alacrity unusual for a creature of his bulk, and for a moment hovered mere inches above a cowering Ponar. "Where is she now?" he whispered, the sound reverberating, crashing through his mind like a thousand knives.

"Will...you...hurt...her?" Ponar cried out, holding his head between his hands as blood poured out his nose.

Brague backed off, and the pain subsided. "If Rai is what I suspect she is, then she will be untouchable to me. Though it is nearly impossible that one such as her holds the key. But as I said, there is an investigation to be conducted first. I must find out what she is, and what she knows, definitively."

Ponar rose and walked towards the hulk of the Assessor, wiping the tears from his face as he stood his ground mere inches from the Juggernaut's mandibles. His fears had passed, blown away with the pain. His mind was scrambled, but he trusted in Rai, in whatever she had become.

Ponar could not stop the Juggernaut in their search for Rai. Brague would not yield. Perhaps if he worked with the alien, Ponar could improve things for the rest of the Durmah.

"I met her on the beach this morning as she emerged from the ocean." The Assessor stilled, perhaps due to Ponar's aggressive stance? "She was herself, as before, but also something more. She knows what she is now, and where she's going. If I help you find Rai, will you help me remove the Temples from power?"

The Assessor did his odd grin, revealing his sharp teeth as he pulled back his enormous mandibles. "I could rip it from your mind instead. It would please me greatly."

"Except you wish to change the Temple structure already. I'm not asking for anything you're not already going to do. I'm requesting you promise to make it happen."

The sensation of chimes rolled through Ponar's body as the Assessor drew himself up on his rear legs. Had he pushed the Juggernaut too far, or would the alien, as he suspected, respect his display of willpower? More blood gushed out Ponar's nose, but he made no effort to clean it up, and it sullied the pristine white carpet.

"Kill me, and you'll never know where she went. Not fast enough to stop what she's planning."

The pain stopped, and Brague lowered himself and came nose-to-mandibles with Ponar. "I do not lack that level of control, monkey." He made the twittering noise again that Ponar was beginning to associate with what, laughter? " I will agree to your demands, but only because they suit my own present course of action. Now, before I make things uncomfortable for you again, you said you know where she is going?"

"Yes. I don't have any idea where this is, but Rai did. She said it's called Sebaiya?"

Brague made his happy purring sound. "I know where that is. You have done well, and I am pleased." He keyed the terminal on his arm and brought up the transparent screen. A moment later, one of his lackeys appeared on it.

"Set a course for the coordinates I'm passing in now. I want to be there by morning. Plan on a small crew to survey the site. I will give more directives at that time."

"It shall be done, Assessor," the on-screen head bowed, and then flickered out.

Ponar listened in awe and frustration. How did this alien know more about Az'Unda than he, a citizen?

Brague laughed. "You reek of irritation. Perhaps because I have access to your original colony records? Yes, I know where your people first landed, which would be the city named Sebaiya. I'm sure there's all sorts of interesting old equipment and things lying about up there, don't you think?"

"You'll take me with you, won't you?" Ponar asked.

"Oh, of course, I will. I'm sure your sister misses you. Doesn't she?"

Ponar paused. "Well, I do want to see her again."

"Oh, she told you not to follow her, did she?" Ponar nodded. "What's the rest of the story? You said she was *something more?* More than the rest of you, you mere humans?" Ponar nodded again, against his will. "What words did she use, now that she understands herself?" Brague remained close, and his mental hold even closer.

Ponar met his eyes, Brague's black, unreadable eyes. "She used one word, but it meant nothing to me."

"I know many words you do not."

Ponar swallowed. Hard. "Vidaaquar."

Brague didn't move. Didn't breathe.

"I think I said it like she did? But there was more. She could change forms. It wasn't just the word, it was a transformation," Ponar replied.

Everything was so still; Ponar didn't know what to do. He had no idea how to read the Juggernaut, but could he hope Brague would find Rai and ... help her? Or would he destroy them both? Ponar could only hope the Assessor's interest didn't include killing Rai.

Finally, Brague spoke again. "Did she say what she was doing? Did she explain what her plan is?"

"Vidaaquar's planning on wiping out the colony, although I don't know how."

"Then it is good we will rendezvous with her. She will have all of our assistance to complete her mission," Brague replied. He seated himself upon a couch and picked up a fruit and bit into it, appearing quite pleased with himself.

"Wait, what?" Panic speared down Ponar's spine. "We can't let her kill the humans. She's one of them!"

"No, Ponar, she's not. Not anymore. She's something quite extraordinary now, and we will assist her with anything she pleases. Unless I'm wrong, Vidaaquar's a being of great grace, and she will ascend to an eminent position amongst my people. And...I'm rarely wrong. Now, try one of these fruits with the purplish flesh. Trust me, they are quite delicious."

CHAPTER 23

Matriarch Natre entered the council chambers and steeled herself for the scene before her. The crowd had gathered, as was customary, with the Elders seated in a semi-circle ready to hear their petitions. However today, the assembled masses pressed wall-to-wall, and Natre had to push her way through to reach her appointed seat. From the tenor of the grumblings and the undeniable musk in the air, the crowd teetered on the cusp of turning brawl.

Of course, there had been fights in the streets over the past few weeks, despite the early curfew. If Natre wasn't careful, things would soon degenerate into outright riots. The fear of the Juggernaut was a dominant force. No one yet knew their intentions.

When she took her seat, she motioned Journeywoman Camille close to her ear. "Fetch the Guardians.

I fear we'll need them to rout this crowd before the day is through."

The look of shock in Camille's eyes wasn't lost on her. "Matriarch?"

"Go, now. We have others to transcribe." And with that Camille scurried off, never one to disobey orders.

Looking over the crowd, Natre noted the Durmah Sept leaders were in the center, but they hadn't brought a large retinue. However, many of their business associates stood close at hand. Weavers, potters, craftsmen, all Septs they did a fair amount of business with were here to back them up. This was no casual crowd.

"The council is open to hearing the voice of the people," Matriarch Natre intoned, formally opening the daily session. "I see we have a large crowd today, but I trust we can keep things organized, and everyone will have their say. Who would care to present first?" Natre's eyes leveled with Kait Durmah's. She wasn't a gambler.

Kait Durmah stepped forward, flanked by Stoi and Laan, her eldest brothers. Despite her frail appearance and tear strained eyes, she was a powerful woman in Raven's Call. "I demand the return of my son, Ponar."

Natre sighed. "Regretfully, that is not within my power to give."

The crowd stirred, rumblings of discontent filled the air as the acrid scent of tempers rising filled the air.

Both Stoi and Laan drilled her with eyes filled with hate. Kait alone retained her decorum.

"Perhaps then you can explain to me, Matriarch, why my son and why the people of Az'Unda, are being given over to the Juggernaut?"

Natre hesitated. How best to release all blame from the Temples, and squarely on the Juggernaut? "During your son and Rai's last trip, they crossed paths with a Juggernaut scouting party and managed to evade them. Now, this might appear to be a positive outcome, but the Juggernaut do not take kindly to losing their prey. They came here for samples of the Az'Undan ecosystem, and our effect upon it. Including human specimens." She let that sink in a moment, hearing a few gasps around the room. "Rai, for reasons I do not comprehend, took her own life, and that put us in a precarious position with the Juggernaut ambassadors. However, they assured us if we turned over Ponar then they would consider no further retribution upon our people."

Kait was stunned into silence. Instead, Stoi spoke up. "You're blaming Ponar for all of this?"

"No, do not take my words in this light, Sir Durmah. He is an unfortunate who crossed paths with the Juggernaut. But we Matriarchs were unwilling to risk the entire population of the planet for one life, dear as he is to your family. We do understand your loss."

"You understand?" Stoi roared, his face flushed

with anger, hands gripped into fists at his sides. Laan mirrored his posture. "You cannot begin to understand our pain at the loss of two cherished Septmates. How soon, and in what condition, will Ponar be returned to us?"

The tension in the crowd was palpable to Natre, at the moment Camille returned with a handful of Guardians. The Guardians stealthily circled the room, while Camille worked her way back to Natre's side through the crowd.

"Sir Durmah, the Matriarchs do not presume to give orders to the Juggernaut."

Kait broke into tears, hiding her face in her hands. This undid her brothers and unsettled the crowd.

"So, they are to keep him?" Laan asked, his emotion-laden voice a mere whisper, yet it carried throughout the crowd. "Indefinitely?"

"We can hope for his eventual return, once the Juggernaut's curiosity is satisfied. However, no statements or promises were made on their part to this effect," Natre explained, well aware this information would only inflame their tempers. Stoi glared at Natre in pure contempt. There was no question where Sept Durmah and the Temple stood now. If she couldn't pacify the Durmah, they might feed the insurgency against the Temples. The last thing Natre needed right now was another crisis. She'd chosen an awful time to step into the role of Matriarch.

"And if they want more? How many of us will you

give?" asked Allen Carle of the Potters Sept. "How much of our blood will you spill to appease them?"

Matriarch Natre rose from her chair, and she noticed the Guardians all stood at the ready. "Fellow citizens, these are the Juggernaut. We don't yet know their reasons for being here, but I believe they seek to know if we have caused damage to this planet. It's a routine check the Hegemony does of new colonies." This was a possibility and the least potential threat. This story would keep rioting to a minimum.

"The Matriarchs have agreed to do whatever necessary to appease the Juggernaut." The crowd grumbled, irate. "To do any less will earn their wrath, and perhaps get us wiped off the planet. So be angry if you must, but yes, I will hand over as many citizens as they require until they leave our space. Because until that time, we are all at risk. And the sooner they leave, the better for all Az'un."

The crowd quieted, like a lull in a storm as her words hit home, and they pondered their fear of the aliens. Had she done it? Calmed some sense through the enraged beast? But no, she felt the emotional tide shift before the first hateful words rang out.

"KILLER!" someone from the back yelled out, inciting a series of similar epithets. Then she felt before she saw the Guardians shift into gear, hearing the whistle of tranquilizer darts thud into the soft skin with her enhanced hearing.

Natre and the Elders were escorted out of the

chambers by Camille and a pair of Guardians, while the assembled crowd continued to scream. Let them wail and moan. Her arguments would sink in, and her words would spread. Many would fear the Juggernaut. That couldn't be helped. But her words would hold weight; hopefully enough to maintain a semblance of order through the next few days or weeks. Natre wracked her mind; what could she have done differently? Although she regretted handing over Ponar to the Juggernaut, it was the least bad option. She'd prepared for the worst while hoping for the best. Not that the Durmah would agree with her.

If they were lucky, the Juggernaut would have satisfied their curiosity with Ponar and moved on. Perhaps Ponar would even be returned, if he'd cooperated and been of enough use to the Assessor. If they weren't so lucky, no one would have a care in this, or any world to speak of.

CHAPTER 24

Graeber led his horse through the abandoned city with care, unsure if any of the Core had beaten them there. The scans showed nothing, but it was possible he was being jammed too.

"I'm not picking up anything either," Bauleel confirmed. She and Rilte looked exhausted, but then, Graeber expected he did as well. They'd ridden hard, and the horses looked ready to collapse.

"Somehow, and I'm not complaining, but I'd expected Sebaiya to be, well, larger." Rilte took a long pull from his canteen. This city was in the higher reaches, and they were all feeling the thinner air and associated need for more water intake.

Looking around, Graeber tried to see Sebaiya with new eyes. The buildings were old colonial functional style, which meant no beauty, just small boxes built of sheet metal scrapped from ship parts. The roads were all straight and narrow, and the city sat next to a large stable cave complex where the colonists stored supplies and vehicles. After 600 years, many of the buildings had suffered some wear and tear, and yet some still stood tall and proud, a testament to the building materials.

"We're just making a simple pickup, and then we're heading out on a shuttle before anyone can catch up to us."

"Graeber..." Bauleel held her head in her hands. Her horse trailed behind his own.

"This isn't up for discussion. I'm not leaving it here."

Rilte looked back and forth between the two of them. "Leaving *what* here?"

"Nothing!" Bauleel snarled. She refused to look at either of them. "Just make it fast. I feel like something is on our trail. I don't care what the scans say."

His gut instinct agreed with Bauleel, and it didn't matter what it was, they needed to be gone before it arrived. Graeber picked up speed and threaded his way through the cobwebs of the city. He hadn't been back here since he'd left the device, but now he felt like an archeologist hunting a relic on an ancient, dead planet. He might as well have been; no one had been through this city in generations.

Soon enough he found the tumbled down shack just as he'd left it. He handed off his horse's reins to Rilte.

Graeber pulled out the tracking device he'd carried with him these many years and confirmed he was at the right place. Then he deactivated all of the fail safes and alarms. It wouldn't do to have the package blow up in his face just as he retrieved it. Throwing away the tracker, he pulled apart the shack, displaying his inordinate strength with no care to who saw the rubble heap after he was done. It had served its purpose.

"I had no idea you were this strong," Rilte exclaimed.

Graeber shot Bauleel a sidelong look. "And here I thought you were going to explain to your friend all about our differences."

"I described the Methuselah treatments," Bauleel replied. Her flushed cheeks told Graeber what he needed to know. She hadn't told Rilte everything.

"You know, before Rilte goes on this joy ride with us, you might want to make sure he understands the full impact those had on us after we colonized."

Bauleel narrowed her eyes at him. "I thought you were against me sharing all of that."

"Things have changed. He's got a right to know before he throws in with us. He might want to turn back if he knows the full truth."

"I doubt that," Rilte had sidled his horse up against hers, and rubbed her leg with his hand. "If the Juggernaut have their way here, there won't be much left anyway. I know what I need to know." The affection in his expression was mirrored in his scent, a cloud of hope and caring.

Graeber laughed bitterly. "You'll regret those words." He'd reached the bottom of the structure and wiped clear the surface, revealing a metal door lock. He wiped his hand clean, well clean enough, on his worn leathers, and activated the lock. A small cavity slid open, and within it laid a box, which he scooped up. Graeber returned to and mounted his horse.

"Let's keep moving." Bauleel and Rilte brooked no argument.

As they threaded their way to the caves, and escape, Graeber opened the metal box, which was only a half meter square and fifteen centimeters thick. Graeber pulled out the contents and tossed the box to the ground.

"What is that?" Rilte asked. "It's like one of the of mass storage devices we used in the lab. Why would you be hiding something like that?"

"You're a bright man, Rilte. I can see why Bauleel likes you. And, I'm not going to discuss my belongings. This is mine alone to take care of."

His tone of voice left no room for argument, and so they rode on in silence, reaching a clearing with a couple broken down land transports stripped of all available parts and left to rot. The storage caves laid just beyond the clearing.

The winds turned, and Graeber caught a familiar scent on the air. He wasn't the only one.

"'Terem!' Bauleel called out. "Show yourself!"

Terem emerged from behind one of the broken-down transports, on foot and travel-worn. Despite his continued plague-ridden state, he appeared relatively stable. Relatively.

"Why did you follow us?" Bauleel demanded.

Terem approached a short distance but didn't come too close. Whether that was to appease the voices in his own head or to not frighten them, Graeber couldn't be sure.

Terem rubbed his arms and shuffled his feet. "The others came after me, just as you said they would. I hid from them, and then when I heard what they planned to do to you, I followed. I had to warn you. You warned me.

"Go on, Terem," Graeber replied.

"I hid out, and listened." He smiled. Considering Terrors could take any shape, Terem could have heard the most private of conversations. "They said they were going to 'skin interrogate you to find out the truth,' and then 'execute you if need be.' I didn't like the sound of that. Thought you deserved to know."

Bauleel had turned milk-white. "Thank you, Terem, for coming to warn us."

"What's a 'skin interrogation, Bau?" Rilte asked, his brows furrowed.

"We in the Core, we have the ability to read thoughts through touch. Especially when many of us work together to overwhelm another's mind. It's not at all pleasant, but very useful. They can rip whatever they want from your mind." A violent shiver ran through Bauleel as she finished describing the process.

"It's not going to happen," Graeber declared. "How far are they behind us?" he asked Terem.

"Hours, perhaps less. I hurried as fast as I could, but they are fast too."

Graeber nodded. He urged his horse towards the caverns.

"Wait! I'm coming with you! That's my price!" Terem yelled.

All three stared at him in disbelief. "You've got to be kidding me," Rilte replied. "You tried to kill Bauleel."

Terem shrugged. "I'm sorry about that, ma'am. I'm different now. I swear I am. And if I stay, the Guardians will find me. You know they will."

"They will pursue you," Graeber replied. "However, they also have the Juggernaut to deal with right now. You're resourceful, go to ground while they are distracted."

"No, I don't want to wait and see what the Juggernaut do either. I've heard them talking. How fearful they are. I'm coming along." He began to shake, beads of sweat dripping from his brow, his firm control hanging by a thread. "Please, have mercy on me. I don't know what I'll do if you say no."

"It's statements like that, Terem, which aren't encouraging to us." Bauleel shook her head. She turned to Graeber. "Do we have any options here?"

Graeber's lips formed a hard line. He hadn't fought Terem, but he'd read all of the reports, knew the instability, and also knew the traditional Guardian weapons were mere insect stings compared to the Terror's constitution. Could they slow him down long enough to slip away? That was the real question. Perhaps subterfuge was the better method? Tell him yes, and then give him the slip at the last minute? It wasn't Graeber's style, he preferred outright combat any day, but he preferred living overall.

"I see only one. Terem comes with us," Graeber said. Rilte and Bauleel looked incredulous, but both thought better of it after he cast them a hard look.

Terem fumed. "You're lying. I can see it layered all over you. Thinking you can give me the slip later?" Terem grew claws and his teeth became razor sharp.

Well, wasn't that unexpected? Mind-reading had been left out of the reports, much to Graeber's chagrin. Of course, there hadn't been many survivors to make reports, had there? Graeber dismounted and prepared for Terem's attack. His horse backed off, smelling the change of tension in the air.

"You two, head for the Andromeda shuttle. I prepped it fully when I was last here. It's fueled and in working order. The coordinates programmed into the system will take you to the colony ship, and from there you can take the time to make your plans."

"We're not leaving without you," Bauleel replied. "I can fight."

"But Rilte can't pilot worth a damn, and you can."

"Not leaving. Not without you." Bauleel's jaw was set firm. Damn her and her sister, neither could be swayed once they'd made up their minds!

"If I kill you, they'll take me with them," Terem said, a wide, terrifying grin revealed rows of sharpened teeth he'd manufactured for the fight. "They don't have the will to resist me."

"You willing to bet on that?" Graeber replied, only to set Terem further off his calm. Graeber palmed the strongest tranquilizers he had, the ones he'd brought along just in case Terem had followed. They could at least give them a few precious minutes.

Terem didn't bother to answer. He lunged and shifted to all fours, leaping towards the Guardian. Graeber moved in a semi-circular pattern away from the others, flanking Terem and throwing the tranq darts as he went. Each one struck exposed skin, driving home a full dose. Terem didn't bother to shake them off; he kept coming at full speed, undeterred. When Graeber ran out of darts, he pulled out two medical-grade laser scalpels he'd been saving. He'd overridden the internal safety protocols, and now they each cut a thin but deadly eight-inch blue swath of light through the air. They weren't quite a match for Terem's nasty claws, but hopefully, they'd give Graeber a chance. Assuming he didn't manage to slice himself with one first.

As they neared each other, two things became

apparent. The sedatives had minimal effect, and Terem wasn't in the least intimidated by the scalpels if his deep laughter was any clue. Terem looked the part of a lion, wild hair, on all fours with sharp claws, and serrated teeth. And now, as the two clashed together, Graeber had his first surprise for Terem.

The two clashed together, and the laser scalpels did their job, slicing into one of Terem's arms and the other into his midsection, but he didn't appear to feel any pain. Then again, neither did Graeber as Terem's claws ripped apart his shirt, but couldn't manage to pierce his toughened skin. Terem also bit down, hard, on Graeber's shoulder with his massive jaws, but again, couldn't break the surface. The sound of teeth cracking rang through the air.

The two rolled, and blood flowed, but it was all Terem's. After a few moments, Terem withdrew and licked his wounds. The skin knit back together in seconds, no trace of a scar remained, just smears of blood stuck to the skin.

"How's Graeber able to do that?" Rilte asked Bau.

"This is another of our...special talents," Bauleel replied.

"But in the Technicians wing, Terem almost killed you."

"He caught me by surprise that day, and I was out of practice. Graeber does this daily. He never got soft like me. It takes constant training to be an expert."

Terem screamed a guttural, beastly sound. "You

will not win!" He shifted more, the claws retreated, as did the giant maw of a mouth and sharp teeth. He looked more like himself again, but thicker, stockier. He went at Graeber again, swinging wide. The first few blows the Guardian dodged but suddenly Terem moved and rained blows down upon him like a thunderstorm, and he was tripped up in the intensity of the tempest.

Stunned, Graeber recovered and swept Terem's legs out from under him. Terem hit the ground with a sizable shudder. Graeber was bruised, despite his 'talents' and the brevity of the attack. Nonetheless, he managed to pull himself up to deliver some strikes with the laser scalpels, but they were now useless. Terem had turned his skin to stone as well, so the blows glanced off. Thinking quickly, Graeber made a jab to Terem's left eye and rolled away.

Terem howled. At least that method had been effectual, but as both of them worked their way to their feet, it was evident this would be no quick battle.

Then, Graeber became aware of another person approaching them at speed. He heard a scanner alarm go off a moment later. From the confused look on Terem's face, he felt it too. But what?

He looked to Bauleel, who already had a scanner out. "What is it?"

Her face displayed her confusion and fear. "I've no clue, but it's moving fast, it'll be on us any..."

Like a shock wave, both he and Terem were

knocked back flat on their asses. When Graeber looked up, there was a creature, no that wasn't right, it was a woman crouching over Terem, gently stroking his face. Comforting him. She had him pinned to the ground. Nice trick.

Graeber scrambled to his feet and approached, unable to keep away, despite the warning bells going off inside his head. Whatever, whoever this was, he instinctually knew this threat far surpassed Terem.

"Shh, Terem. Be still now. Be at peace." Her voice was disconcertingly familiar, but when she spoke, the air trembled around her. He'd never heard anything like it. Every cell in his body heard her words, and it calmed him too.

He couldn't see her face from this angle due to the hooded robes she wore, much like a Guardian's but shinier and more iridescent, as she was perched over Terem. His gaze flickered up to Bauleel and Rilte; they had the full view. Rilte was fascinated in awe of this new arrival. Bauleel's face was one of horror, and she shook her head in disbelief.

Bauleel's look nagged at Graeber, reminding him of something, but he shoved it aside for now.

Graeber watched as Terem transformed back into his normal, teenage self. Tears poured out of the boy even as he healed. "I'm so sorry. I didn't mean to hurt him. I didn't know." Terem sat up, pleading his case.

"That's all right. You had your directive. You did well. I will quiet your voices. Make it easier for you."

Again, her voice was melodic, full of song, and Graeber felt it in his bones, in his mind, and in his skin.

She slid her hand down to his chest, and Terem sighed in relief. Right before he turned inside out and fell into a puddle of gore on the ground. Bauleel screamed, hiding her face for a moment, but unable to turn away. Rilte turned pale as a moon flower.

No, whatever this was, it was certainly going to be far worse for them than Terem had been. Graeber checked the distance to the caves where their transport of escape awaited. Yet he understood due to the creature's speed, there wasn't much hope for them to reach the caves.

And yet it had killed Terem, which, in turn, helped them. Was that a coincidence? Graeber blew out a slow breath and did his best not to think too far ahead. Over planning a response to an unknown entity could remove you from fighting the present beast. He had to stay in the present.

The creature stood, still facing Bauleel and Rilte, and dropped the hood of her cape. At the sight of her auburn hair, Graeber's breath caught in his throat. *No.*

"Sister, yes? I'm glad to see you well." This time, her voice lacked that melodic ring, and he recognized it all too well. When she turned to him, Graeber still didn't believe it, but he drank up the sight of her. She appeared as Rai Durmah all over again. "By the moons, he beat you bloody." She walked closer to him, and Graeber took equivalent steps backward.

Rai got a stricken look on her face and stopped her approach.

"Who are you?" Graeber demanded, not allowing her displayed emotions to sway him. This creature looked like Rai, but her abilities spoke volumes to the contrary. "I know who you look like, but who are you, really?"

"I'm Rai. I'm still who I used to be." Her gaze met his, and he saw something there, something alien he couldn't name. "Whatever else I have become, *I* am still here."

"So I gathered." Graeber glanced over to the remains of Terem, which had quickly decomposed from blood and bones into a dirty looking heap of organic matter, and then back at Rai. Whatever she'd done, it was a quick reformative process. "Why are you here?"

The look of pain in her eyes humanized her, despite her actions. "I just saved you from Terem, and you think I'm going to hurt you?"

"The thought had occurred to me, yes." Graeber saw no reason to lie her and suspected she would know if he was.

Rai's eyes glistened, but no tears fell. "I came for my memories, which you're holding now." She held out a hand. "I'm ready to be whole again."

"How did you know?" But no, whatever she'd become, that something extra, must have scanned it off of him. What was she now? How dangerous? How much more dangerous would she become if he handed over the data block? Kilawren knew all the colony history, all of the history of the Core. "No. You're not Kilawren anymore," Graeber shook his head. "And I will not hand over her memories to whatever alien force resides within you."

CHAPTER 25

"I can see more now, beyond what the eyes see." Rai took a few steps forward. Graeber held his ground. "I will be her again. *Myself* again."

"No, I'll destroy it first," Graeber replied. Resolutely, he moved his hand towards the data cube, meaning to trigger the internal-destruct mechanism, which would render the internal components useless.

In less than a heartbeat, Rai was on him, hand placed gently on the crease where his neck met shoulder in an intimate gesture. The pressure was minute, yet Graeber was rendered immobile from the neck down.

Direct skin contact evoked the feelings he'd tried to avoid since he'd taken Rai's memories, however willingly, from her. He steeled his system as her emotions slipped under his skin and shocked him worse than he'd care to admit. His long-suppressed cravings for everything Kilawren had surfaced. By the look of recognition in her eyes, she knew it.

"You do want me back," Rai pressed, her words expressed through the skin link into his mind.

However, as their thoughts slid against each other, entwined together in a most pleasurable way after so long denied, Graeber couldn't help but notice they weren't alone. Whatever shared this space in Rai's mind, it was a hulking behemoth barely contained, just waiting to step back into the foreground. Graeber kept a wide berth and marveled at Rai's mental fortitude.

"You, I will support and aid. But you're not alone. I don't understand what this other means."

"I don't entirely understand either. Vidaaquar is an ancient power. Humans awakened her. I found her. She wants me whole, my memories restored, and so she allows me to speak with you."

"Why not just kill me like you did Terem and take what you want?"

Tears slipped down Rai's cheeks. *"If that's what she wanted, it would be."* Graeber knew that's how little power Rai held and how it terrified her. *"But Vida is pleased with me, and she feels you may be useful later. Don't make her rethink her decision. Please."*

"Vessel." The melodic sound rang through his mind, and he knew it came from the other. It filled him with foreboding.

Rai shook her head. *"Vida, have a moment's*

patience! Graeber, I will be restored. There will be a time for your concerns later."

Rai slipped her hand under his cloak, retrieving the data cube from where he'd stored it. She held it between them, the simple black box that held her past. Her memories. "Without returning them to me, what were your plans for these?" she asked aloud.

Graeber didn't utter a single word. He closed his eyes. "I'd planned to destroy them."

Rai slipped back into his mind, effortlessly. *"Tell me you don't want this. Tell me you don't want Kilawren whole again."*

Graeber's eyes sought hers out, and he strained against the hold she kept over his body. Rage boiled his blood, knowing whatever else laid inside that fragile shell of her mind that Kilawren was lost to him. *"It was your sister's idea to neuter you like this. If I'd had my way, we would have fled and taken our chances amongst the rogue planets, far away from the eyes of the Hegemony."*

"Thank you." Rai cried again, feeling the raw emotions roiling within him. *"I don't know what I can give you, once Vida has her way, but there will be some room for negotiation. Surely."*

But Graeber felt the emotions she tried to hide, which flowed in both directions. Rai lived and expressed herself at Vidaaquar's whim. His heart ached in response to Rai's admission.

Rai broke the bond and stepped backward, raising the small black box to her chest between both hands.

"You'll need a terminal interface to upload the data, there's one in the ship," Graeber gestured towards the cave complex.

Rai's words were once again melodious, her eyes dark as pools. "I have no need of your primitive technological assistance." Her finger pads and palms transformed and molded to the storage device's contact surfaces. It made no sound, but the flat surface lit from within, blue lights blinking as data was accessed, retrieved, and downloaded. Rai's eyes glowed throughout, and she stood stock still, digesting the massive array of information. Six hundred years of knowledge gained in mere minutes, what would that do to a psyche?

More concerning, what did Vidaaquar want with that knowledge?

When she was done, the cube crumbled to dust in her hand, never to be used again. Rai crumpled to the ground, head in her hands, shaking uncontrollably, with her eyes wide open. Graeber rushed to her, unsure of how the reintegration may have affected her.

"Graeber!" Bauleel yelled. "Don't!" He stayed his hand, looking to her and Rilte. They'd tied off the horses and approached but kept a respectful distance.

"She might not be able to control her responses right now," Rilte said. "Please, be patient. I doubt whatever is happening now will cause permanent damage, but she could destroy you in a heartbeat without even intending to."

Graeber grudgingly nodded and moved to join them. But his eyes didn't leave Rai's twitching form.

"I gather it's really her, my sister?" Bauleel asked. Graeber nodded. "But what happened to her?"

"It calls itself Vidaaquar," Graeber answered.

"It behaves like a Terror. Or a stable mutation," Rilte replied.

"Or like one of the Core," Bauleel added. "But then that's what we are. Stable mutations, with the aid of the Methuselah treatments."

Graeber crossed his arms and turned towards them. "You don't understand. You haven't been in there. It's not one of us. This is like us, of the same mettle even, but on a whole other scale. It'll squash us like ants."

Bauleel frowned and pursed her lips. "It doesn't have to be a bad thing. She could have killed you just now, and didn't."

Graeber gave Bauleel a harsh look. "Have you been reading the latest transmittals?"

"No," Bauleel replied. "I didn't want to chance anyone finding our location on a back-trace."

Graeber fished out his comm pad and handed it over, his lips pursed into a fine, thin line. "This one is secure. Read the last three days' worth of communiqués. Note the line of destruction headed directly towards us. Now that Rai's here... Rather, now that

Vidaaquar is here tell me what you two make of that?"

Bauleel and Rilte scoured the logs. Bauleel paled, and Rilte rubbed his stubble down with both hands. When they were done, Bauleel handed the pad back with a look of disgust on her face.

"So many lives lost. What do you think its purpose is?" Bauleel asked.

"Per the message she sent out via Ponar at Jeweled Cove, she's here to wipe out the colony. Now she's here and whole with Kilawren's memories. But what does that gain her?" Graeber asked.

Rilte put his hands on his hips, an exasperated look on his face. "Our entire colony history, for one, even the original intent of the settlement when you set out on your mission. It gets her everything. Everything she needs to understand the human colonists, from start to finish."

All three turned to stare at Rai, whose shaking had ceased. She lay still, apparently dozing, but Graeber doubted she slept. Vidaaquar had already decreed an end to this colony. Would she seek out other human colonies as well? What had he done in handing over Kilawren's memories? What other choice had he had?

Rai opened her eyes and turned to face them. Standing up, she walked over to join their conversation. Rai moved with slow deliberation, seeming to take some care not to startle them.

Graeber studied her for outward signs of changes.

"Your eyes are hazel now." No longer green. And your hair is darker, longer, as Kilawren's was, but you still have your auburn curls."

"Yes, I suppose I would look different. Although I've regained my past, I haven't given up my new parts. It's all me," Rai explained. She looked vulnerable, the alien absent again. Was that a good sign, or was the behemoth busy planning?

"How do you feel?" Bauleel asked. "I was never sure how, technically speaking, this part of the process would work, assuming we could do it. And this wasn't at all how I'd imagined it would go."

Rai gave her a half-hearted smile. "A little shaky. The memories feel like a dream, and altogether too real, and too much all at once. There's just so many of them, reintegrating it all in chronological order's hard. It'll take me time to sort it out. I'm sure Vida will have it worked out before I do."

Graeber shifted uncomfortably at that notion. "But it's all there?"

Rai's eyes met his. "Oh yes. I know who I am again. I know who the two of you are, and who you are to me. But I have no clue who you are, Rilte. However, I see Bauleel claims you for her own." To which her sister flushed. "And that's good enough for me."

"Should we call you Kilawren now?" Rilte asked.

Rai shook her head. "No, that was my old life. I've become something new. Kilawren remembers being sentenced to death by the Core. She remembers being hunted by them, and when she ran, you drew the blade across my neck," she said to Graeber.

"Like I'd have let them rip you to shreds?" His words were ice. The others had been intent on savaging her, tearing her to pieces. With a single, damning stroke he'd thwarted their butchery.

Rai nodded. "And I remember you, my sister, reviving me, and concocting this scheme to remove my memories and shift me into another form."

"It worked for a time. We kept you hidden. In your new form, you behaved differently. Mostly." Bauleel wrung her hands.

"I didn't want you to try and save me, and I should have told you that. I should have made you both let go," Rai replied. "It would have been safer for you."

Graeber swore and grabbed her by the shoulders. "I should have run with you then. Gone far away from all this madness. We can still run now. Everything is at the ready."

A look of profound sadness overcame Rai's features, and she tilted her head to the side. Her hand slid up to cup Graeber's face, and she pulled him into her thoughts.

A profound sense of visceral need surrounded him and images, memories of Kilawren's life, kept flashing by at random intervals. Were these remnants of the reintegration process? It took every ounce of self-control not to act on the intimacy of this moment she'd invited.

"I may have her memories, but I am no longer your Kilawren," Rai said. "She died back in that forest, and only shadow memories and reflections remain of the person you once loved."

Graeber felt profound loss at her words, knowing them to be accurate through their skin bond. "I understand."

Rai nodded, and then a flash of iridescence colored her eyes. "The Core is upon us," Rai said.

Graeber's heart skipped a beat. "We have to flee them!"

Rai shook her head. "Look, deeper." She opened a window into her depths, and he glimpsed Vidaaquar...amassing herself? Growing larger, denser. "Yes, that's correct. She's preparing for them. We have nothing to fear. Besides, I see through Vida's mind's eye that they bring weapons. They anticipated your attempt to escape and are prepared to shoot down the transport ship, if necessary. Your attempt would have failed in death."

Graeber cocked his head. "You wouldn't be coming with us?"

"Vida isn't done here yet. I am her vessel. That she's allowed me this time to talk with you all is a gift."

Graeber's temper flared. "Still, I am not okay with you being her instrument of torture."

Rai's hands dropped, and she pushed him away. "Turns out, Vida's not much of a negotiator."

"How soon will the Core arrive?" Bauleel asked.

"They've entered the town, and it hasn't come up on your scanners because they are jamming the signal. But as I said, you have nothing to fear. Vida has *rewarded* me by sparing you."

Bauleel moved forward and hugged Rai, and after a moment Rai responded. "Thank you." The words rushed out of Bau. "It's good to have you back. In whatever form, for however long. I'll never regret what I did, I'm just sorry for what it's cost you."

When they separated, both were teary-eyed. "No regrets, Sis. And it's not over. Not yet."

"There they are." Graeber pointed to the clouds of dust kicked up by horses coming around a corner a few blocks away. The Core moved quickly, thinking their quarry would attempt to run.

"Stay behind me. Or don't. I'm fast enough now, it won't matter. Just stay close together," Rai directed.

"I don't like you doing all the fighting," Graeber replied.

"Only because you can't stand missing a good fight," Rai smiled up at him. "But this won't be a fight. This will be a schooling. You've read the reports. I heard you talking. I doubt it will come to that, but I don't know what all Vida has planned. Regardless, I'm in no danger, and neither are you."

And somehow, Graeber took a sick form of pride in her words.

CHAPTER 26

Rᴀɪ sᴍɪʟᴇᴅ ᴀᴛ Gʀᴀᴇʙᴇʀ ᴀɴᴅ ᴛʜᴇ ᴏᴛʜᴇʀs, ᴇᴠᴇɴ as she felt Vida pushing to the surface within her consciousness. Rai caught an inkling of Vida's plan. She didn't understand it all but knew better than to fight or question.

"I'll be changing forms. Let me take the lead. Whatever I say, go with it. They seek traitors, but we will give them one of their own." Their eyes were full of questions, but soon her flesh shivered and slid, remolding and stretching into her new shape. Her hair darkened and lengthened, even her robes shifted. She shook out the kinks from the change, and couldn't help but meet Graeber's eyes, knowing he saw Kilawren in the flesh again.

"I don't miss that look on you." His voice husky, his eyes yearning for the past.

"It's just for show," she replied. Graeber shrugged.

"Please remember, I may sound like me, but Vida will be in the foreground, so don't be fooled. I'd recommend you keep your distance, just in case she gets... irritated."

"Noted," Rilte replied. "We'll look pensive and intimidated by their big guns and scary threats of interrogation while forgetting you can turn them all into slime in a heartbeat."

"I don't think you're taking this seriously. Vida wants them held accountable."

"For what?" Bauleel asked.

"*All will be revealed,*" Vidaaquar answered in melodic tones.

"And...there she went, and here they come. C'mon, all, let's look properly contemptuous." Graeber folded his arms and stepped up next to Kilawren, who shot him a questioning look. "What? Of course, I'd stand by her, *your*, side."

In return, Vida inclined her head in assent.

Inside of Rai, Vida waited. Her sheer power amazed, as always, and Rai felt no fear as over four-dozen riders descended upon them. At that moment, a thought occurred to her, and she initiated an internal conversation with her ever-present companion.

"Vida, why have you kept me? Now that I'm whole again, you have my memories; you have all the answers you need. Yet I'm still here, and not pushed into some small box in this 'vessel' either."

She sensed the tinkling of Vida's laughter. "Would you prefer I snuff you out?"

"Of course not! It's just, I wish to understand."

"You were not complicit in the crimes of your founding colonists. You tried in earnest to understand me, and you have served me well. Thus my boons to you and your companions."

"For which I'm forever grateful. You speak of crimes? Is this beyond the destruction of your planet?"

"It led to the destruction. Be still, child. And you will see. There is a traitor among your founders, and you were not the one."

This left Rai to ponder, and she willingly released her body to Vida. Not that fighting would have done much good, but it would have worn Rai out.

Soon they were surrounded, and by Vida's mind's eye and with Rai's knowledge, she knew five of the members were Core with about four dozen Guardians to back them up. Graeber's sister Raza, Tinker Somnu, Taessen, Cerry, and Rebea. Vida supplied these names, and knew the Guardian's names too, but didn't bother to enumerate them. The Core members dismounted and came to stand face to face with them. And why not? They weren't a threat, after all.

"It appears we have two surprises today," Chieftess Raza said. "We come here hunting down Terem, and instead we find ourselves a very much alive and well traitor. I must say brother, and Bauleel, you're keeping poor company."

"Terem is dead," Graeber replied. He gestured to

the remains on the ground at the far end of the clearing. "We were able to take him down together."

A couple of Guardians dismounted, pulling out their scanners to inspect the remains. All waited in tense quiet while they crouched over the spot, focused on their readings. "It's confirmed, this is, well was, him," one of the women called out.

Rebea sighed. "That's one less worry. He did enough damage on the way here."

Vida suppressed a rumble of amusement. "*Oh, they thought he'd done all that? Hadn't we'd been clear with them, Rai? Fools.*"

"How were you able to manage it, just the three of you?" Raza asked.

"Technically, there are four of us." Graeber motioned to Rilte. Raza stared at her brother blankly. All knew Rilte wasn't trained for fighting, and he couldn't have been of any material aid. "You shouldn't discount him, sister. His wit alone is invaluable."

Raza's eyes narrowed, and Rilte fought hard not to laugh, but Bauleel shot him a hard glance, and he regained his stoic composure.

"Many thanks, Guardian. I'm glad I am appreciated," Rilte replied.

The Core members observed them carefully, sensing something was off.

"Guardians, search the area for other threats and secure the perimeter. We intend to hold private council now," Raza informed her staff, and the four dozen Guardians formed a perimeter, leaving the group to talk amongst themselves. "And now, for this other matter before us. How long have you been keeping Kilawren in hiding, Graeber?" Raza asked.

"I suppose it doesn't matter how long, does it, Raza?" Graeber answered. "The fact that it was done at all is damning enough, yes?"

"Indeed it is," Somnu replied. "Have you no shame for violating our group's mandate?"

Graeber grinned. "I don't live in the shadow of your shame."

"You're mad!" exclaimed Rebea, face flushed in righteous anger. "And you, Bauleel. You stand by his side, with a Technician you abducted from the Guild. Are you complicit in this act?"

Bauleel walked forward to stand next to Kilawren. "Actually, it was my doing in the first place. Your mandate was unfair, so I defied you. Graeber only helped me cover it up."

"Oh, and just to clarify, I wasn't abducted," Rilte spoke up. "I insisted on the trip. Bauleel needed the medical attention and the assistance..." His voice trailed off under the withering stares from the Core members. Bauleel took his hand in hers and gave him a reassuring smile.

"And here we thought we'd have to interrogate you to get to the truth," Cerry replied. "Instead you stand there, willing to lay it all out for us, knowing we'll condemn you all in a heartbeat. You've condemned yourselves. Except you, Rilte, we'll take you back to the Guildhall. You've done no wrong, except being led astray by this despicable lot."

"Yes," Somnu replied, looking quite solemn, "I'm afraid we have no choice. Today Bauleel, Graeber, and Kilawren must die."

"There's only one problem with that solution," Kilawren said, speaking for the first time.

Anger flared in Somnu's eyes, but he held his tongue.

"What problem?" Raza replied.

"We aren't the only traitors here," Kilawren replied.

"Oh, fancy that," Rebea said. "We came here to see if Bauleel and Graeber might be responsible for the luna berry taint. What do you want to bet they plan to blame it on someone else in the Core?"

Bauleel and Graeber exchanged glances, but Kilawren kept her eyes on their accusers. "There's the issue of the berry taint, but that's not what I speak of. I uncovered a threat to us, to our colony, and if the Juggernaut discover the cover up, the consequences will be grave beyond your comprehension."

Rebea shifted, confusion painted across her angular features. Rage burned in Somnu's glare.

Taessen broke the silence. "What did you discover, and how?"

"I came here and sifted through old records to unearth the truth. I suggest we do a group skin interrogation. I can pass along the information, verify my sources as accurate, and establish that none of you were the ones who committed the crime."

Kilawren held out her arm, bare skinned, and offered all to touch. Graeber and Bauleel laid hands upon her upper arm, a testament to their faith that Vida wouldn't destroy them as she had Terem. Rai was moved by the depth of their trust, and continuing friendship, despite the current circumstances. The other Core members shrank back, although Raza appeared to be fair game, she no doubt wanted to move with the others.

"I will not be judged by a traitor!" Cerry replied. "Show us this information source, and we will judge for ourselves."

"Alas, there is no more time," Kilawren answered.

"Don't be silly, take us to the data terminal!" Somnu ordered.

"I'm afraid you're out of time. Submit now, or things are going to become much more uncomfortable for you," Kilawren replied.

Raza looked at her with fear in her eyes, and Kilawren knew she'd won Raza over, save for fear of retribution by the others. The other four were enraged.

"We will not be ordered around by a traitor! Especially not by one who's supposed to already be executed!" Rebea exclaimed.

Kilawren dropped her arm. "Fine, it's too late now anyway. We have guests."

CHAPTER 27

"Guests?" Taessen asked.

Kilawren pointed to the sky. "A Juggernaut shuttle is arriving, although it's been jammed on your sensors. Raza, call in your Guardians so they don't get injured in the disturbance. The shuttle will have a small team on board, so keeping the humans together will minimize casualties."

Raza looked puzzled, but pulled out her communications device and sent orders to her team.

Kilawren turned to Graeber, Bauleel, and Rilte. "The Assessor is coming, and if I give him the Rai he's looking for, that should put him in a more favorable mood." She shook her head and body loosely, like you'd shake out your stiff joints, and transformed back into the form of Rai.

Graeber's face fell, resigned to her transformation.

Vidaaquar heard a body hit the ground and turned

to see Cerry flat on the ground, having fainted dead away. Somnu appeared ten shades of livid, while Raza was holding her head between her hands. Taessen and Rebea stood dumbfounded, unsure of what to make of Kilawren turned Rai. The gathering Guardians tensed, awaiting Raza's order to strike at Rai.

The Juggernaut shuttle landed in the open clearing in front of the storage caverns. The humans regarded it with extreme fear as if this was the worst thing that could be happening.

"You don't need to worry about them," Vidaaquar spoke, her melodious voice carrying easily across the crowd. *"But stay close, and don't even dream of running. You can't outrun me. Nothing on this planet can."*

Vidaaquar walked a short distance towards the shuttle, with Graeber close on her heels.

"You're not concerned about the Juggernaut, the most powerful race in the universe?" he asked.

"Oh, are they now?" she laughed.

He gave her a confused look. "Do you know anything about them?"

"Oh, yes, I would say I do." Vidaaquar nodded. *"Although I am a bit out of date. It has been a few millennia since I've connected with another of my kind via the hive mind we share. I've been busy here, for eons, terraforming this world and shaping it to my will until I was interrupted by your people."* She emphasized this with a finger poke to the chest. *"I knew the Juggernaut at their inception."*

Graeber shrugged off this sophisticated reply. "Still, won't they complicate things?" he asked.

"They will. When the Juggernaut discover your founder's crimes, they are likely to wipe your colony off the map." Vidaaquar answered.

This visibly unsettled Graeber. "Not all are responsible."

"No, but it's no different than what I was planning."

"There's another way. Punish those responsible and use those remaining for source components." He touched Rai's arm. "This vessel has served a purpose, after all. Perhaps others could as well. We're all just material to be molded, yes?"

Vidaaquar smiled, pleased at his insight. *"You're bright for a human."*

"I've lived a long time. It's given me more time to mature." He smiled back and dropped his arm, and they both watched the Juggernaut envoy approach. They had a human in tow. "That's Ponar Durmah," Graeber said.

"Rai recognizes him as well. He appears in good health."

They waited a few minutes in silence for the Juggernaut to approach, not wanting their conversation to be overheard by the envoy. Stillness hung in the air as the envoy came to a halt, Ponar and Assessor Brague face to face with Vidaaquar and Graeber. The rest of the Assessor's retinue held back. Vidaaquar recognized Brague from the communications bursts which kept floating through the sub-stream around the planet.

"Rai Durmah, the rumors of your death were greatly exaggerated, I see. That will need to be addressed at a later time. I do appreciate your escort handing you over into my care. Are you ready to depart?" the Assessor asked.

Vidaaquar was aware of Graeber folding his arms and taking a sharp intake of breath next to her, but a short glance reminded him to keep his tongue in check.

"Assessor Brague, it is a pleasure to look upon a Juggernaut after all this time. Welcome to my territory. I offer you safe passage." She spoke in her usual lyrical tones, but this time the words reverberated, and she used the full range of her multi-dimensional speech capability, layering in messages only for the Assessor. Including, "my precious one" and "the humans are the intruders" and "let us deal with them together."

The Assessor cocked his head, and switched to his native tongue, also multi-dimensional by design. *I came searching Rai / You wear her form, yet imply, and appear to be, much more / Please, be direct, and if you are who I hope you are, you will have my entire fleet at your disposal.*

Vidaaquar smiled, but it was a smile filled with distaste. *If you search the oceans, you will find my Seed Marker / Or do you require miracles? / Acts of destruction? / My ability to speak to you, as such, should quell your fears, mighty one.*

A look of wonder overwhelmed Brague's eyes, and he rocked from side to side. *No! / There was no Seed Marker! / Our scans would have detected!*

Your scans are flawed! / And the humans hid the marker / I do not know how, but I will have a confession today / Do your scans again, and be thorough this time. Full visual scans off of the Jeweled Cove area. You will find me!

The Assessor ordered the oceanic scans via his arm console, his voice an angry tirade echoing throughout the meadow. The human Ponar cowered at his side, silent through this entire exchange. Vidaaquar sensed Rai's concern for Ponar but also knew he was in good health and had not been abused. In fact, he looked forward to this day with great fervor. He too wanted revenge, just of a slightly different flavor. Well, well. Perhaps she could serve up enough to satisfy the lot of them.

Next, she heard the Assessor open a private channel to his Queen Klimitzi, he shielded himself and told her he thought he'd found one, after all this time. The Queen was astonished and was sending a personal envoy to verify. The planet was to be deemed a sanctuary. And so on, and so forth. Vidaaquar realized she was stunned by their communications, and Rai empathized to console her.

To be found? Were her kind somehow absent? Busy, yes surely, that must be the reason. Too busy to be bothered.

The Assessor finished his call and turned to Vidaaquar. *I have ordered the scans / I will inform you promptly when we find your Seed Marker / Until then, it would be my utmost honor to continue the interrogations for you / I am quite skilled / I offer my humble service.*

He bowed and offered his neck, the proper sign of respect to a superior. However, Vidaaquar's temperament had darkened from overhearing the Assessor's conversation. Vidaaquar stepped into his space, the ground under her feet shattering and crumbling in direct response to her mood, and gripped his upper carapace with hands strong as steel. Her teeth elongated into razor-sharp weapons. She bit a few millimeters deep into his vulnerable, exposed folds, just to get her point across. To the Assessor's credit, he didn't flinch, not one iota. His pulse held calm and steady under her flicking tongue. The Assessor's retinue, stunned, began to raise weapons, but he waved them off, and Vidaaquar growled in approval. Rai within was mortified, yet awed. Who'd ever witnessed a petite redhead cower a Juggernaut before? Not that it was *her* doing, of course. Ponar, however, was terrified, held in place by one of the Assessor's Juggernaut.

Vidaaquar pushed him away, not ripping the vulnerable folds of his neck, and retracted her teeth. He did not move. *"You may give your Queen Klimitzi my regards when next you speak."* His eyes rose to hers in shock, unaware she'd been able to hear everything through his impermeable shield. *"You may observe my work, and assist as I see fit / Do not interfere with me / My thanks for returning Ponar / He will be of use."*

Assessor Brague brought himself up to his full height, his motions stiff. *"You truly are a Progenitor / Praise be to this day / I am honored beyond words to be in your presence / I did have promises to Ponar / They must be kept."*

Vidaaquar tilted her head, ignoring the honorifics. *"What promises to the human? / Let's hope you can keep them."*

Brague guffawed. *"No worries, honored spirit / He despises the way women are used as lowly breeders here / I am shocked you perpetuate a system which limits their influence and shortens their lifespans / I promised to destroy the Temple system for him."*

Vidaaquar turned to Ponar and smiled, shifting back to human speech. "It's good to see you again, Ponar. I understand you wish to see the end of Temple service. You'll have that by the end of the day. All that, and perhaps a bit more."

Ponar scuffed his feet nervously under their scrutiny, but who wouldn't? "Rai?"

"Yes, and no," Vidaaquar replied. "When she jumped off that tower, she found me in the ocean. She liberated me, and I saved her from drowning. We are bonded together now." She turned to the Juggernaut holding him. "Release him. He will come with us willingly."

The Juggernaut soldier turned to the Assessor, who barked an order, and then they complied, releasing Ponar.

"Now, we find ourselves the traitor," Vidaaquar announced, leading the envoy back to the awaiting group of Core and Guardians, who looked none too happy to see them return.

Despite Rai's secondary seat of power within her own body, she now contemplated the utter irony of the power shift she'd witnessed since the last time she'd seen Ponar. Back then, she was a simple girl, with little power within her own Sept, and now she was, what, a vessel to a Progenitor, whatever that was, with an entire fleet of Juggernaut ships backing her, and another on the way.

Again, she wasn't *exactly* in charge. But she did at least get a front row seat.

"Progenitor," the Assessor politely continued in human speech, as she had shifted over to it, "how do you expect to find the traitor? The colony is over 600 years old. Whoever committed the crime is now long gone."

"Ah, that's where you're wrong, Assessor. And you will call me Vidaaquar, or Vida if you prefer. I am not one for titles. I insist."

The Assessor's mandibles clattered, but he recovered gracefully. "Then, by all means, Vida, you must call me Brague."

At this point, they'd rejoined the Core and

Guardians, who waited wide-eyed. The five Core sat in a small circle while the Guardians occupied a separate and much larger patch of ground. Bauleel and Rilte stood off to the side, watching to see that none attempted to escape. Graeber and Ponar joined them.

"You see, Brague, the original crew took Methuselah treatments to increase their chances of surviving the initial trip to the colonization site. Thus, the original traitors are likely still among us."

"You're a liar! They did no such thing!" Rebea exclaimed. Cerry and Somnu sat and fumed next to her. Taessen held his head in his hands, and Raza stared wide-eyed at Vida.

"Don't bother," replied Rilte. "I've done scans on Bauleel myself, and Vida here has examined my mind. You can't make her un-know the truth of it."

Rebea turned shades of red that should have been impossible for a human, but held her tongue, realizing she'd lost the argument. She slumped in resignation, a host of words held behind her lips.

"Methuselah treatments?" Brague roared, and Vida shot him a warning look, which he ignored. "No, Progenitor, my pardons, Vida, this goes against the Hegemonic law, and renders their colony charter null and void."

Vida smiled the sweetest of smiles. "So? Render it void. Tear it up. Consider the settlement of Az'Unda no more."

Brague paused, and then pulled up his communications console. Cerry and Rebea began crying, desolate at this outcome, while Somnu was even more incensed. Despite the language barrier, you could hear the relish in Brague's voice as he delivered the news to whomever he spoke.

"But Brague," Vida interrupted.

"Yes," he paused, turning back to her.

"Keep in mind; I have marked this planet as my own. And I claim all inhabitants upon it as my property, to do with as I see fit. If I wish them relocated, I will ask it of you."

His form grew stiff. "I can also dispose of them for you. I do have resources at the ready. Surely they were not in your original design matrix?"

"No, they were not, but my initial efforts to remove them altered their genetics to a small degree. Some more than others." She eyed Bauleel, Graeber, and the Core members. "But do not concern yourself with such trivial matters. Any I feel are superfluous, I can render down into their material components." She gestured at the pile, which had been Terem, and as Brague comprehended, he shivered in appreciation. The Core members and Guardians appeared visibly shaken.

"As you wish. But concerning the legalities, the colony charter will be declared void, and the planet a fitting sanctuary to the Progenitor Vidaaquar. Sanctuary Vidaaquar." He bowed low, the scent of victory rolling off of him.

Rai took the opportunity to roll her metaphorical eyes.

How long had it been since he'd seen one of her kind, Vidaaquar wondered? But that was a discussion for another day.

Vida nodded her assent to the Assessor. "Now, Graeber, please identify for Brague, the locations of all Core members so he can retrieve them for us now. I wish to interrogate them all at once."

"Don't!" cried out Taessen.

"Why?" asked Graeber. "Are you the traitor?"

"Of course not!" Taessen shot to his feet. "But we can't expose all of us to them like this!"

Graeber placed a hand on his shoulder to calm Taessen, but it had no visible effect. "Look, I know all of this is a lot to take in, but Vida's in charge now, and we're not."

"That's fine for you, you're one of the enemy's pets! What did she offer you to sell out your own kind? How little did it take, eh? *You're* the traitor!"

Graeber took one calm, level look at Taessen, and decked him square in the jaw. Taessen crumpled to the ground unconscious.

Graeber, face calm as stone, fished his comm unit from his gear and keyed up the necessary files, and walked the group over to Brague. "This data lists all of the Core members, all of the founding colonists. They aren't always attentive to their private comm units, we keep these hidden, so you might need to make some sort of special announcement to get their attention, and then wait for them to get online. Regardless, they keep the comm units close at hand, and only they can unlock them. They will attempt to flee, but their faces are identified."

"And Brague," Vida interrupted, "tell your men that once cornered, they may try to run, and shape-shift their faces. They have that gift from me. However, it won't occur to them to shift their scent. So key first to their scent, and then they can't elude you."

Brague chattered in anticipation of the hunt. "We will not fail. All Core members will be rounded up within two solar hours." Brague accepted the unit and went to work, returning to his shuttle. His envoy remained to keep guard over the prisoners.

Bauleel stepped up to Graeber, reached out to touch him but then thought better of it. Vida could see the waves of anger emanating off of him as he reacted to Taessen's remarks.

"The real traitor here was the one who hid the Seed Marker from all of us," Bauleel said under her breath to Graeber. "They kept us from making an informed decision on where to set up our colony. They brought this day to pass."

"Agreed," Graeber replied. "But that's not to say we haven't acted selfishly, is it?" His eyes met Vida's, and thus Rai's. Vida faded in contemplation, allowing Rai into the foreground.

Rai searched her heart for regrets and found none.

"No regrets." The words formed in her mind, and she saw instant recognition in Graeber's eyes. Interesting. She smiled at him, and he smiled back, but his heart wasn't in it.

"Vida is taking a meditative break, and we have some time before the Core is rounded up. Perhaps we should get some rest and eat?" Rai suggested.

"I suppose we have some rations left in the saddlebags," Bauleel replied. "Let me grab them."

"No, wait," Ponar said, speaking just above a whisper. "Vida is a Progenitor, a venerated species to the Juggernaut. Rai's her vessel. You three are her esteemed companions, yes?"

"What are you getting at?" Graeber asked.

"That you're not understanding your present status, my friends. I've been on their ships. I've seen their wealth. Their prosperity. I say we avail ourselves of their hospitality."

CHAPTER 28

"I think you've spent a little too much time around our dear Assessor, Ponar," Rai said, eyebrow arched.

Ponar audibly, at least to Rai's hearing, ground his teeth. "I fought for you up there, Sis. It wasn't at all pleasant, but I know how they think. Perhaps even better than you or Vidaaquar. He said his entire fleet is at your disposal, didn't he?"

"Well, yes, but his offer meant military force," Rai replied.

"Like I said, I know them better. Watch." Ponar walked up to one of the envoys dispatched outside the shuttle, knowing the Assessor had gone inside. Rai exchanged glances with Rilte and Bau. "The Progenitor's vessel and her chosen companions require sustenance and a place to rest, while the Core retrieval operations are taking place. Please inform the Assessor," Ponar stated in a matter of fact tone, and instead of waiting, he turned and walked back over to them. The envoy entered the shuttle for a few moments, and then returned to his post.

Rai and the others waited a few minutes, but nothing happened.

"What are we waiting for, again?" Rilte asked.

Ponar smiled and pointed to the sky. "Something like that." A second, larger ship descended, sleek lines running the length of its pearlescent, ovoid form.

"What style of ship is it? It's not a shuttle, and not a war cruiser either. I've seen specs on those," Bauleel asked.

"How would I know?" Ponar replied. "But I'm certain it's some hidden treasure."

A bell reverberated through Rai, within Vida, yet Vida remained in her meditative state. Graeber shot her a look askance, and she knew he'd felt echoes of it too. Rai could only shrug, not knowing what the signal meant.

The ship landed, and the five of them walked towards it. The top of the ship was blanketed with windows, visually open to space like a solarium. A panel slid open, and a pair of slender, dainty Juggernaut emerged.

"Please, will the vessel follow us so we may be of service to you and your esteemed companions?" The pair genuflected, chests scraping the ground, and then trundled back inside along a short ramp.

The *vessel* and her honored companions followed the two odd Juggernaut into the ship. Rilte clapped Ponar on the shoulder on the way in. Rai sensed Graeber's nervousness. He looked down at her, caution and caring warring in his glance.

"They can't hurt me, remember?" Rai whispered. "I don't even think they want to."

He looked away. "Let's suppose Vida can hold off an entire Juggernaut armada if she needed to. What if they didn't want to hurt you? What if they want to keep you? Keep *her*?"

Rai felt a chill travel down her spine. What if Vida wanted to be kept? But, surely not? Az'Unda, or whatever she called it, was her home, or at least her project. She wouldn't abandon it. Would she?

They entered the vessel and were greeted with the finest of perfumes and, as the panel slid shut behind them, the increased humidity alerted them that this was no ordinary sterile ship.

Rai felt Vida stir, but she didn't rise to the surface. "What class of ship is this?" From her recovered memories, Rai knew of no such Juggernaut vessel.

One of the diminutive Juggernauts approached her and bowed low. "Progenitor, I am Caretaker Traken, and this is my assistant Kaanee. We humbly serve upon this Sanctuary class starship."

"I know of no Sanctuary class starships amongst the Juggernaut fleet," Rai replied.

Traken rose, momentary surprise quickly wiped from his features. "Of course, Progenitor. We keep them secret and tell other races we use these vessels to grow crops. In truth, they are traveling monuments to your race, memorials to the impact you had on our inception. In times of need, any Juggernaut may come here to seek guidance. However, while you are here, your group will not be disturbed. Now, we have taken the liberty to prepare a feast for you, and there are also places to rest. We are hopeful you will feel at home."

"I am honored, Caretakers Traken and Kaanee. Please, escort us to the feast," Rai replied.

Traken led them on a labyrinthine path towards the center of the vessel, decorated with a wide variety of plants, stacked stone placements, fountains, and arcane carvings upon cut metal slabs of varying shapes which levitated in the air. All walked along quietly. The energy of the space demanded their silent awe, as if talking would violate some implicit code.

Rai took all this in, waiting for some sign from Vida. After all, this was a monument to her species, and yet she remained curiously reserved. Or perhaps she just chose not to share her reactions with her vessel? Rai had no way of knowing.

After a few minutes, they reached the center of the ship and saw the promised feast table laid out in front of them.

"Now, this is what I'm talking about," Ponar said, walking straight towards the food.

"*Wait.*" Vida's voice rang out. Her eyes were fixed upon the column in the middle of the ship, identical to the one Rai had discovered in the depths of the ocean. Rai recognized it at once; both she and Vida knew it from their personal experience.

"What's wrong?" Graeber's voice at her ear, reassuring.

Rai walked forward even as she felt Vida stall and hold back within her. Odd, now *Rai* was the brave one? "It's a Seed Marker. Well, part of one. You can see where it's been cut at the top and bottom."

"Yes, Progenitor," Traken replied, chittering in joy. "All Sanctuary ships carry such a token, in case we find you again."

Rai looked at him, keeping the question out of her eyes, and certainly not voicing it. She felt Vida's pain sear through her. *Where are my people?*

"Thank you, Caretakers. We will take our feast in private. Now leave us," Rai said.

"If you need anything," Traken replied, "please summon us from the communications array." He gestured to a panel located at chest height next to the doorway into this room.

"I asked you to leave," Rai replied.

He bowed low. "There are sleeping quarters," he said as he retreated. "May we show you?"

"I can find them on my own," Rai replied.

"Of course you can, great Progenitor. My apologies. It has been some time."

Some time? Vida's confusion rippled through Rai's gut.

The Caretakers left, groveling all the way out the door.

"Well, dig in everyone," Rai said. "And thanks, Ponar, you were right about the Assessor."

Rilte took a seat at the table. "It's not our usual fare, but I can't say I'm feeling picky at the moment." He dug in without complaints, and Bauleel and Ponar joined him.

"You're not hungry?" Graeber ran a hand down her arm and watched the way she stared at the Seed Marker. "What's your plan?"

"The markers store information on Vida's people."

"And?"

"They serve as a living history, but can also store consciousness, as the one on Az'Unda did for Vida," Rai explained.

Graeber frowned. "Don't you think if this one had a sentience within it, that it would have already found a vessel, as Vida did?"

"Exactly," Rai agreed. "Vida wants to know where her kind went, but it also scares her."

His face softened, and a lip curled up. "Something scares the invincible?"

"I know, it's oddly comforting to discover she has a vulnerability."

"So, what is Vida going to do?"

Rai regarded Graeber, reading the tension in his form as impatience. She knew he wanted to talk, as did she, although not with the outcome he was hoping for. Rai used her mind's eye to seek out the mentioned sleeping chambers, and indeed, there were plenty available and easily accessible.

"Vida is sitting on her butt. I think she will be occupied for a while contemplating the universe," Rai replied. "Perhaps we could eat privately? We have a lot to discuss."

Graeber nodded. "Talking would be great. But first, I think you need to go and touch that Marker. Vida can get her information and stew on what it means."

Rai's eyes widened. "You want me to force her hand?"

"Well, *your* hand, actually," he chuckled. "Come on, while we're unsupervised."

"What if whatever she sees upsets her? We have no idea how she'll react."

Graeber turned her to face him. "Could you have gone on, not knowing your past?" he asked. Rai shook her head. "As I understand it, this is a history book for her race's past. Just read it. Vida has lived for millennia, I have faith in her resilience."

Rai shrugged, and before she lost her nerve or the possibility for Vida to rise up to stop her, she walked straight up to the Seed Marker and put both hands on it.

At first, her vision faded to black as the energy of the Marker seized her. Her external senses shut down, as her mind's eye connected to the latent power of the stone. The monolith illuminated, both within her and itself. Ancient scrollwork lit up along the depressions of the Marker, and Rai was conscious of the others approaching, awestruck.

"Stay back. I'm not yet aware what may be contained within," Rai said, her voice a sweet harmony, despite Vida's continuing decision to stand in the wings. She felt her friends, and the Caretakers, who'd returned to witness this seeming miracle, look on with anticipation.

Full of focus, Rai opened the book before her, pulling Vida along on her journey. Sucked into a cavern of knowledge, data streaming all around her, Rai could have been lost, but she held tight onto the stalwart Vida.

"Explain to me what I'm seeing." Rai kept her tone unemotional. Yet demanding.

"It's a Seed Marker. It's broken."

Right. "How much remains?"

"There," Vida pointed to an area of blackness, where the data flows cut off abruptly, *"and there, it has been severed. This is a quarter of the whole."*

"Does a sentience reside here, as you did at the one I encountered?"

Vida made a noise of disgust. *"No, they would have left before this atrocity was committed. No Progenitor would allow such a thing to occur. An incomplete Marker does not permit the full story to be told."*

"Do you require a Marker? To house yourself?"

Vida mentally chuckled. *"Of course not! We may rest within them, and we store project history and our travels within them, but we are independent. This one was abandoned and then desecrated by the Juggernaut."*

That didn't bode well for the Juggernaut, did it? "I think they intended this ship as a tribute to your race, Vida. This looks something like a Temple. Perhaps they come here to worship and seek comfort in their last vestiges of connection to the Progenitors."

Vida's sad expression touched the core of Rai. Within moments Vida's disgust transformed to rage. Vida reached up her arms to the walls of the Marker and arcs of blue lightning danced between her flesh and the polished stone. Rai's eyes glowed incandescent, mirroring the raw energy's color.

Information poured from the Marker into Vida, while Rai gleaned snippets as it rushed by her consciousness. Another world, another colony, not Juggernaut at all. The monolith represented another failed experiment, but the details weren't recorded within this segment of the stone. Frustration and abandonment were etched into the very crevices, and the weight of sadness crashed down upon Rai as Vida kept extracting and pulling every morsel of data she could find. Nothing would have been enough to satiate her curiosity.

Rai sensed Vida's tipping point and knew why the Progenitor had been so quiet and withdrawn. The absence of others of her kind was foreign to Vida. Although they lived at great distances to one another, the connections formed lasted millennia. This broken marker, and the Juggernaut speaking of her race as lost, had created an abyss within Vida herself, which could not be filled with the contents of this broken relic.

"There are no answers here. Only questions." Vida's eyes raged, their blue fire staring off into the distance.

"Vida!" Rai yelled, drawing her dark, wild visage upon herself. "We will go to all of the Sanctuary ships. You will make the Juggernaut show us all of the Seed Markers they have. We will unravel the puzzle of what happened to your people. I promise this to you."

The light went out in Vida's eyes, and her arms dropped to her sides. No more lightning crackled. She held up a hand, and illuminated scrolling text flowed above it. *"You can read as well as I can, Rai. Even in my language, I have seen to it. Here it says my sister failed in her mission. This Progenitor feels that our time has passed and went to join others who shared her convictions. They felt it was time to step aside and be separate from interfering in the ways of the natural order."*

Rai read the words and felt the sadness and regret inherent in them. The Progenitor who'd written them felt they'd not only failed but also done great harm.

Sorrow filled Vida's eyes, and Rai echoed her

emotion. "Again, I promise you, we will find your people."

Vida dropped her arm and the text dissipated into the air in swirls. "*The Juggernaut have stated my kind have been gone for some eons. I am a monument of another age. You owe me nothing.*"

CHAPTER 29

Brague paced back and forth before the display console in the empty transport shuttle as he waited for it to cue up the connection to Queen Klimitzi. He'd cleared the ship of his staff to ensure his conversation with the Queen would remain private despite using the full-screen display. It would be like they were talking face to face. A thrill of anticipation shuddered down his carapace.

The display chimed, and Brague struck an appropriately humble posture, neck bared, back straight, and eyes down.

"Assessor Brague, I am pleased to hear from you again so soon. I hope this is good news?"

Brague straightened and looked upon his Queen. She was veiled, and her slight form reclined, resting upon many pillows. "Yes, my Queen. When last we talked, there was a particular subject here, a Rai

Durmah, who appeared to have been touched by Progenitor technology. I can confirm for you, beyond any doubt, that this was the case. More so, she has become inhabited by the Progenitor, unlikely as that may be for a lowly human."

The Queen bolted upright. "What proof have you of these blasphemous statements?"

"Let me replay what I have witnessed. Then judge for yourself, my Queen."

Brague keyed his arm terminal and uploaded his data files to the open connection, encrypted of course. He watched them replay for the Queen, and he observed her reactions throughout. She took her time, not asking to have anything skipped over. Eventually, the feed finished, and the Queen reclined again and sat in silence for a time, contemplating.

"I am well pleased with your efforts, Assessor. You are to be commended."

"Surely I am at the right place at the right time," he deferred.

"No, it is more. So much more. You have been given an opportunity to be an instrument of light for our people. Whatever else you do, befriend the Progenitor. Give her whatever aid she desires. Become as close to her as she will allow."

The Selector, the Hunter, in Brague railed at the thought of catering to anyone's whim. But he was, above all things, a servant to his duty and more so, his curiosity. "If I may ask, to what end, my Queen?"

"You must find a way to bring her here. To me. I need an audience with her. It is imperative to our race."

Brague understood he couldn't question why. There was a palpable desperation clinging to the Queen's words. What was so important here?

"I will placate the Progenitor, befriend her, and bring her to you."

"Above all, do not risk angering her. We cannot lose her. This is imperative. Too many have been lost."

Abruptly, the connection terminated, but Brague had his orders. And his questions.

CHAPTER 30

THE LIGHTS AROUND THEM DIMMED AS THE SEED Marker went inactive. Rai opened her eyes and stood with her hands against the Marker, face damp with tears, her friends and the Caretakers standing in silence behind her. She searched, panicking, stepping back from the stone. Had Vida stayed in the Marker? *But no that couldn't be, she'd require an intact Marker as a home.* After living with the Progenitor for only a few weeks, the intensity had made it feel like a lifetime, and now the silence echoed within Rai like a hammer.

"We are honored, Progenitor," said Caretaker Traken. "That was a beautiful display. I have never seen the stone glow before. The patterns will stay with me to my end days."

Rai wiped the tears from her face and turned to face her audience. The activation of the Marker had been visible. How much, if any, data had been broad-casted, or was is simply a light display?

"Traken, leave us to our meals and rest period. Alert us when the Assessor is ready." Emptiness ached through her, and Rai crossed her arms protectively across her midsection.

Traken bowed low, groveling adeptly from a life-time of servitude, and exited the room backward. Bauleel snickered, and Rai didn't blame her, she would have found his display cute if she wasn't so upset. Once Traken was well out of view, Graeber was in her face, not touching, but seeking her eyes.

"How bad is it?" His eyes bored into her. Bauleel and Rilte kept their distance as if sensing the delicacy of the matter.

"Hold on a moment," Rai replied. "I'm not sure." Rai closed her eyes and focused internally.

She went down, and down, and down... And there Rai found Vidaaquar, in the depths of her mind, in the dark, still as a statue. Still as a marker stone.

"What are you doing?" Rai asked her.

Vida sat unmoved.

"Are you giving up?" No response. "Since when does a Progenitor give up? What am I supposed to do with this mess?"

Vida did not move. Did not respond.

Vida had become a stone wall within her mind.

"Great. Now I'm stuck with a mess the size of a

mountain, and you're, what, grieving? Fine. Sit here and pout. I'll deal with this without your help!"

Rai shot back to consciousness filled with frustration, her anxiety edging on panic.

"All you all right?" Graeber asked.

"I'm exhausted. Do you mind if we take some food to a room and eat there?"

Graeber's eye's narrowed for a moment. "Do you know where the rooms are?"

Rai nodded. She focused a moment and activated the in-floor lighting leading to two different bedroom suites, located close to each other.

"Neat trick," Rilte smiled in appreciation. "So, did her Profoundness have a meaningful conversation with the rock?"

"Vida managed to extract all available information. There was nothing of interest to our situation, just history from another Progenitor's operation." Rai sidestepped Graeber and grabbed a plate, filling it quickly, not particularly caring what it contained. She didn't need to eat, but the notion of filling her stomach was a comforting distraction.

Rai turned to leave, almost slamming into her sister.

"I'd like to talk about our plans," Bauleel said. "I know Vida wants to teach the Core a lesson and she's considering wiping out the colony. We four need to negotiate with her. Now, before things get out of control again."

Rai gripped her plate tighter, willing the helplessness to not show on her face. Moons, she was so, so tired.

"Rai needs to rest first, Bauleel," Graeber's voice cut in. "We're all in need of a little time to wind down after today's events, don't you think?" There was an undeniable 'you do not want to challenge me on this point' edge to his voice.

Bauleel's amiable expression turned grim, her brows drawing together and lips thinning. She looked every inch the Matriarch she once was, and more than willing to challenge Graeber despite his firm stance. Neither was used to being told what to do.

Rilte stepped up next to Bau. "The man's got a point. Tensions are running high at the moment. Why don't we find out how lovely these Sanctuary accommodations are?" Rilte asked.

"I simply don't want to run out of time. The Assessor could have the Core assembled in a matter of hours," Bauleel replied. Rilte reached out and placed an arm around Bauleel's shoulders, and she in return leaned into his touch, relenting if only for the moment.

Rai couldn't help but pick up on their chemical signatures with her enhanced senses. She was surprised Bauleel had become so close to a non-Core member, and that she'd been able to open herself up to anyone. But perhaps that was exactly how Rilte had gotten past her defenses. How could Rai be anything but happy for them?

"There will be time. I promise you," Rai replied. "Vida will delay them if necessary." Could they hear the lie in her voice? When would they suspect? Rai just needed some time to think.

"Good enough for me," Rilte replied. "See you both in a few hours." Rilte pulled Bauleel along by the hand down one of the lighted paths. Bauleel cast a meaningful look over her shoulder.

"Don't stress about it right now, Bauleel," Graeber called after them. "We'll work it all out. Go." He turned his full attention to Rai, and his look of concern only intensified. Wordlessly, he took the plate of food from her and gestured to the other lighted path.

At the end of the gravel lane, they reached a tall, arched doorway, which opened into a spacious suite decorated in earth tones and devoid of the jungle plants from the main Sanctuary area. The center of the room contained a squat but large square bed, there was a shower in one corner, and an eating area consisting of a short table surrounded by a bench covered with over-stuffed cushions.

Graeber placed her plate on the table. "Why don't you eat first?"

Rai sat at the table and picked at the foods on her plate. There was comfort in eating, although Rai didn't have to eat much anymore. Not since Vida had moved in. Rai took a tentative bite.

"I'll be right back." Graeber had walked out the door before her mind had processed the words.

Rai ate, curious what he was up to. In a few minutes he returned, drinks in one hand and a bundle of plush fabric under one arm. She couldn't miss noticing the wild quality to his eyes.

"We're in luck. Traken had some hominid-shaped sleeping robes on hand. They aren't perfect, but I think they'll do. I had him take some to Bauleel and Rilte too."

"That's thoughtful of you." Rai shoved the food around on her plate, having only eaten about a quarter of it.

"I look after my own. You know that." He dumped the robes on the bed. "Not hungry?" She shrugged, and he set down water and a wine bottle in front of her. "Do you drink anything anymore?" He forced a grin, but it was slight and touched with worry.

Rai realized that, despite having her memories back, and despite knowing she'd been bonded to this man for multiple human lifetimes, they were not the same people they were before. Rai had no idea where her future lay and doubted Graeber would find a path alongside her own.

Rai shrugged her shoulders. "I don't get particularly hungry or thirsty anymore. Not since my transformation. But eating makes me feel more ... normal. It's a comfort."

Graeber opened a water bottle and took a long pull. "May I sit next to you?"

"Yes." Rai patted the bench beside her, and he

lithely slid onto the roomy seat. His substantial presence, so familiar in Kilawren's memories, stirred a level
of comfort reminiscent of long-lost home within her
being.

"Tell me, Graeber. Are you afraid of me? Of
Vidaaquar?"

He barked out a laugh. "I have never feared you. I
can't even conceive of such emotion with you."

"How can you be so sure? I have no idea what Vida
or the Juggernaut have in store for me."

"They don't matter. I will not lose you again. And I
have nothing to fear from you," Graeber replied. He
reached out a hand and, after a brief hesitation, Rai
took it in her own.

Rai didn't shut him out, and their mental connection deepened, two minds brushing past one another
along a dark corridor. "You don't know me anymore,
Graeber. Not who I am now. Or even, what I am."

"I agree, you are no longer the Kilawren I knew and
loved. But Vida is a layer of you. Rai is another layer,
one I have also known for a time, although less well.
Vida is another layer of you, and I accept all that you
are, in this present moment. If I didn't, I would not be
worthy of your trust nor respect."

"Vida could erase me at any time." Rai took a
moment to probe for Vida's consciousness, yet she
remained distant and still as stone. "I cannot predict
her actions."

"I can feel your anxiety, your confusion," he

replied. There were no secrets between skin talkers. "Rai," he spoke in a whisper, and she met his eyes, hers full of frustration, his full of wonder. At that moment, she calmed, his presence steady and steadfast. "Open to me."

Her gut twisted, knowing what he asked, wanting to give it, but unsure she was willing to strip herself bare to him yet.

"I told you, I'm not afraid of you. Of what you've become."

Rai nodded, and let down the last of her shields. Defenses she didn't even realize she'd been gripping tightly to, and then Graeber's mind flooded into hers. In turn, her mind flooded into his consciousness, and they blended together, feeling what the other felt in each movement, each breath. Every touch amplified and echoed between them, an awareness shared.

Rai felt his focus as a thirst long unquenched, awaiting reconnection with the one he'd lost long ago. Rai reached out with a part of herself to fill his void, and she felt him strengthen, become more like her. Less human, more Progenitor.

None of that was of consequence, however, as Rai was lost in the timeless space between them.

"I feel, different," he said. "Energized. You gave me something. A part of yourself? Of her?" It was less a question and more a statement of fact.

"I felt you needed it. It won't make you like me. Well, I don't think so, at least." She frowned.

"We'll see." Icy blue eyes pierced hers, and she felt him probing. Felt him encounter the solidity of the dormant Vida, his eyes filling with questions. "What happened in the Marker?"

Rai's eyes erupted with unbidden tears. "Let me show you." She pulled up her memories of the entire episode, replayed it in her mind, including her attempts to rouse Vida afterward. Graeber's face grew grim.

"Who'd have thought our invincible Progenitor could be so fragile?" he replied. Rai felt his compassion for Vida, and for a moment they both marveled over the kindness they felt for a being who'd caused so much destruction. "Are we concerned for Vida because she's an asset to us in negotiating with the Juggernaut, or has she influenced our perception of her in some way?"

"I don't know how we could know if Vida modified our awareness? And yes, Vida being unavailable for this meeting leaves us in a tight spot, doesn't it? The Juggernaut expect a Progenitor to perform in short order." Rai knew the tide of her panic swelled just beneath the surface, surging to break free. "What do we do when they return?"

Graeber smiled. "We give them their Progenitor." He looked at her meaningfully.

"We fake it? *I* fake it?" Rai asked.

"Yes, and if we play it right, we get an outcome more suited to our liking."

"That's a dangerous game. Vida could awaken at any time." A shudder ran through Rai. "And her wrath is fearsome."

"I'm willing to risk it. The alternative is worse. Consider telling the Juggernaut the Progenitor has gone dormant, and they can do as they will with the planet. What then?" He stroked a hand down her cheek, but the truth of his words cut deep.

"They'd declare this planet a Sanctuary, just like all the rest where they've discovered Progenitor relics. They'd destroy our colony, wipe out all evidence of human existence, and keep us as some sort of lab rats." Rai shuddered.

"They'd keep you, Rai. You're a relic to them. The Core? Perhaps they'd keep some of us for experiments, but the Assessor was quite clear in his opinion of our use of Methuselah treatments. Without Vida to speak up to protect us..."

"There is no other option," Rai resolved. Too many lives hung in the balance. "But can I do all of the tricks a Progenitor does? She'd just begun to show me her abilities."

"You lighted the way to our rooms without her help. How'd you do that?"

"Her, my, mind's eye. I suppose it's a part of me now?"

"I wager it's hardwired into your new physiology, not her consciousness."

"You're right. I do have access to Vida's tricks. At

least the ones I've seen her use. Even if I'm like a child using them compared to her expert hand."

Graeber turned her towards him, eyes dark with worry. "What about the move she used on Terem? Can you do that, if you have to?"

Sorrow filled her heart. She hated having to admit it, especially to him. She nodded. "I already have."

His expression became grim, "No, that's good," he replied. "Because you will be called upon to repeat that particular performance. And soon."

A shiver ran down her spine. "I can and will if it means saving the colony." She placed a hand on his chest, savoring in the feel of his heartbeat, his breathing, and their connection. "For now, let's keep this secret between us, agreed?"

"Agreed. I wouldn't want to put any strain on Bauleel, and I fear it's beyond Rilte's ability for subterfuge."

Rai frowned. "That's my concern. One slip, and we could be ground to bits underneath the might of the Juggernaut Empire."

"We won't slip up. Not this time. Not working together."

Rai curled up against him and pushed the negative thoughts away with the grounding of his energy. They would succeed because the price of failure was too high.

CHAPTER 31

RAI, AWAKING FROM SLUMBER, SENSED THE coming of the Assessor with her mind's eye. She goaded Graeber to alertness. "We must wake the others. Brague is on his way." He sensed her knowing through their contact, and didn't question further, rose and dressed. Rai stood and examined her sleeping robe, adjusting it to sit squarely on her shoulders.

"You're not going to wear that?" he asked, pulling on his leather pants.

She shot him a sly grin. "Of course not." Focusing, she transformed the elements in the robe into a layered silken gown in oceanic blues which hugged her form, yet fanned out in layers around her calves and elbows. With a shake of her head, her auburn curls fell into place. She left her feet unshod, prefer-ring the contact and knowledge gained from contact with the ground.

"All women would envy your newfound talents." He buttoned up his shirt, shaking his head ruefully.

"Aye, but not the price I've paid. Let's go."

He pulled on his boots and grabbed his cape as they walked out the door. Rai steered them to the room Bauleel and Rilte occupied and knocked. Moments later they answered, fully clothed.

Rilte noted her change of clothing. "Clever trick."

"Is there still time to discuss our options?" Bauleel asked, anxiety weighing down in her voice.

"Yes, the Assessor just now finished gathering the Core members," Rai replied.

"That doesn't give us much time to negotiate with Vida." Bauleel's hands worried at each other.

"Rai had conversations with her last evening, and I believe we have come to an arrangement," Graeber replied.

Rilte perked up. "Well, that's good news then, yes?"

"What sort of an arrangement?" Bauleel asked, wary.

"She has relented on her insistence to destroy the colony," Rai replied. "The Temples and the current breeding methodology have to go. I don't see a way the Juggernaut would abide by it otherwise. But Vida feels she can now incorporate the humans into her overall plan."

Bauleel let out a long breath. "That's a huge relief!"

"Wait." Rilte was guarded. "What exactly is the 'overall plan'?"

"She's been transforming the planet into beings like herself. Like me. Humans will be a part of this change," Rai explained. "It's the intended natural order on this planet."

Rilte shook his head. "You're asking too much. I've seen what it can do unchecked to the adult mind. Terem is a prime example."

"To the adult mind, yes. If children were raised to be shifters, it could be different. And those of us in the Core fared well through the change." Rai met his gaze, and the anger percolating within. "You need to understand, what's in the bio-system here, it's not going away. Vida's changes can't be fought, only accepted."

Rilte's fear bubbled under the surface. Bauleel's hands fidgeted. "But humanity will lose something in this process, becoming something different. New. Many will reject the change. Vida will not bend on this?" Bauleel asked.

Rai's heart went out to Bauleel, but she and Graeber had been over the possibilities all night. Removing the changes Vida had wrought on the planet was simply beyond Rai's understanding and abilities. The colonists would have to adapt.

"Will she stop the plague? Can we at least get that much?" Rilte spat out, face flushed.

"That is agreed." Rai nodded, keeping her face calm. Could she instigate such a change on her own? Much hinged on her ability to not only imitate the

Progenitor role but also wield Vida's powers with deft precision.

Within her mind's eye, she felt the presence of the Assessor board the Sanctuary ship. "We must go now. He approaches." Rai turned and faced Graeber, and for a moment her mask slipped, and she knew he saw into the panic floating under the surface.

Graeber reached up and cupped her shoulder. Through the skin bond, his thoughts were clear. "*Never forget the Progenitors are invincible, untouchable to the Juggernaut. They may challenge you, but they will never seek to harm you,*" he communicated. "*Show them no fear, for you are the vessel of their creators.*"

Rai's eyes dropped, and she mentally touched Vida's stone cold shoulder. "*Yes, I'm a walking Seed Marker and specimen, all rolled into one indestructible package.*"

"*You're indestructible?*" His lips twitched in a hint of a smile.

Rai laughed. "*Maybe?*"

Graeber pulled his hand away, breaking the connection. "We'd better get going," he replied. At least he'd lightened her mood.

"What was that all about?" Bauleel asked her, voice lowered.

"He told me a joke to lighten my mood. And it worked," Rai smiled at her sister. "Don't worry too much, today will be hard, but I have a feeling Vida will cooperate."

"I hope you're right," Rilte replied. "The fate of the colony depends upon her edicts."

"As she's well aware," Rai replied, turning away from them both to stem the tide of questions and advice. They meant well, but they also didn't know the full situation, and it was better if they played along as if nothing had changed.

Rai swept out of the room without further discussion, and the rest followed, Graeber closest behind her. When she neared the central area of the ship where the Assessor awaited her, she walked right up to him and met his gaze fearlessly.

"*All is in place, Progenitor,*" Brague inclined his head.

"*I am aware / Let us proceed,*" Rai spoke, using the Progenitor's gift for multidimensional speech. Without waiting for a response, she swept past Brague and headed for the exit via the ship's circuitous route. Everyone followed her, but Graeber came alongside.

When their eyes met, he had an unspoken question for her. "*I understood you back there. How?*"

"*The energy sharing?*" she replied with a smile. "*It's a good thing, now you'll understand all of the Juggernaut.*"

"*That's a definite edge.*" He kept his smile contained to his eyes, and soon they both refocused on the path ahead.

Outside of the ship, a new day had dawned, and with it, more Juggernaut and their transport ships crowded the area. Yet Rai knew with her mind's eye where to go. No doubt Brague would lead them, but she needed to prove her abilities, lest they are questioned later.

When other Juggernaut she didn't recognize saw her coming, they backed away, bowing and groveling to clear her path. Her image must have been circulated within Brague's crew. They reached the area where the Juggernaut had corralled the Core members. The Guardians had been kept in another group, except for the few who'd been Core themselves, like Graeber's sister Raza. The Juggernaut guards parted, and the four humans and the Assessor entered the area, facing a now irate group. The grumbling and whispering started when the crowd saw who was colluding in their captivity.

Brague stepped forward. "Let me be quite clear to your feeble minds. You will listen without complaint to the Progenitor. Her word is law to me, and my word is law to the Hegemony." He stepped back with a flourish, leaving her the proverbial floor.

Rai heard the whispers of 'Progenitor' rise up from the amassed Core gathered. In truth, just over two dozen of the original colonists and crew remained, and all stood beside or before her now.

Whispers of 'traitor' and 'murderer' followed close behind. Rai met their gazes, one by one. Some had defended her, some had abstained, but most had condemned her to death. They had all been colleagues, many friends, at one point. Rai no longer considered any of them worthy of her regard. Bauleel and Graeber alone had earned her trust. Either the Core would accept her offer, or they would perish. The time when she would have had misgivings over their potential fates was long past.

"Yes, I still live, yet I am not as I was before." Rai allowed her voice to ring out in the dulcet tones the Progenitor used, reinforcing her alien otherness. "Bauleel and Graeber saved the body of Kilawren and brought her back, shifting her into this form to hide her as Rai Durmah."

"They should be punished for breaking Core mandates," Matriarch Natre's voice spoke clear and fearless amongst the crowd.

Rai waved her off. "Your law holds no sway with me. Besides, they are my chosen vessels for when this body no longer serves. As some of you may be, if I so choose."

She watched faces pale as her words sank in, eyes shifting between her and the Juggernaut guard. The realization that the Core was no longer in charge had finally hit home.

"My purpose today, however, is not to seek out a new host. When human ships first came to my world, I noticed you and fought back. Yet you survived and became what you are today. However, as you surveyed my planet, some of you found my Seed Marker. You knew what it meant, and you hid it, denying my authority."

"Have you found proof?" Chieftess Raza asked, fear present in her eyes. Did she fear for her brethren, or herself?

Rai sought the answer, found it and turned to Brague. "Present the evidence, Assessor."

Brague bared his mandibles. Rai knew this to be a display of joyful anticipation. He bowed before motioning waiting guards forward. They carried a cumbersome and sea-encrusted contraption forward and laid it next to Rai, then returned to their positions.

"Where was this was found, Assessor?" Rai prompted.

"Approximately five yards from your Seed Marker, Progenitor," Brague replied.

"And the purpose?"

"To block the transmissions and detection of the Seed Marker from space vessels in orbit. It was effective. We were unable to find your marker without the precise coordinates you provided."

"And the technology?"

"It is in keeping with scavenged parts from the colony ship, both in the manufacture, age, and molecular structure."

"My gratitude, Assessor."

"I am your humble servant, Progenitor." Brague inclined his head and stepped back. The scent of his joyful anticipation laced the air.

"Now, I will hear from you. Whom amongst you placed this device to hide my claim on this world so you could use it as your own? Admit your crime, and make the penance easier on your brethren." Rai stood stony-faced, meeting the gamut of expressions.

"I, for one, will not be judged by the traitor who should be dead, not walking among us!" Taessen shouted out, face flushed. Others grumbled and echoed his sentiments.

Rai's eyes narrowed, and she took a long, slow breath. Crumbling now would be easy. These were the ones who had hunted her down through the forest. Clawed at her, thrown her to the forest floor, and beaten her to within an inch of her life before Graeber had stepped in and drawn the blade across her neck himself in the act of mercy. Her eyes flickered to his, and she knew he shared her mind at that moment, and it bolstered her strength.

Rai lifted her left foot and slammed it upon the hard-packed dirt. A shudder rolled forward through the earth, toppling many within the cordoned area to the ground. After the tremor had passed, she spoke softly, but her words carried true.

"Heed my warning: I'll learn the truth, no matter the cost. You have seen the destruction I have brought to your colony so far. I am willing to do whatever necessary to find the one, or group, responsible for planting this device. You may even wish to hunt them out amongst yourselves. After all, if not for their lies, there would be no plague, no deaths, none of this. The fault rests on them. I'll give you a few moments to consider my generous offer."

Rai turned her back on them and walked towards the Assessor. The tenor of the conversations behind her had changed, however. She now scented fear and panic ripe on the breeze, and the keen desire for self-preservation had reared its ugly head over the previous camaraderie.

"What will you do if a confession doesn't occur?" Bauleel asked she stood stiff, a sign the anxiety of the crowd was eating at her.

Brague's mandible's chittered. "They will break. I feel the inevitable approach. None innocent of the crime wishes to feel the brunt of the Progenitor's wrath. If you watch, you can even see the moment where the tension wave will crest, and they will set upon each other like wild beasts during a hunt." His eyes scanned the group, the skilled marksman that he was. "There, see the one named Wraen? He's pushing for skin interrogations and will have his way, or there will be bloodshed. Mark my words," he chattered in excitement.

Rai drew her eyes to the scene he pointed out and had to agree. Widening her focus, she watched how the others reacted, and who refused to get into the fray. From her memories, she knew the Core members were an argumentative bunch. All wanted to get their perspective heard. She looked to Graeber and Bau.

"Is it just me," she asked, a corner of her lip curling up wickedly, "or is a conspicuous someone not jumping into the fray?"

Both eyed the crowd for a moment. Graeber caught it first. "Somnu. He isn't saying a word, and he's standing on the outskirts, holding his cape around him, protecting his skin from contact. He's the only one holding back."

"It could mean nothing," Bauleel replied, "but let's focus on him and see what surfaces."

Rai nodded. She walked back towards the Core, and they quieted, fearful of her approach. "I have decided you are to begin skin interrogations."

Chieftess Raza stepped forward, skin pale, yet brave enough to face her. "How would you like them conducted, Progenitor?"

Rai honored her with a slight smile. They were family, after all, and if she had her way, Raza would emerge unharmed. "I would like as many hands as possible on the subject. As you haven't come up with names on your own, I will pick them for you in the order I deem fit. You will begin with Somnu."

"No!" Somnu shouted, and he sprinted to escape, but the Juggernaut guard dragged him back into eager arms. There would be no escapes today. "I reject your judgment! Traitor! Traitor!" he screamed and pointed an accusatory finger at Rai before he was flung to the ground.

His Core compatriots didn't take his behavior as a

positive sign either. Soon his cape, shirt, and pants were ripped from him, leaving small gouges and scratch marks weeping blood. They left him his under-garments, but he writhed in the dirt, attempting to escape the touch of so many seeking hands. Of course, who wanted their mind bared for all to see? It was one thing to be freely given, as Rai and Graeber had the night before. To have others rip into your conscious-ness was an act akin to rape. Rai forced herself to not cringe as memories of her own, so similar attack, by the same Core members played out before her now.

She could show no weakness, brook no mercy.

The Core gathered around him, and he tried to shove them off, but their strength was too much for him, and their perseverance too determined.

Rai walked up to the group, but they took little notice of her. "Chieftess Raza, will you open to me?" Rai asked, holding her hand out.

Raza had her hand on Somnu's foot and nearly jumped out of her skin at the request, focusing on getting into his head, and not in the world around her. Her expression was guarded. "Will it hurt?"

"No, I only wish to observe the group mind, and what is uncovered here. I will not delve into you, nor will you be allowed access to mine." Rai had seen Vida block before, thus knew how it was done. Vida had used it with Terem, so he hadn't known his fate beforehand.

Raza held Rai's gaze for a moment and then offered

up her hand up. Her eyes sought and met Graeber's, Rai saw secondhand through her mind, and he nodded to his sister in reassurance. Raza looked back to Rai's face, and Rai felt her uncertainty and distrust, and the resignation underneath. Then Raza looked back to Somnu and refocused on him.

For Somnu's part, he'd ceased struggling, except in moans and grunts. He'd retreated inside his mind and was trying to keep them all out, hiding out as if it were a fortress of steel. His mental shields were impressive, to say the least, and it made Rai wonder how long he'd trained at secret keeping over the years.

For minutes the group pushed and prodded, trying to force down his internal barriers, but they held tight.

"Progenitor, we may not be able to breach his defenses. Some minds are too resistant and will shatter rather than open under pressure," Matriarch Natre spoke up, a sheen of sweat on her brow.

"I will have his mind open to us. The fact that he refuses damns him further." Rai stepped forward and laid her hand next to Raza's, gaining skin contact. Keeping her mind blocked from intrusions, she slid into the mass of thoughts around her and felt others begin to withdraw. "No, all of you will remain. I require you to witness. Graeber and Bauleel, join us as well." When she felt Bauleel and Graeber's touch join the fray, Rai continued.

Snaking through the gathered minds, Rai wound her way to the bottom of the literal heap where Somnu had hidden inside himself, walled away. He'd done an impressive job of shutting his mind off from the Core, but the walls wavered at Rai's indirect approach. Rai remembered the way Vida had molecularly disassociated so many beings and buildings. She tentatively, carefully, brought this skill to bear on Somnu's mental wall, unwinding just a few of the bricks holding his mental walls together.

Destabilized, his wall fell into shreds, and Rai withdrew to the edges of his consciousness, not wishing to cause further damage. But she'd wrought well, and his mental walls fell, leaving his mind naked to the will of the Core.

They wasted no time. Although this wasn't a standard procedure, it was a skill not forgotten over the passing of decades. Rai took no part in the deconstruction of his thoughts. It was important that any information gleaned from the Core members today be of their making. They needed to see the truth of their deception, of the fate they'd brought upon themselves, for themselves. This was essential above all else.

So Rai watched and waited. The Core was ruthless in their hunt, and the hunt was, as Somnu's behavior had predicated, fruitful.

However, his betrayal swept further than even Rai could have anticipated.

The memories of him discovering the Seed Marker were as fresh as yesterday. A great find, to be sure, and one he and his then partner Treus knew meant voided their colony charter. Somnu had argued with Treus, and on the way back to Sebaiya, Treus had met with an unfortunate end, and Somnu had reported him missing at sea. When Somnu had gone back to 'search' for Treus, he planted the device to block the Seed Marker's signal, thus allowing the Colony Charter perfunctory validity.

"Why the risk?" Rai breathed out.

Somnu's eyes flickered open, meeting hers. "I thought them a myth. You're a myth. Why endanger our colony for a stupid myth? We didn't have the resources to make it to another, better location. We were stuck here or somewhere much worse. It was worth the risk."

Rai arched a brow, and his eyes closed again. No eyes turned towards her. All were still focused on Somnu. This was not his only secret. It was felt. Known. The Core dug deeper.

Somnu's memories revealed how he directed the construction at Jeweled Cove, insisting upon the high walls and great tower overlooking the sea. A tower which would be used to watch for any visible activity from the Seed Marker far below. When a hundred years had passed, Somnu himself wrote the orders to abandon the tower watches, declaring the seas safe and of no potential threat to human life.

He'd been wrong, of course, but the revelation damned him further.

Again the Core dug deeper, sensing yet more.

And menial details bubbled by, Rai ignored them, so did the others. They cared not who he'd slept with over the years, who he'd pilfered from, and what minor lies he'd told to cover his identity within the Core.

But when they lifted the image of him placing the thallium-laced devices into the luna berry swamps, a collective gasp arose from the crowd, and his eyes shot open, wild with panic.

"I didn't intend anyone to get hurt! The stockpile of berries and storehouse checks should have caught the tainted batches in time!"

The atmosphere around him had turned into a dark miasma, as the Core members delved for every tidbit of detail regarding this new transgression. They were nothing if not thorough, and their anger stoked with every passing moment.

"Yet you sought to frame Graeber and myself with your crime?" Bauleel accused. Her thoughts moved within the stream of the others, welcomed now, while before she'd been held separate and apart. "You came here to accuse us of the very acts you committed."

Somnu turned vicious, perhaps realizing he had nothing left to lose, his gambit lost. "You and he deserved to die for defending the traitor. You were never part of us! And now, it's clear you never followed our mandates! Kilawren's experiments defiled us, robbed us of our humanity and treated our children like animals. She slaughtered them for nothing!"

Matriarch Natre stood tall, a grimace upon her

face, brushing her hands on her robes. Could she brush away the offensive mind she'd crawled into? "No, instead you killed and maimed innocents to draw guilt onto another? I had to witness and tend to the injured personally. I speak for everyone here: you disgust us, Somnu."

The images of the injured and dead filtered from Natre to the others, courtesy of a light hand upon her calf from another. The tension within the group mind ratcheted up another few notches. Rai, or rather Kilawren, remembered the sensation all too well. The Core was about to issue a mandate.

And it was time to remind them of their place.

"I have heard enough," Rai announced, her voice echoing through the air and minds of those gathered. All eyes turned to her. Yet she waited.

"What is your will, Progenitor?" Graeber asked, setting the tone.

Rai had remained where she was, at Somnu's foot, connected to the group mind. Yet no emotions played over her face, and she refused to mirror the rage displayed by so many others. Rai was Progenitor and alien, Core no longer. Somnu's betrayal of them did not impact her emotionally, but she felt the searing heat of Bauleel and Graeber's anger.

Had residing with Vida for so long changed her fundamentally, despite Vida's current disposition?

"Somnu allowed human settlement upon my world in violation of the treaty, and in return, I wrought damage upon all of you for centuries. He further violated Core and colony laws, causing the deaths and maiming of others," Rai proclaimed

Rai rose and stepped backward in slow, measured steps. All eyes watched her in anticipatory silence. "I will unmake him with a single thought."

"That is too merciful a death for his crimes," Matriarch Natre replied.

"I well know the lack of mercy the Core shows traitors," Rai replied, leveling a stare at each of them in turn. "My decision will not be swayed by your rancor."

"When will you carry out our sentence?" Matriarch Natre asked. Her anger was a palpable force.

"Now," Rai declared.

Rai had the option of terminating a living being as Vida had relatively painlessly extinguished Terem. However, Terem had been the unfortunate result of Vida's plague--Somnu had been the cause. Somnu's actions had brought immeasurable pain to the colonists of Az'Unda.

Rai knelt and placed her hand squarely on Somnu's chest.

"If I deserve to die for failing the human race, so do you!" Somnu exclaimed, and then spat at her. "You'll get your due, Kilawren. No one can outrun the consequences of what they've done, or who they've become."

Rai had listened to his speech, grinding her molars. When he paused, likely awaiting some biting retort, Rai set the skin of his chest on fire through mere contact and the intention of her will. She stood and took a couple steps back as the immolation spread to engulf his entire body.

Somnu's screams rang through the valley, and Rai was impressed that only Rilte flinched and turned away, while Bauleel and Graeber watched, expressions of mild disinterest schooled upon their faces. The frustrated bloodlust on the faces of the Core members was not lost on her; Rai's actions had thwarted a greater punishment at their hands. The Juggernaut took an even more unashamed interest, grunting, and keening along with the Somnu's screams, but they did not break rank.

If she didn't grind him into nothingness, some part of his consciousness might remain, and over time, reform. Despite the seeming brutality, it was merciful in the end because there was a finality to it. Perhaps Vida wasn't as vicious as Rai'd assumed earlier. Perhaps disintegration was the only way to extinguish the shapeshifters she'd created.

Rai stomped her foot, and the earth trembled and rippled. The ripple rolled forward, and Core members leaped out of the way. When the ripple reached the remains of Somnu, what was left of him was unmade and sank into the ground, erasing the evidence of his death and preventing any possibility of return.

"I am impressed with your handling of the situation, Progenitor," Brague said. Rai gifted him with a slight smile and returned her attention to the Core.

CHAPTER 32

"WHAT IS TO BE DONE WITH THE CORE NOW?" Natre asked. She thrust her chin forward and continued, forcing a fearless manner that her scent betrayed. "We have been cleared of initiating our Colony against the treaty. Therefore the other humans and we are free of wrongdoing, are we not?"

"I agree, Somnu acted alone," Rai replied. "Yet I am left with a species not in the scope of my designs. It presents difficulties I am under no obligation to deal with."

Natre paled, and she wasn't the only Core member to react so. However, they all remained quiet. Expectant.

The Assessor stepped forward and bowed low. "It would be my pleasure to eradicate the vermin from your territory if that is your wish, Progenitor. It would be a simple service for all your kind have done for my people." His formal offer made the knees of more than one Core member quake.

"Your offer is most generous, Assessor. However, I cannot accept. You see, as I study these creatures, I realize they are no longer fully human."

He straightened, surprise stiffening his joints to his full height. "How so?"

Rai had stayed up all night working out a solution to minimize the human deaths and also pacify the Juggernaut thirst for vengeance. Could she now deliver it? Further, would both sides accept her resolution?

"My attacks on them, via the plague, as they called it, have modified their DNA and RNA patterns. Thus, I have begun to change them into my image just as I've changed the rest of this world, just at a different pace. If they cease fighting me, then I stop attempting to destroy them via the plague, but rather integrate them into my bio-system. Then they may stay."

"Despite the fact they are interlopers?" Brague's voice was raised, and she knew his blood boiled. The Juggernaut believed themselves to be chosen. Special. Watching humans be selected by a Progenitor for use must be profoundly disturbing to him.

Rai turned on him then and raised herself to his height. "I am content using whatever flotsam and jetsam presents itself to meet my goals. They are biologic material, as your kind once was. I shall mold them. I shall give the directives. And if they do not comply, they can return to the constituent matter from which they came, and I will find an alternative material to shape."

The Assessor shifted back and forth on his feet, fighting the urge to bow in acquiescence. "You're assuming their makeup is sufficient to the task. I can assure you we have found human DNA quite lacking," Brague countered.

Rai blinked, and then advanced with inhuman speed on the Assessor, knocking him to the ground with a force that sent dirt flying. She sat on his chest and pinned his carapace into the dirt. "You doubt my abilities to transform lowly pond scum? Your race was once not much more than insects, as I recall."

His eyes leveled with hers for many minutes. Rai scented his need to fight as his muscles rippled beneath her, but he managed to keep his temper in check.

"I do not doubt your prowess, Progenitor. I'm sure when you are done with them they will be barely recognizable to their inferior human ancestors," Brague replied.

Rai sprang from him and turned to the gathered Core members, who awaited an answer to Natre's, and now Brague's, question. She ignored Brague as he regained his composure. Rai's point had been made, and he was willing to bow to her will, at least for now.

Natre held her ground. "So, you do not intend to discard us?"

"No," Rai replied. "I shall instead incorporate you into my ecosystem."

"And what of the plague?" Natre asked.

"The plague shall be no more. After all, why would I destroy my own cherished creations?"

The Core members breathed out a collective sigh, yet Natre stood tense. "And what *modifications* will you require of your newly acquired creations?"

Rai smiled, as she'd imagine Vida would. "You in the Core know best. You took the full brunt of the changes with the plague when you first arrived. I'd hoped to overwhelm you with too many changes at once, and yet some of you survived. Some even thrived. I'd assumed most would perish, while a small few would transform, aligning themselves with my grand design. Those who survived failed to develop as I'd hoped. Many of you have not yet embraced your abilities as shifters. You may fear your potential, yet I have made you what you are."

A stir went through the crowd as they digested her words.

"But the plague made us into shifters. You said you're going to take the disease away." Raza asked. "Isn't *that* the plague?"

"Oh yes, the *plague* will go away. The dead will no longer rise up into Terrors, I will see to it. But you will cease giving plague medicinal to everyone. And the rites of Temple service for your young women ends now. From here forward, the Temples will be used for healing and settling legal disputes only. Births may happen at the Temples, but not conceptions.

"Thank you, Vida," Ponar whispered. Rai looked his way and briefly inclined her head. A promise kept.

Taessen approached, wringing his hands. "You don't understand, Progenitor. In the initial outbreak, many went insane when they turned. They couldn't cope. They didn't know how to handle this new existence. And the breeding programs we have today, it's just so the women don't shift while they're pregnant and lose the child. We aren't cruel. We've made choices to safeguard, not harm."

Rai raised her hands, signaling she'd heard enough. "I do not place blame, Taessen. However, we must move into the future together. Your kind must evolve. Some of you have, to no ill effect, and you stand here now. Taessen is correct, some may be too old, their minds too inflexible to change. I will offer a compromise."

"My edict stands, but any Az'Un who does not wish to stand under my protection, to share in the evolving DNA of the Progenitor, may opt out. However, when they do so, they may neither marry nor have children. Their line will end with them."

"What if they already have heirs?" Natre asked.

"So be it, but no more," Rai answered. "And their spouse, if they choose to embrace my offer, is allowed to remarry and continue breeding. You can expect to live longer lives without your medicinal and with the natural boost from what I have to offer."

Furtive glances met this last news, and Rai knew

she had them hooked. An overall improvement in the quality of life and they just had to put up with becoming shifters? How bad could it be?

"How will you enforce this?" Raza asked.

Rai smiled. "All of you shall be my ambassadors. I will instill within you the ability to harmonically shift their resonance with me either on or off. Your mission will be to visit all of the colony in the next month and determine their willingness to accept or reject the change."

"And I suppose any who are unable to handle the change, who end up at the Temples due to mental instability, we can turn them off for their own safety?" Taessen asked.

"As you see fit," Rai replied. "But be warned, once my gift is removed, the modification is a permanent one."

"I suspect that will be a comfort to most," Raza said.

"For those who fear, yes." Rai paused and clasped her hands together. "I am concerned over your volatile natures, and I believe it important to utilize the Guardians to protect the colonists as they adapt to their new skills. Please direct your formularies to develop inhibiting brews to tamp down the expression for those who need more time to acclimate."

"Wise words, Progenitor," Natre replied. "We will see it done."

"And what will you be doing while we're acting as

your Ambassadors?" Raza asked eyes keen on Rai. Raza hadn't missed a beat, had she?

"That is Progenitor business, but you will not see me frequently. I intend to have Ponar act as my liaison if he is willing? My host assures me he is trustworthy." She turned a confident smile towards Ponar, and though startled, he smiled back.

The Assessor had an eye on her. No doubt he'd ask her what business she had in mind soon enough.

"Once I know the full details, I am sure, for the good of the colony, I won't be able to refuse. You did grant my request, after all, Progenitor, for which I am eternally grateful," Ponar replied.

"My thanks for your indulgence, Ponar." Rai turned back to the assembled Core members. "Now that I have gained your assent, we will travel to the Seed Marker, where I will make the necessary adjustments to alleviate the plague, including the humans in my overall ecological plans."

"For the sake of expediency," Brague interrupted. "May I offer my vessels?"

"I was about to inquire," Rai replied. "And perhaps they can clean up along the way?"

"A most excellent suggestion." Brague directed things efficiently, and soon people were in motion, being loaded onto shuttle transports.

Rai approached Chieftess Raza. "Raza, please direct the Guardians to return to the cities and outposts on the horses they brought with them. They are of no concern and will take orders as needed from you as per usual. There is no need for them to travel with us."

"They will be happy to depart," Raza replied. She stepped closer and lowered her voice. "May I ask, how often is the Progenitor in charge of this host body? I only ask because it seems your mannerisms are at times familiar."

"Vidaaquar is always in control. Sometimes Vida is more ... occupied than others, as she is now. But she is ever present, just under the surface."

Raza kept the smile on her face, but it left her eyes, and a shudder passed through her skin. She looked to Graeber, and a knowing look passed between them before she turned in haste and walked away.

Rai steeled herself. Let Raza mourn for her and Graeber. Keeping the truth secret was paramount.

Assessor Brague approached her, and Rai could tell from his scent and posture that he'd regained the poise lost during their earlier encounter.

"Would you prefer to travel via the Sanctuary ship, Progenitor?"

"You may return to addressing me as Vida, now that we are apart from the masses, Brague. And no, let us travel by a smaller ship. Although the Sanctuary ship is a beautiful and appreciated haven, it's too large to land safely at Jeweled Cove."

"As you wish, Vida. Will you need the Core

members nearby to affect the changes you discussed?" he asked.

"Yes, after I modify the Seed Marker, I will need to touch each one. Ponar here as well. Then the necessary changes will be complete."

Brague genuflected. "I would be honored to escort you to the landing site."

"I would not deny you." Rai allowed him to lead them to his ship, and he led them to a small lounge area on board and then left.

Rai breathed a huge sigh a relief, and it wasn't lost on her companions.

"What, is Vida napping out on you?" Bauleel asked, concern sparkling in her eyes.

"Yes, you could say that. Vida's been a bit preoccupied. I had to improvise here and there."

Ponar crossed his arms and leaned back against the counter holding beverages and snacks for their comfort. In many ways, he knew Rai, better than anyone else in the room, as they'd spent the most time together over the past few months.

"A little?" He raised a brow. "I know that look on your face. Spill it."

"This room is not *secure*, brother," Rai replied, tapping her ear.

A tense moment of silence filled the room, filled with furtive glances.

"There is another way." Bauleel stepped forward and held out her hand. The Juggernaut had no way of monitoring a telepathic skin bond conversation. Even Rilte and Ponar, who lacked the innate skill, could be brought in via the active skills of the others. Ponar and Rilte clasped hands with Bauleel, then all three looked at her expectantly.

"They need to know. Now is as good a time as any," Graeber whispered into her mind.

"It could endanger them," she countered silently.

Graeber nodded. *"Possibly. They could also help cover more creatively if they know the whole story."*

Rai sighed. "All right," she said aloud. She and Graeber joined the others clasping hands with Rilte and Ponar to form a circle. Within moments the group mind formed, haphazard at first, but Bauleel, Graeber, and Rai reined it into stable and cohesive form. Now they had a place for conversation away from prying eyes and Juggernaut recordings.

"I am going to show you something, recall something for you, but you must remain calm. Agreed?" Rai asked. The others nodded, except Graeber. Then she replayed the incident with Vida and the encounter with the Sanctuary's broken Seed Marker in her mind. Rilte gaped in segments, but otherwise, everyone kept their composure.

"So, that's really what she's like?" Bauleel asked. *"Vida's remarkable."*

"Sure, and she's an immutable stone at the moment," Rai replied, the anger an unmistakable undercurrent in her mental wavelength.

"Wait, today, you're saying she was like that, all day today?" Bauleel asked.

"Yes." Rai shifted her feet.

"So you have access to all of her powers, even when she's like this?" Ponar asked.

Rai met his gaze. *"Yes. And the Juggernaut can never know she's not in charge. Otherwise, they will step in, and the fate of the colonists on Az'Un will go poorly. Very poorly."*

Ponar shook his head. *"So all of those ideas, the agreement with the Core. That was you, not Vida?"*

"Well, yeah," Rai replied.

"And you sentenced Somnu to death?" Bauleel asked, her emotions were conflicted, partly supporting Rai's decision, partly despising her for acting alone.

"I had to act the part, Bau. You know from being within the group mind of the Core: they saw his guilt, they knew he'd planted the device and doomed the colony to Vida's plague, they agreed with my conclusions and edict." But the emotions roiled in her gut, reacting to Bauleel's disapproval.

"I know you did what you had to do," Bauleel replied. *"But if the Juggernaut discover their precious Progenitor is dormant, they will step in and cleanse this world of the human taint. But what do we do when she awakens and learns your actions?"*

All eyes were on Rai. *"You don't appear to understand. Vida knows exactly what I'm doing. At every moment. At times, she reacts like I've struck a chord within her. Yet, she's made no move to stop me. She's effectively made me her proxy, while she quietly watches from the sidelines. She's been free to take action, yet she refuses."*

"And when she does decide to act, what then?" Rilte asked. *"Well you can't know, and neither can we, so I vote we move forward and do our best to salvage what we can of our society. I, for one, think you were brilliant out there today, Rai. My only question is: can you actually turn off the plague?"*

"I am pretty confident I can," Rai replied. *"Otherwise I'll have to come up with some sort of creative or impulsive Progenitor-style reason to not fix it."*

"You'll do your best, and we'll support you. Of course we will. What you negotiated is in the colony's best interests," Graeber said.

Everyone chimed in with their agreement.

"Did you have to declare that all humans accept shifting as a part of their DNA?" Bauleel asked. *"It drove a lot of us insane when it hit."*

"Because they didn't know what was happening, or how to do it safely," Rai replied. *"Now they have teachers. And perhaps only the youth will fully accept the change, and the adults will take medicinals to temper the effects. All I know is this is what Vida had planned all along, and we disrupted her plans. I am endeavoring to do right by all parties."*

Rai felt a wave of respect flow over the group mind

from Bau. *"Then you made the correct decision,"* Bauleel replied.

"I am wondering what your plans are?" Graeber asked.

"Pardon?"

Graeber's hand clasped hers more firmly. *"You showed us the entire recollection of Vida's time in the Sanctuary ship's Seed Marker. I got the impression it gave you some ideas."*

"Well, it did, actually. Once I reprogram the Seed Marker, it will function on auto-pilot. Ponar, if you are willing, you can act as liaison with me and let me know if everything is going all right."

"I've already agreed to do so," Ponar replied, cocking an eyebrow in curiosity.

"And then I'm going to find out why the Progenitors gave up being Progenitors and where they went into hiding. I hope to reunite Vida with her own kind."

This was met with shocked looks and emotions and a resounding chord from Vida that echoed through the group mind.

Bauleel frowned. *"So, did Vida like that idea or hate it?"*

"I have a sense she is aligned with the concept," Rai replied. *"So, I know you three were willing to leave the planet before. Will you leave with me now?"* Rai asked Bauleel, Rilte, and Graeber.

"We'll likely get a Juggernaut escort the entire way. You know that, right?" Graeber asked.

"*I have accepted that eventuality. However, it does mean room, board, and fuel will be provided free of charge.*"

"*And what if the Juggernaut doesn't want the Progenitors found?*" Rilte asked.

Rai frowned. "*But, they're like gods to them.*"

Rilte frowned. "*Some folks are quite happy with dead gods.*"

Rai shook her head. "*I'm still going. It's a promise to Vida. With or without you three.*"

"*I'm with you,*" Graeber replied.

Bauleel and Rilte shared a long look. After about a minute of private mental conversation, Bauleel said, "*We're in.*"

"*Thank you. All of you. Now, we just have to live through the next few hours, and then the stress will be off,*" Rai replied.

"*How do you figure that?*" Graeber asked. "*If we venture among the Hegemony, you will have to keep up your charade for months, perhaps years.*"

Rai sagged a little then. "*Yes, but no one has seen a Progenitor for millennia. They don't know what to expect. Away from here, no one knows me. Neither the old nor the new me. There's less association to who I am, more on what I am.*"

Graeber nodded, and she felt his compassion for the stress she was under. "Come, let's have a snack before we get there. It's still a long day ahead of us," Graeber said.

CHAPTER 33

RAI STOOD ON THE BEACH OF JEWELED COVE, Graeber on one side and Assessor Brague on the other. The Core was being brought down to the shore, but there was no rush, as it was known Vida would need some time at the Seed Marker. She stared out over the waves, steeling herself for the task.

"Is there anything else you need to be readied before you return, Vida?" Graeber asked. He didn't touch her, but his scent was a comfort to her nerves.

"No, you've both proven you understand my directives the first time around. I will consume ocean life on my return trip to ensure I have adequate energy reserves available for the task."

"I would be happy to prepare you a feast, Vida," Brague replied.

"My thanks, Brague. However, you misunderstand

the scope of the sustenance I will require for this effort. Another time, perhaps?"

Brague drew back, stiff and wide-eyed. "Whatever you wish."

Rai's lip curled up in a smile. "I'd best not wait any longer. I'll return when I have completed the changes."

Without looking back, she walked towards the ocean. Rai barely remembered her emergence weeks ago. Vida had been in total control at that time, Rai the overwhelmed and traumatized host. Rai assumed she could find the Marker on faith. Faith that there was enough Progenitor stamped into her makeup for her to not only find it but also activate and program it on her own.

Rai reached the surf and waded out into the icy water. Knee-deep, she transformed her hands and feet into webbed flippers and gave herself an all-over scaly makeover to aid with swimming. Next, Rai added a second set of transparent eyelids to protect her eyes from the salt water and gills to breathe. When she could think of nothing else to change, she leaped into the water.

For a long time, Rai swam away from the land and down, deeper and farther from the shore. When she crossed paths with a living animal, no matter the type, she'd consume it in the manner of a Progenitor. Rai'd stun it with a simple touch, dissolve it to a molecular state, and then absorb it through her skin. She'd seen

Vida do it so many times and it had never failed to disgust her. However, Rai assumed it provided necessary nourishment beyond eating simple meals. And what she was about to attempt would require a high degree of energy.

Rai continued to swim deeper and further out, and after a time her patience ran low. She focused with her mind's eye and yet nothing presented itself. She knew the Marker was no longer shielded, so why was she not able to sense it?

Could Vida be blocking her?

"Vida, you need to allow me to go to the Marker. I need to fix things for the colonists. I won't let this go. Let me do this one thing, and then we can leave your Marker alone. *Please.*"

For a few moments nothing happened, and Rai wondered if her plea had fallen on Vida's stone deaf ears. But then Rai became aware of a distant hum that reverberated through her bones. In her mind's eye, the exact location was a pinpoint, not far ahead.

Lesson number one: even dormant Progenitors had immense power and ability to exert their will.

"Thank you, Vida."

Rai swam with confidence and soon stood on the silty ocean floor before the Marker. Despite the lingering butterflies in her belly, she placed both hands upon the stone, and it lit up, amber lines tracing grooves within the surface, expanding outward from her touch until the entire stone blazed in color. At that moment, her mind linked into the Marker's neural network and Rai lost awareness of her body.

The internal neural map was similar to the one on the Sanctuary ship, except it was much more extensive because it was complete. Rai recognized this Marker was still functioning in an almost living capacity because it was plugged into the living, breathing planet of Az'Unda. The Marker continuously monitored the entire ecosystem and all life upon Az'Unda. This wasn't just a rock stuck in the ocean floor. It served as a complex nexus, regulating all life on the planet.

Rai searched and discovered how the Marker tracked different species. She got more than she bargained for, however. Each one displayed a history and planned future timeline. *The Progenitor was directing the evolution of all species, flora, and fauna, upon the planet.*

No wonder the Progenitors were seen as gods by some, Rai mused. They had perfected a form of terraforming surpassing all others and had no moral qualms using it.

Rai searched for and found the species information on her human colonists. They were, not surprisingly, blacklisted as a foreign element with all other species ordered to seek and destroy.

Attached to the human colonists was a linkage to the virus which caused the plague. Rai pulled up the virus and asked it to deactivate. Nothing happened. She asked it to detach itself from the human hosts. Nothing happened. She asked it to die. Again, nothing.

What was she doing wrong here?

The threads from amber datasphere moved all around her in a rhythm of life and synchronicity. Except she didn't understand how to direct the flow to her use. Why?

And then it hit her. *She wasn't thinking like a Progenitor.*

Virus, she commanded, *mutate.* Instead of attacking the humans, strengthen their immune systems. In response, the virus shifted and changed before her very eyes, becoming something new, different. *Shifting.*

Rai focused again on the human species, and where they had been marked as a foreign element she now marked them as native. The system morphed to accommodate this change, and soon the display included projections of human DNA integrated with native strands within a few generations. Images of these future people were displayed for review and approval. They appeared very similar to the present, but they'd adapted to the shifting their Core counterparts took for granted. These humans would be formidable foes for the Juggernaut, thought Rai with a smirk. Rai approved the changes and the datasphere set the new course in motion.

Next, Rai identified the Core members in her mind and queried the datasphere on how to gift them with the ability to shut down the mutation in the now native humans at will, but only as requested with specific intent.

The system offered the options of marking the hominids as foreign or terminating them. Neither appealed. Rai countered with a request to cease mutation efforts and retain human's native status. The system churned for a few minutes and then gave Rai an acceptable response. The Marker informed her it had aligned the Core members systems to deliver the appropriate messaging to the human's system on cue. There wasn't anything left for Rai do to except explaining to the Core members how to enact the upgrade.

Looking around, Rai let out a heavy sigh. Her mission here was complete, but she wasn't quite ready to leave yet, for she had a secondary goal. Her promise to Vida. Reaching her mind out in all directions, she opened herself to the datasphere.

"Show me your history. History of this planet, history of Vidaaquar, and history of the Progenitors, please. Whatever you've got. I need it all."

There was a slight pause, and then the amber datasphere pulsed, flaring in intensity. A moment later, information poured into Rai like water down a parched throat. First, the history of the planet, which was extensive and went back before Vida began her work. Then the diaries of Vida slammed into Rai's consciousness all at once. Thousands of years' worth of information, too much to digest all at once, and then Rai was filled with a mountain of data which she briefly recognized as the Progenitor history she'd requested.

It was too much, but the datasphere *wouldn't stop.*

Everything went black.

Rai felt the warm sun on her skin, heard the pounding surf echo off the cliffs, and the murmur of voices in hushed tones.

Her eyes shot open.

She laid on a blanket on the sand surrounded by Juggernaut and her appointed 'entourage.' What the moons had happened?

"You're awake," Graeber stated. "Are you in need of anything?"

Rai met his gaze confidently. "No, I'm quite fine, thank you." She sat up and looked around. Brague stood just a few feet away. Both had been anxiously waiting for the Progenitor's reawakening, it appeared. "Thank you both for attending to me."

"We fished you out of the ocean a few hours ago," Brague replied, motionless, revealing nothing, except his implied suspicion.

Rai let out an exaggerated sigh and stood up, making a display of straightening her dress and then modifying the colors into tones reminiscent of the sunset. She'd reverted to her pre-transformation clothing at some point after she'd passed out underwater.

"I'm afraid I underestimated the capacity of this vessel." She shrugged. "Nonetheless, my task is accomplished."

Brague remained very still. "I checked since you returned apparently unconscious. The plague virus remains active."

A smile ghosted across Rai's face. "You doubt me, Progenitor? For shame. As I've stated, I completed the mission."

"But the virus..." he replied.

Rai placed her hands on her hips. "If you must, please rerun your scans on the virus. You will discover it now functions towards another purpose. I would tell you what, but that would ruin all the fun of running the scans, now wouldn't it?"

"I...suppose," he stammered.

"Now, where is the Core? I assume you have them gathered? It's imperative I speak with them." Rai arched a brow and tapped a foot impatiently.

"Allow us to escort you, Vida," Bauleel replied. "They are camped out on the beach up near the road overlooking the Cove."

"Good. The sooner I am done here, the better," Rai replied.

Bauleel led the way, although Rai knew it, as it was helpful to have a guide through the mass of Juggernaut crowding the beach. Graeber was close at her heels, and Rilte and Ponar followed at the rear, yet none spoke. She sensed the tension, and the questions they must have, but now was not a safe time to resolve them.

They climbed up the rough-hewn steps in the cliff wall of the Cove and soon faced the group of Core members gathered in a makeshift encampment at the top. Although they were only here for a short while, the Core had demanded decent accommodations, and gotten them, for many tents framed the space and tables with food and wine had been laid out as well. While she'd been busy at the Seed Marker, they'd been busy managing their lives via their comm units and negotiating with the Juggernaut. At her approach they gathered, eager to resolve this business and return to their normal lives.

Rai envied them.

"Thank you for your patience," Rai addressed the crowd in Vida's melodic tones, ensuring her voice would carry to all. "The plague virus is no longer a threat to your existence. In fact, it will now add a boost to all human immune systems. This will be a benefit as they adapt to the new shifter DNA."

"And if they choose to opt out?" Matriarch Natre asked. "How do we handle them?"

Rai raised a hand and placed it on Bauleel's head for example. "It's very simple. You stand as I am now, and the one wishing to renounce their claim to this soil states aloud, 'I am not of this land.' Let it be understood there will be no retribution for this act. The planet will simply no longer recognize them as a native organism needing inclusion via mutation, but neither will it see them as a foreign body needful of destruction. They will revert to an inactive status. You will be responsible for rendering them sterile. Is that understood?"

"Why entrust that to us?" Natre asked. "When you can do so much, why not be in control of all of this yourself?

Rai sighed. If not for the mystery of the Progenitors, she would indeed stay here and ensure the colony's transition. "I wish to see if you can be trustworthy. My host felt your healers would know the best methodology in this matter."

Natre inclined her head and bowed, a rare homage from the haughty Matriarch. "We are honored with your trust."

Rai turned to a nearby Juggernaut drone. "Will you convey my command to the Assessor? Make sure the Core members are escorted home with all due haste." The drone bowed and activated his communications terminal. Rai didn't bother to listen in, knowing he'd diligently recite in detail, or replay recorded video, everything that had transpired here for Brague's amusement.

Rai's back spasmed, and she fought to bring it under control. "Now, I must rest, for the journey was difficult for my host. I entrust this mission to you to oversee my purpose on this world. You can expect my emissary Ponar to report on a regular basis. You will report to him as you would to myself, without reservation. The Juggernaut will assist in your travel needs."

Rai turned to walk away and stumbled, but Graeber caught her arm and steadied her. "You're unwell," he stated, speaking in low tones, concern and distress laced in his tone. "We need to get you out of the public eye."

"Back to the Sanctuary ship?" Rai suggested. "Did they bring it here?"

Graeber gave a curt shake of his head. "Let's use one of the tents. It's closer and less likely to have prying ears."

They commandeered a tent at the edge of the encampment which was already abandoned and closed it up tight. Rilte waved off one onlooker, explaining the Progenitor needed time for quiet meditation. By the time Graeber got her to the sleeping cot, her legs had given out entirely, Rai's limbs spasmed in short, uncontrollable bursts.

Graeber crouched down next to her and held onto her arms, his emotions sliding from concern to anger and back again.

"She has myoclonic jerks," Rilte said. "With her Progenitor strength, she could break one of your arms."

"I'll take that risk," Graeber growled in response. "What's happening, Rai? First, they pull you out of the ocean unconscious, and now, you're losing control of your body. What happened down at the Seed Marker?"

He pushed at her mind, but Rai shut him out, slamming shut the door.

"I, I," Rai stammered, "I got the plague stopped. Then the other change was done. It's all done. The humans are safe."

"Yeah, we figured that out," Ponar replied. "What did this to you?"

"I did." Rai felt tears run down her face. "I made a promise to Vida to find her people. I needed to know what she knew."

"You downloaded the Marker," Bauleel replied, intuiting her sister's dedication. "All of it."

Rai nodded as another wave of spasms hit her body. "At first, it went smoothly and then I just blacked out. I woke up on the beach."

"There's no way your brain can handle that much data, by the effects we're seeing. You have to ask Vida to delete some of it," Rilte replied.

"Even if I wanted to..." Rai said.

"Vida is, of course, helpful as a rock," Graeber spat out. He took her face in both hands, making Rai focus. "In your current state, Brague will not allow you to go on this hunt of yours for Progenitors. You will have failed. Do you want this?"

"No! Of course not!"

"All right, then transfer some of the data to me. Do it now, before they come and discover their broken Progenitor. You know the Juggernaut won't tolerate flaws."

"I won't endanger you."

"You'll doom us all if Brague decides the Progenitor is broken," Graeber replied, his tone terse. "I'll take a little risk here."

"But I won't have access to the information anymore," Rai replied.

Graeber frowned. "Sure you will. I'll be here, anytime you need it. Just think of me as offsite data storage."

"And me," Bauleel said. "Spread it out in logical chunks and whenever you need to search for something, we'll link up."

"I'm in as well," Rilte said. "And not just so my girlfriend will like me. It's best if the data load is distributed."

"You're right, this is overloading my neural network," Rai replied.

"I'd help out, Rai, you know I would, but as I'm staying here I won't be around for you to access the information," Ponar replied.

"Agreed. And thanks, anyway." Rai replied.

"How about you watch the door, and warn us if anyone is coming?" Graeber asked.

"Will do."

"Okay, everyone else, grab on," Rai said.

Graeber and Bauleel both took a hand, and Rilte held a foot. Rai concentrated through the spasms and opened herself to them.

Selecting distinct packets of data, Rai passed them

to her peers. She would have been hard pressed to give a technical guide to her process, there was a flow to it not unlike the datasphere formed by the network of their connected minds.

The others commented as she passed the data, as was the nature of the telepathic connection.

"I'm barely skimming the surface of this, there's just so much," Bauleel said.

"I know what you mean," Graeber replied. "These diaries go back millennia. They are well indexed, dated, and tagged multiple ways, but I'm not a computer, how do I search them?"

"I will, later," Rai replied.

"Wait, I get the planetary history? That's a bum deal!" Rilte exclaimed, but he was just ribbing her.

Rai kept the greater part of the Progenitor history, thinking it would yield the most valuable data and be something she'd need to reference the most. Already her mind was quieting, normalizing towards homeostasis, and her muscles reflected the change.

"I think that's enough for now," Rai said aloud. "Does everyone feel okay?"

"We're okay," Bauleel said. "How are you?"

"Improving."

Bauleel and Rilte stepped away, but Graeber stayed near, maintaining the mental connection.

"I've almost lost you twice now." Blue eyes pierced her heart. "Do we have to hunt down this mission of yours? If we stay here, no one will touch us."

Rai propped herself up on one elbow, putting them face-to-face. "Are you so sure of that? So sure everyone is happy with the fate the Progenitor has dealt out? There are about fifty thousand colonists. Are they all going to love the change?"

"Of course not, but at least here we know the dangers."

"And yesterday you wanted to fly as far from Az'Unda as possible. Now, we'll go with the protection of the Hegemony," Rai replied

"And their ever watching eyes. What if you over-reach again, like today? What then?" Graeber asked.

"It won't happen," Rai smiled.

"No?" Graeber scowled.

"No. Because you won't let me. You'll keep me in line, won't you? You'll make me see reason, remind me to be careful, and that not only my life hangs in the balance when I'm impulsive. Right?"

Graeber ground his teeth so hard Rai heard his jaw pop.

"I. Will. Not. Lose. You. Again," Graeber answered, his frustration palpable.

"Understood," Rai replied.

"We're about to have company," Ponar said. "It's the big boy himself, and he's headed straight for us."

Everyone shared a look. Rai swung her legs down onto the floor and sat up. Graeber put a hand on her arm to steady her, but she waved him off.

"I'm much better now. And I must appear recovered from my bout in the ocean. After all, I need to negotiate our passage with Brague. Who knows what his goals are at this point? Now, everyone, game faces!"

Rai closed her eyes and placed her hands calmly in her lap. She heard the movement of Graeber standing up, but he remained close by her side.

Moments later, Ponar opened the tent flap for the Assessor and Brague stepped inside, filling the space with his bulk. Rai opened her eyes and looked at him as if she hadn't a care in the world.

There was a beat where no one spoke. Rai waited for Brague to take the lead, which, predictably, he did.

"I have made the arrangements to return the Core members to their varying points of origin," he said.

"My thanks for your service."

"May I inquire what you are doing, here in this tent?"

"Meditating. It was a convenient location."

His mandibles chattered briefly, but he soon quieted, controlling his outward display of irritation. "May I ask, have you settled the situation to your liking on this planet for the time being?"

"You may ask, Brague. And yes, I am satisfactorily pleased with the outcome to date."

"This is welcome news, Vida." He paused and looked around the room. "Could we perhaps have a private audience at this juncture?"

Rai tilted her head. "But you do. These vessels are

all an extension of myself. Please continue your thoughts."

Brague blinked a few times quickly, before continuing. "If it pleases you, Queen Klimitzi seeks an audience with your Eminence. In person. If you could see fit to leave your planetary oversight for a short time, that is."

Rai smiled coyly. "The foremost Juggernaut Queen wishes a personal audience with me?"

"How did you know she was foremost?" Brague rattled his carapace. "You are the last remaining Progenitor. Of course, she wants to meet with you, you're a link to our past."

"And your future, no?" Rai asked. Could a Juggernaut look startled? If so, Brague just did with his irises narrowed to pinpoints. She'd never seen them do that before. And he was avoiding multidimensional speech in this conversation. Was he attempting to mislead her, or prevent her from seeing his true intentions? "As it happens, I have planned a trip, and thus have need of your services. Perhaps we can trade a visit with your Queen for your agreement to take me where I need to go?"

Brague swayed his head side to side. "Vida, there is no reason to trade, as you put it. That would be a dishonor to my race. The Juggernaut are already in your debt. If you require transport, it will be provided along with the appropriate guards and honors fit to your station."

"You are generous."

"It is nothing. A minor dent in our vast resources. I will escort you, if only for the sheer pleasure of your presence."

Rai allowed a frown to knit her brows. "Surely an Assessor of your esteem has better things to do than being my escort? More important assignments than running a Progenitor on her sightseeing errands and matters of state?"

Brague sighed, the universal signal for frustration. "Sadly, all issues concerning the Queens also concern me. I have risen to the post of consummate politician despite my best efforts." His candor surprised Rai. Or, was he playing her to gain information? "Yet I doubt you wish to go sightseeing after all these years. Tell me, after we visit my Queen, what is your destination?"

Rai rose to her feet and moved closer to him. "I'm not sure. You see, the location of my brethren is something of a mystery to me. I mean to seek them out." Rai watched Brague for reactions but got none.

"I will happily be at your disposal for the duration of the trip," Brague replied. "How soon would you like to depart?"

"My companions need to collect their things. We'll need the use of a transport ship to various cities to accomplish this. After that is accomplished, perhaps we could leave tomorrow?"

"Of course. Would you like any of my troops to

remain planet-side to maintain order after we leave? It would be no drain on my considerable resources."

"That won't be necessary," Rai replied. "Ponar will be staying here, and he will be contacting me via standard comm channels on a periodic basis. If anything critical comes up, we can respond as needed. I also trust in Raza and her Guardians to handle controlling the populace against any uprisings. I expect they'll all be so happy about the lack of the plague and the removal of Temple controls that they won't have time to revolt."

"Be assured, Vida, I will report on our progress regularly," Ponar said.

"I will leave my contact information with you as well," Brague replied. "I can ensure reinforcements are here in the quickest possible manner."

"I'm sure you can," Rai replied. "However, they will not act without my consent."

"Your authority shall not be challenged," Brague replied.

Their gazes met, and an acknowledgment of power passed between them. Yet, Rai felt the undertones. She'd stated what she wanted, but not the entire reason why, and Brague had done the same.

"I'll leave you to your arrangements, then," Brague said. "You may commandeer any available transport shuttle you wish. I will make sure at least one remains in the area available to you. In the meantime, I have an army to extract from your bountiful world. Until tomorrow, Progenitor Vida."

"My thanks, Assessor Brague," Rai replied.

Brague strode from the tent and began barking out orders to his staff. The flurry of activity in response was unmistakable.

"That went well," Bauleel spoke in a whispered tones. "I wonder what the Juggernaut Queen wants with you? A cup of tea?"

Graeber wrapped an arm around Rai's shoulders. "Somehow," he answered in a low growl, "I expect she's got other plans for you."

"Calm down you two," Rai replied. "I'm on a level of a deity to them, right? They won't hurt me. People don't go killing their gods."

Graeber shot her a wry frown and groaned. "You haven't read much ancient human Earth text, have you?"

"No, why?"

"Their old gods rarely had it easy."

Rai kept her calm despite her frustration. She had no idea if the Juggernaut were somehow watching their exchange. "Enough of your moods. I can't help what the Juggernaut want. We'll deal with it when we get there. You never know, it may help with my hunt. Right now, let's go get whatever we can't leave home without."

There was some grumbling all around, but finally, assent.

"And you," Rai looked to Ponar, "We'll drop you off in Raven's Call. I bet Kait's in a snit waiting to see you home again."

Ponar dragged a hand through the hair at the nape of his neck. "Yes, and Kait is going to give me no end of grief over this entire episode!"

"On the upside, serving at the Progenitor's personal Ambassador does have the cachet of making you the most marriageable man on the planet."

Ponar held up his hands. "Oh no, not that again! But, on second thought, you're right. And it will get her to stop bemoaning my near-death at the hands of the Juggernaut."

"See, there's the bright side of the coin!" Rilte chimed in.

They exited the tent and walked towards a nearby transport shuttle, moods in various states of humor.

"Where should we stop first?" Bauleel asked.

"The colony caves to the shuttle I had prepped there," Graeber answered. "I took some time stocking that ship. Seems a shame not to take advantage of it."

"And after that?" Rai asked.

"Perhaps your home at Harper's Sorrow? You might find things of interest there."

"Yes, and then on to Raven's Call," Bauleel replied. "There are things I'd like to get from the Temple. And I'm sure you'd like a chance to gather a few items from the Technicians Guild?" she asked Rilte.

"Yeah, I think I would. Not knowing how long we'll

be gone. Or if we're even coming back, yeah, if we have the time I'd like that," Rilte replied.

"Let's take what's ours with us. Lifetimes may pass before we return," Rai said as she stepped onto the Juggernaut transport shuttle, followed by her friends, bound by a bond beyond friendship.

A bond of mind, thought, and flesh.

Brague stood at ease before the impressively large communications terminal in his private lounge, neck bared, and hands clasped behind his back. One of the screens awaited the Queen's answer. Another kept a close track of the transport shuttle the Progenitor was using to prepare her team for their imminent departure.

With him.

A single chime proceeded the screen flickering to life, and then Brague was face to face with Queen Klimitzi again, except now she stood, veiled in sheer lavender, her pillowed nest abandoned behind her.

"What news, Assessor Brague?"

Brague straightened to his full height. "I leave tomorrow from Az'Unda. The Progenitor and her companions accompany me. We shall arrive within ten of your days to a sub-Latne, depending on the solar flares Iaos is spouting when we pass."

The Queen brought her hands to her lips. "This is most welcome news, Assessor. You are a tribute to your race." Brague inclined his head. "Tell me, how did she agree to this meeting, when so few are willing to part with their home worlds without coercion?"

This fact was news to Brague, and it made him wonder why she hadn't shared it earlier. "The Progenitor wishes to locate others of her kind. Her 'brethren,' as she calls them. She became aware through contact with me that my race hasn't seen a Progenitor for generations. She appears curious where they've gone." Some of this was information he'd gotten from reports given by Caretaker Traken on the Sanctuary ship.

Klimitzi stepped closer to the screen. Her hands were still held high, fingertips touching. "Tell me, did you allow her onto the Sanctuary ship?"

"Yes, it seemed an honor befitting her." Brague tilted his head down low, braced for argument.

"And by the reports of the Caretakers, did she interact with the Seed Marker on the ship?"

"Yes. Was this inappropriate, my Queen?" Brague kept his frustration in check. If this was something he wasn't supposed to have done, it should have been dictated clearly up front.

Klimitzi held up a hand to forestall his questions and then steepled her fingers again. "And after her interactions, did she behave the same as before?"

Brague searched his memory. "Yes. On every count. There was a time the Progenitor overloaded the capacity of her host vessel, but that was the host, not her, failing. When she revived, all was as normal again."

"How remarkable. This Progenitor is different than the others I have encountered. More resilient. I can't wait to meet her."

"I shall bring her directly, my Queen. Her quest to search for her brethren can wait until after your visit."

"Yes, Assessor. I'm glad you understand the situation." The Queen turned and laid down upon her nest of lavender silken pillows, before again squaring him directly with her gaze. "And for your exemplary efforts, you shall be justly rewarded."

"I am honored, Your Excellency," Brague replied. *Could he hope for the ultimate of rewards?*

"And Assessor, I feel it would be a shame if the genes from a male of your esteem did not make it into our lineage. Therefore, after you introduce me to the Progenitor, you will be given a short leave during which you will be granted breeding rights during your stay."

Brague bowed low, overwhelmed by the bestowed honor. "I am grateful beyond words, my Queen."

"As you should be. Few are afforded such an elite right. Now, I leave you to your task. And be mindful of your passenger."

"I assure you, my Queen, her safety is my utmost

priority." Brague rose to his full height again, affronted by the perceived slight.

"Of course, Assessor. That's not what I was referring to. Rather, as the old eldritch saying goes: when the old gods awaken, take care, for they are 'oft times cranky. Beware that you stay on the friendly side of this one, lest she bites."

"I will heed your words," Brague replied.

"And I look forward to greeting both of you, face to face. Give the Progenitor my warmest regards."

The screen flickered off.

For many moments Brague was so caught up in the rush of being awarded breeding rights, something every Juggernaut male fought tooth and claw for his entire career, that the entirety of the conversation hadn't yet processed. But when Brague thought back over the conversation, two questions kept rolling around in his head.

The first was: how old, exactly, was Queen Klimitzi?

The second was: the Queen has met other Progenitors? When?

The End

Want more? Sign up now for updates and I'll send you
a newsletter exclusive extra!

AUTHOR'S NOTE

If you loved the book and have a minute to spare, I would really appreciate a short review on the page or site where you bought the book. Your help in spreading the word is greatly appreciated. Reviews from readers like you make a huge difference to helping new readers find similar stories.

Thank you so much for reading and supporting my work!

Candice

P.S. If you'd like to know when my next book comes out and want to receive occasional updates from me, then you can sign up for my newsletter at candice-bundy.com. I promise I will never sell your email to the daemonic marketing hordes.

The Stolen Legacy Series

Forbidden Fates

Entangled Essence

Hidden Hearts

The Shadow Series

Shadow in the City, A prequel novella

Twinned Shadow

Poisoned Shadow

Shadow Underground

Caught Between Worlds Series

Smoke and Daemons

(*previously published as Daemon Whisperer*)

Other Works

Ripples, a novella

Open Rack, a contemporary short

WRITING AS CR BUNDY

The Depths of Memory Series

The Dream Sifter

Dreams Manifest

For a list of my full catalog of available titles, visit my
Amazon Author Central page.

ACKNOWLEDGMENTS

Thanks to Zippy Wizard Redaction for their editing and proofreading services.

And to my friends and family who've been a source of unending strength, laughter, and wine over the years: thank you for the inspiration.

ABOUT THE AUTHOR

Candice lives in Denver, Colorado with her son and their cat Newt. A professional hedonist, rabble-rouser, winemaker, and goat-herder, she adores archeology and mythology. Candice focuses on habit hacking to meet minimalist, health, productivity, and positive mojo goals, and sometimes even blogs about it. An unrepentant epicurean, she grows heirloom tomatoes and ferments a variety of sauerkraut, sourdough, kombucha, pickles, and water kefir.

If you would like to know when she has new books out, please sign up for her newsletter at candicebundy.-com. Or, email her at candice@candicebundy.com if the mood strikes you.